# DAYZEE DAZZLE

## AND THE

## *CADAVER COLLECTORS*

Other Books by Edward Allen Karr

**SERIES: Thrills N Kills in the Hills**
(Racy, Comical Horror in Beverly Hills)
Dayzee Dazzle and the Kildare Killers – Book One
Dayzee Dazzle and her Manic Mansion – Book Two
Dayzee Dazzle and the On-Set Onslaught – Book Three
* * * *

**SERIES: Socrates Lewis Stories**
(Psychological/Religious Fiction)
Crosswinds – Book One
Crossovers – Book Two
* * * * *

**SERIES: Fringes Of Infinity**
(Contemporary Fantasy Fiction)
Lin Finity and her Mayhem Rising – Book One
Lin Finity in Holding On – A Novella
Lin Finity and the Words Unspoken – Book Two
Lin Finity and the Islands of Time – Book Three
Lin Finity and the Flights to Forever – Book Four
Tayo Tersoo and the Hunter of Souls – Book Five
* * * * *

**SERIES: A World So Close**
(Middle-grade Fantasy Adventure & Coming of Age)
Jayden Blue and the Gift to Imagine – A Prequel
Jayden Blue and the Sword in his Shadow – Book One
Jayden Blue and the Call of the Wings – Book Two
Jayden Blue and the Lair of the Iron Lions – Book Three
Jayden Blue and the Journey to Val ka'Yoom – Book Four
Jayden Blue and the Forest of Night Fallen – Book Five
Jayden Blue and the Wait of the Sun – Book Six

* * * * *

# DAYZEE DAZZLE

## AND THE

# *CADAVER COLLECTORS*

---

## Thrills N Kills in the Hills
## Book Four

### Edward Allen Karr

LAKESIDE LETTERS, LLC

Lakeside Letters, LLC
30628 Detroit Road, #247
Westlake, OH  44145

This is a work of fiction. Names, characters, businesses, events, and incidents are the products of the author's imagination. Any resemblance to actual persons, living or dead, or actual events is purely coincidental. Certain long-standing institutions are mentioned, but the characters are imaginary. The opinions expressed are those of the characters and should not be confused with those of the author.

Dayzee Dazzle and the Cadaver Collectors
Thrills N Kills in the Hills Book Four
©2024  Edward Sechkar.   All rights reserved.



First Edition, 2024
www.LakesideLetters.com

Cover design by JD Smith Design

ISBN-13:  978-1-950886-28-9

She'd called them over her shoulder and then resumed her study of the deathhouse where Chang had been mauled. From leaning over the hood, both palms flat on the clean metal, Kenzie's skirt had traveled up, revealing more generously her long, toned legs.

"Oh, my, Sissy. That's not acting. Those legs are real."

"Strong, too, Sis," said Sophia. "When she pinned me down upstairs, back when we were trying to kill that first assassin, I—"

Marilyn giggled and said, "That's a good word, Sissy: 'assassin.' Two asses, your and hers, and then the word 'in.' I could take some guesses what that all adds up to. Ask me. I dare you."

"Girls," said Dayzee, "Kenzie might be right about this all getting out of control. We can give some careful attention to all of our asses later."

From Chapter 5 – They Really Are on Fire

Table of Contents

# Chapter 1 – We'll Have So Many Cadavers

"Dammit, I'm losing track," Dayzee said as she leaned her back into the heavy wooden door of the Prism bar on Sunset Boulevard.

She scoffed at the traffic streaming past, oblivious to her and the Kildare Killers standing in the Southern California sunshine. Her tiny black skirt and short, high-heeled black boots left a lot of distance to show her black fishnets. She shook her head a couple of times, sending her thick, wild blond mane off of the shoulders of her tight, low-buttoned white blouse.

She looked down at the severed head that she was cradling in her arms like a newborn.

"I mean, whose head is this?"

She looked to her left and met the disinterested bright blue gaze from Sophia, who smirked, resumed her study of the street, and said, "Like it matters. It's just the one Mack handed to you on the way out."

Sophia leaned back into the building's brick wall and lifted one pointy black heel up against it, shortening her black skirt even more. Between her red blouse and the sunlit wall, her long, straight, silky black hair hid from the light breezes.

"Yes, Sissy," said Sophia's twin sister, Marilyn, and Dayzee turned to the right to catch a sight of her equally bright blue eyes as she leaned forward to address Sophia. "Getting any head is probably a good thing. But maybe Dayzee should return it? Trade it in for something more fun?"

The breezes were enough to flutter around the bottom hem of Marilyn's very short and tight white dress. Her classic, wavy blond hair teased gently in the gusts and when she noticed that Sophia had placed one heel against the wall, she also put one of her white high heels up.

Sophia leaned forward and said to her sister, "Sis, that could work if Dayzee had a receipt. But when heads get lopped off and passed around, no one takes the time to—"

"Girls," Dayzee said while holding the head out in both hands, shaking her head at the sight of its blinking eyes. "This head isn't our biggest problem."

She dropped it onto the concrete, causing a sharp cracking sound and a squirt of slime through the neck.

"Sheesh," said Sophia.

"He's still winking at me, Sissy."

"Of course, Sis. Even when they're dead and—"

"Girls, we need to figure this out."

She kicked the head toward the curb, and two young men passing by started kicking it along with them like it was a soccer ball. They'd never slowed or even laughed.

"Only in Beverly Hills," Dayzee said, shaking her head at the detached head being bounced away along Sunset. "I just had to get out of there. Those Collectors are just too—"

"What about the potion they promised us, Dayzee?"

"Oh, Mare, it can't possibly be worth—"

"Supplying them with cadavers?" said Sophia. "Before the sun sets on your mansion in the Flats, you know we'll have so many cadavers that—"

"Fia, we don't know that. Can't we possibly have just one day without a bunch of dead bodies everywhere we look?"

"Well, Dayzee," said Marilyn, "I looked in your freezer once to get some waffles, and there weren't any dead guys in there."

Dayzee frowned before turning to her right, toward Marilyn.

"Mare, that might be the one place where—"

Sophia scoffed and said, "I bet there's one in there right now."

"Good one, Sissy. Yes, or maybe just a head?"

"Look for head, and you'll find it, Sis," Sophia said with a smirk. "Frozen head is better than none at all."

"Those two gentlemen just got some head, and they weren't even looking for it."

Dayzee had been looking from one twin to the other, shaking her own head, and she said, "Mare, that's just silly. They never stop looking, even when they don't know they're looking."

"Hey," said Sophia, "how much of that super potion can we get from those creepy Cadaver Collectors if we just trade a head?"

"Sissy, I don't think a head counts as a cadaver. What do you think, Dayzee?"

Looking out across Sunset, Dayzee puffed up her cheeks and let a deep breath slowly seep out.

"Mare, Fia, I'll vomit right here if I imagine either of those two Collector creeps getting head."

Sophia nodded and said, "Good one, Dayzee."

"Sissy's right, Dayzee. And so are you. I don't want an upset stomach again like when I had those baby squids swimming around in me."

"Sis, it was probably just some tiny eggs, that's all. The only one with squids squidding around inside was Cliff."

"Oh, girls, Cliff. Or Dirk. I don't even know anymore. But he's back at the mansion setting up for our reality show, 'Kildare in The Hills.' We should probably get back there."

"And do what?" said Sophia. "Just leave those freaky Collectors and our chance at snagging some of that super-orgasmic potion?"

"I want super orgasms, Dayzee," Marilyn said with a pout.

Sophia smirked and said, "And I want to watch her when she has those, Dayzee. We'll just have to figure out some kind of deal with them."

"Okay, fine. I can't argue with you girls. And I can't even imagine how agitated you'll both be after getting your fountains of youth with that special potion."

"You too, Dayzee," said Marilyn. "And Sissy and I are both going to be right there to see it."

Sophia scoffed and said, "Hell, we'll help."

"First," said Dayzee, "we need to get back to the house. A couple of drinks there should help."

At the sound of a loud slap, all three looked to the left. The head was rolling back toward them, and the two men waved before turning and continuing their walk.

The head's eyes spent a second looking at each of them.

"He's trying to—"

Marilyn laughed and said, "Sissy said 'he!' That head by itself is still a 'he!'"

"Yeah, Sis, but he, the head, is trying to think of a pickup line for a time like this. Can't do it."

"Damn. Only in Beverly Hills," said Dayzee.

*　*　*

Dayzee tipped forward from someone inside the Prism giving the door a shove, but she leaned back into it.

"No way. Those creeps are trying to follow us. No way am I letting them out."

"Um, Dayzee," said Sophia, "maybe some normal human type of person just wants to get out of there?"

"Sissy's right, Dayzee. It might just be a human."

"Oh, fine. Let's let those freaks,"—she turned and pulled the door out—"face the sunshine and—oh, it's you, Kenzie."

Kenzie leaned enough to look through the narrow opening. Her long brown hair hung straight down to one side as she looked from Dayzee, to Sophia, then Marilyn.

"Yeah, it's me. Who'd you think it was? Those weirdos at the bar?"

Dayzee opened the door all the way and said, "We didn't know," as Kenzie exited and took a spot beside Marilyn.

"Oh, wait just a second," Sophia said before whistling loudly once. "Let's have a look at you."

She gestured for Kenzie to step away, then closer to the curb so that they could all see her. Kenzie grinned and complied, then turned to face them.

"Wow, that's a sight," Sophia said while looking her up and down.

Kenzie wore high red heels, a short red skirt, and a tight black blouse. She'd neglected to button it up enough to keep three pairs of appreciative eyes from staring at a generous portion of her breasts treating themselves to the sunshine.

"Oh my," said Marilyn. "That's how you dress as a barmaid?"

"No, silly," she said to Marilyn. "I'm leaving for an audition. I'm an actress, remember?"

Dayzee grinned and looked to her left, where she saw Sophia staring straight ahead, her face locked in a smirk.

She looked to her right and saw Marilyn studying the sidewalk, shaking her head slowly.

Then, looking again at Kenzie, she said, "Of course, Kenzie. Everyone around here is. Before you run off to that appointment, though, we could use an experienced limo driver."

Kenzie frowned at her and said, "Me? I've never driven a limo around."

Marilyn leaned out and said to her sister, "Oh, Sissy, she still doesn't remember."

"Remember what?"

Sophia said, "You took a hit to the head, and—"

"Not that head," Marilyn said, pointing at the one that was now looking up at Kenzie. From up close. With a view from right below her skirt.

Kenzie, looking down first with a smile, then a frown, said, "Oh, I'm feeling kind of funny. Something about that Halloween decoration on the sidewalk maybe."

"Yeah," said Dayzee, "that's what it is. Mack was cleaning up and wanted us to take it."

Sophia said, "Hey, is it making you remember anything? Anything about heads?"

"Or just, 'head?'" Marilyn said with a giggle.

Kenzie looked at each of them and said, "Oh my God. I'm starting to remember all kinds of crazy shit."

"Dead guys walking all around?" said Dayzee.

Softly, Marilyn said, "I still say they were dancing."

"Mountain lions ripping heads off of everyone?" said Sophia.

Marilyn giggled once and said to herself, "Big cats looking for head."

"Oh," said Sophia, "yeah, Sis is right. How about this, Kenzie: say 'damn lions,' alright?"

"Uh, why would I do that?"

"Humor me?"

Sophia saw that Marilyn was clapping silently, staring intently at Kenzie.

"And humor Sis?"

"Fine. Damn lions. Ooh, that's weird. I felt like I was about to . . ."

All three girls were smiling and staring at Kenzie.

"Hey," she finally said, "who are those two new freaks that were at the bar?"

Dayzee lost her smile and said, "Wait. What do you mean, 'were' at the bar?"

"Well, last I saw, they were sniffing around by that statue guy."

Nodding, Marilyn said, "They sure do a lot of sniffing."

"Chattering, too, Sis," said her sister. "Remember those teeth? Sheesh."

"Oh, God," said Dayzee. "They're sniffing around the portal. We have to get back to the mansion."

"I don't remember anything about any kind of portal or any other—"

"There's no time for that," said Dayzee. "We need to go, and you're driving!"

"But I have an audition that I—"

"No, no, no," said Dayzee. "You're back in the show with us."

"Kildare in the Hills," said Sophia. "All of us."

"Maybe even Kozy?" said Marilyn.

Kenzie turned to her, squinting, and said, "Kozy. I remember that name."

"We'll figure that all out later girls. Right now, we have to move!"

# Chapter 2 – Take This More Seriously!

Dayzee hooked Kenzie's arm and said, "Walk with us, Kenzie. See the limo over there?"

"That shiny one? Wow, it's spotless. Nice that you got it detailed."

"Not the way you think," said Sophia. "It's a special process."

"Yes," Marilyn said, walking behind them with Sophia by her side, "very special. If it wasn't for those Collectors, our limo would still be covered in all kinds of—"

"Leaves," said Dayzee. "Bugs and mulch and dirt too."

"Oh," said Kenzie. "So, who detailed it? Someone that collects limos?"

Dayzee turned enough to wink at Sophia.

"She's kind of a sweet kid too."

Then, to Kenzie, she said, "Let's just say that we have someone on speed dial that can clean up any kind of pesky, annoying—"

"Or bloody!" said Marilyn, causing them all to stop.

Quickly, Dayzee said, "We're hoping for no blood. But, um, in these memories of yours that are coming back . . . anything about blood?"

Kenzie stopped, and the three girls stopped with her.

"Uh, no. Not yet anyway. Something about a hat, though?"

Marilyn clapped quietly and said, "Yay! You know who's coming back!"

"Sis, we don't know for sure that—"

"Who's coming back?"

"No one, Kenzie," said Dayzee. "Let's get back to the house. Girls, we have so much to figure out that we might have to call Mack with an emergency booze delivery."

"I bet he could deliver all kinds of good things," said Sophia.

Marilyn said, "And die trying."

* * *

"I do kind of remember driving this limo around," Kenzie said while swinging open the driver's door.

"Might not have been this one," Dayzee said as she claimed the front passenger seat. "We kind of burn through them."

"Burn, Sissy," said Marilyn. "We sure do burn through . . . things."

"Like, yard guys, Sis? Film crew guys?"

Dayzee saw the worried look on Kenzie's face and said, "We're just kind of demanding, that's all. It goes with being such famous film—"

When she saw Kenzie's eyes bug out and point at the dashboard, Dayzee looked too. A finger was lying there oozing into a red puddle.

The twins, sitting up against each other in the back seat, leaned forward to look too.

"Damn lions," said Kenzie. "Hey, why did I say that again?"

Dayzee pointed at the finger and said, "Because that's what they do. They're always ripping things off of—"

"Why didn't the Collectors suck that up too?" said Sophia.

Then, she looked at the small body parts ground into the carpeting beneath her and her sister's heels and said softly, "Sheesh."

"Oh my, Sissy. They're not very reliable."

"Girls," Dayzee said, holding the finger up for emphasis, "this was inside. They didn't take the time to suck up all the—"

"Vacuum up, you mean?"

"Yeah, Kenzie. Uh-huh. Sure."

Dayzee tossed the finger onto the sidewalk and powered up the window.

"You're just leaving that on the sidewalk?"

"Kenzie, this the Hills. That's the least of the weird stuff that happens around here."

"Always some kind of thrill," said Marilyn.

"Anyway," said Dayzee, "I'm ready. Kenzie, you have the wheel. Do you remember the way to my house?"

Sophia smirked and said, "Without those Collectors, she could have followed the trail."

Kenzie spun around to look in back and said, "What trail?"

"Sissy's just being funny," said Marilyn. "Home, James."

"That's funny, Sis."

"I remember the way. And who's James?"

"No one, Kenzie. Can you please get us all back to the Flats?"

"Sure. Even though I'm not a driver. Or a barmaid. Not really."

"Yes, you're an actress, Kenzie!" said Marilyn.

*  *  *

With Sophia and Marilyn whispering in the backseat and Dayzee watching the Sunset Boulevard scenery, Kenzie took the sweep left on the way to Dayzee's mansion in the Flats.

"I'm starting to realize something," she said.

The twins stopped to listen, and Dayzee turned toward her and said, "Oh, and what might that be?"

"That head back at the Prism. It wasn't—"

"The head you were looking for?" Marilyn said with a giggle.

"Sis, are we sure she was looking for head? I mean, those two soccer players—"

"Fia," said Dayzee, "they weren't soccer players until they got some head."

"And just like any other guys," Marilyn said, shaking her head, "when they were done, they just kicked it out somewhere."

"No," said Kenzie. "No, listen to me. That wasn't a decoration, was it? God, it was looking up my skirt!"

"Who wouldn't?" Sophia said with a smirk. "Give me half a chance."

"Oh, Sissy, you've had way more than half a chance. It started when we were all driving home, and you and—"

"Sis, maybe not now, alright?"

"Sure, Sissy. Later, I'll remind you of every little detail that—"

"Stop and listen, alright?" Kenzie said as she turned left onto Dayzee's street. "That head was alive, at least at one time. And that finger, Dayzee? That wasn't any kind of decoration, was it?"

"Well, um, I wouldn't hang it from my Christmas tree."

Sophia snorted out a loud laugh, and Marilyn giggled before saying, "And we're not wrapping up all this yucky stuff back here either."

Kenzie hit the brakes, bringing the long car to a stop.

"Uh, what stuff back where?"

"Nothing important," Sophia said while powering down her window and tossing out a hand. "Accidents happen."

"They sure do, Sissy. All the time around us."

Dayzee turned to smile at the twins and said, "Girls, it's Beverly Hills. Things like that always—"

Kenzie turned to her and said, "Dayzee, no! I'm starting to remember a whole lot of stuff like this, and it's not funny!"

"It's kind of funny," said Marilyn. "Sissy, I like how they were always dancing around, looking for head, then—"

"Sis, they were never really dancing. Looking for head, though? Oh, yeah. Sometimes they even found—"

"All of you!" said Kenzie. "You should all take this more seriously! Don't you realize it could get so much worse?"

They all sat in silence while Kenzie looked at each of them, then she ended up holding Dayzee's calm gaze.

Until Dayzee started to laugh.

"Then, my dear actress Kenzie, we'll just rock and roll with it."

Kenzie stared with no reply.

Marilyn said, "I want some of that potion. Whatever it takes, Sissy."

"Oh, yeah, Sis. That's the only way to dance with dead guys."

Kenzie still stared at Dayzee, her face frozen with wide-open eyes. "It's the Hills, Kenzie. Let's get some booze in you. You'll be fine."

* * *

"Yes, right there," Dayzee said with a beaming smile as she tapped her phone to open the massive wrought iron entrance gate to her estate in the Beverly Hills Flats. "You really did remember."

"Yeah, this all looks familiar. It brings back a lot of memories too."

"Good. Don't let it upset you. We find that if we don't take things too seriously, then, well, they're not too serious."

"Just how much do you remember?" said Sophia.

Kenzie screeched the limo to a stop just inside the gate. They all had a view through the windshield of busy yard guys, all wearing orange jumpsuits, and other men carrying around lighting and sound equipment and cameras.

She turned enough to see Marilyn but couldn't see Sophia. So, Sophia laid her arms on the seat back and leaned over to give Kenzie a view of her big blue eyes.

"I remember your name," Kenzie said with a quick giggle.

"Uh-oh, Sissy," said Marilyn. "Here we go again."

"Wait a second, Sis. Kenzie, what name is that?"

Kenzie paused to look at Dayzee, who grinned and said, "I could say it. But I think we all want to hear it from you. So, Kenzie, what name for Fia are you talking about?"

She held Sophia's gaze for a second, smiling, then grabbed the steering wheel and looked out at all of the activity around Dayzee's mansion.

"Fifi."

"That's my Sissy," said Marilyn. "Well, it was for a while."

Sophia, with a big grin, said, "I did like being called—"

"Girls!" said Dayzee. "Never mind that now. Look!"

She pointed toward the long row of second-story windows, drawing Kenzie's eyes to them. Marilyn and Sophia leaned low and into the front seat to see up through the window.

"Hey, Dayzee," said Kenzie, "how did they get here before us?"

"Uh, they, um . . ."

"Oh, maybe it's not the same ones? Could that be it?"

Sophia said, "They, uh, those . . ."

Marilyn said, "No. That's them. See the chattering teeth?"

"Yeah," said Dayzee, "and they're the same shade of yellow. The only thing that could make this worse is—"

They all looked up at the rapid series of thumps on the roof of the limo, then watched three large female mountain lions pad down the windshield, across the hood, and to the asphalt.

Two more hustled to join them along each side of the car.

The lionesses all paused for just a second, then split up and scurried silently behind the hedges to each side which provided thick walls all along the high iron fence ringing Dayzee's property.

"Oh, boy. Just wonderful."

"And I'm okay with all of that," Kenzie said, then put the car in drive and began idling closer to the house. "You know why?"

All three girls stared and waited.

"Because it's Beverly Hills," she said, still looking up at the Cadaver Collectors in the window. "Things happen here. Crazy things."

Dayzee said, "It's not because, uh, you're an actress?"

"Well, that too."

# Chapter 3 – Already Mostly a Corpse

"No!" Dayzee screamed, "Go that way!"

Kenzie was about to pull straight in toward the row of garage doors, but she did as instructed and turned enough to begin following the curved drive which led to the exit gate.

"Sure. Why?" said Kenzie. "What's the big deal?"

"Because we should just leave. I think we should just run."

"No way, Dayzee," said Sophia. "You promised us some drinks."

"Sissy's right, and I need a swim. Why on Earth would you—"

"That's funny, Sis."

"—would you want to leave your house? Just because those creepy Collector fellows are—"

"One of them is a 'she,' Sis. At least, that's what the 'he,' told us."

"Sissy, we don't even know if he's a 'he.'"

"Girls! It doesn't matter what they are. Can't we just all disappear for a couple of days? I could use some rest. It's been a wild few days."

"No, hold up," Kenzie said as she coasted the shiny black vehicle to a stop near the porch. "I already lost that audition so that I could star in your—"

"You're starring?" said Sophia. "It's not enough to just—"

"No, Fifi," said Kenzie, "it's not enough, dammit."

"Ooh, Sissy, she's a fiery one."

"Oh, like hot, you mean?"

"Uh-huh," said Marilyn. "Yep. Maybe you two could try out your—"

"All of you, stop a second," said Dayzee.

Everyone quieted down and watched able-bodied men, some of them prisoners, taking care of the grounds and setting up for shooting some reality show scenes.

From farther along the drive, Cliff was approaching the limo with a clipboard in his hand.

"Just wonderful. Squid boy."

"He's not really a squid anymore, Dayzee," said Marilyn. "Remember that strange Moe character? That head soup deal?"

"Sis, he never was a squid. He just changed his name because he had one from that comet dug deep into his—"

"What on Earth are you three talking about?" said Kenzie. "Squids and soups and comets?"

"Um," said Dayzee, "blame it on Beverly Hills? Maybe?"

Kenzie just stared out at Cliff as he drew near, and the twins giggled in the backseat.

"And here we go," said Dayzee.

* * *

Dayzee let him rap on the glass before she lowered it.

"Cliff, so good to see you."

"I'm not entirely sure, Dayzee, but I think I might be back to being just Dirk. Is that alright with everyone?"

He leaned over to look all around in the limo.

"Oh, that's good," he said. "Kenzie's back."

Holding her gaze, he said, "I'd love to have you and your brother, Kozy, conniving and scheming and—"

Kenzie blurted out, "I remember Kozy. That was fun!"

Dirk grinned and squinted at the same time, and Dayzee leaned forward to get a better look at Kenzie.

"Just how much do you remember?" she said.

Kenzie pointed up toward the bedroom windows.

"You know what I'm talking about, Dayzee. Oh my God, that was so weird."

"Uh, weird in a good way, at least?"

"Oh yeah, Dayzee. Somehow, some way, we're going to get that going again like when I was, um, different, and—"

"Hey," said Sophia. "Enough with memory lane, alright? Sis and I want to get going on that maniac potion, so we'll need—"

"Corpses," said Marilyn. "Oops. I mean, cadavers."

Dirk said, "I still have no clue what's going on here, and I love it! All of you girls, just do whatever you want. All I ask is that you wait for a camera to do it. Alright? How's that for a plan?"

Dayzee turned back to him and said, "Uh, Dirk. We're not really planning to blow up the rating system just on this reality show, are we?"

"We could. We sure as hell could, girls. But no, you're right. We might have to edit out a few bits and pieces so the old ladies don't have fits and strokes and things."

"Fine," said Dayzee. "You asked for it, you got it."

Sophia got her hand in front of Dayzee and pointed up to the windows.

"Them, too, Dayzee. You know what I mean."

"I know what Sissy means. Those two odd things are in the script somewhere now too."

Dirk said, "I still don't have the slightest idea, but that's brilliant. Who needs writers? They could never think up stuff like this!"

"I can barely keep up with it myself," said Dayzee. "Still, we should probably—"

A lion's roar, followed by a scream, called out from the thick shrubbery near the entrance gate, which Dayzee had closed. All any of them could see was a few branches waving around until they came to rest.

"And, there's body number one," Sophia said with a smirk.

"Oh, Sissy, you mean cadaver."

"Cliff," said Dayzee. "I mean, Dirk. Do you have a head count for your crew?"

"Oh, that's funny, Dayzee," Sophia said while laughing comfortably.

"Thanks, Fia. I try sometimes."

"We tried counting them last time, Dayzee. Remember that?"

"I do remember, Mare. I don't think we know numbers that big."

"What on Earth is going on with all of you?" said Dirk. "I really have no clue!"

"I think I know," said Kenzie, then she turned to look out at the shrubs. "And this, what I just have to do, is for all kinds of reasons."

She powered down her window and leaned out, using her hands as a megaphone.

"Damn lions!"

Sophia grinned while shaking her head, and Marilyn giggled softly and clapped her hands.

Dayzee said, "We're heading for more reality than any audience is ready for."

∗   ∗   ∗

Dayzee and the twins were bringing Dirk toward the few porch steps that led to the front door, but Kenzie was leaning against the driver's door of the limo, scanning all around.

"Hey, Kenzie," said Dayzee, "I don't think saying that has much to do with actual lions."

"She's right," said Sophia. "It's all about you saying 'damn lions.' That's the thing."

"I bet Sissy has a few more things she'd like you to say," said Marilyn.

"Sis, there's no need to—"

"I like her saying 'damn lions' just fine," said Dayzee, then she gave a quick glance up at the bedroom windows.

While Sophia was saying, "If you and Kenzie can get that to work again the way you want, Dayzee, I want a front row seat."

"Ooh, if there's only one seat, Sissy, can I sit on your lap? I want to watch too."

"Sure, Sis. Plan on that even if nothing's going on. Even if there are lots of other seats. We can—"

"I hate to interrupt your indecipherable conversation," said Dirk, "but who in the dreadful reality show called hell are those two?"

Dayzee and the twins didn't even bother looking up.

"That's, um . . . they—"

"What Dayzee means," said Sophia, "is that those, um, particular individuals, that, um, you see up in that—"

Marilyn said, "They're Dayzee's parents!"

Dayzee's face froze in a snarl as she stared at Marilyn. Sophia shook from the laughter that she fought to contain. Marilyn only shrugged at Dayzee, then looked at Dirk.

"This is fantastic," he said. "It's just too good to be true! Yes, good, there are family members here for filming."

He pointed high over the roof and said, "Your guesthouse, Dayzee. Way at the back of your property. That's where we're planting those delightful parents of yours!"

"Uh, they probably should be planted, but I'm not so sure that they're anywhere near being delightful."

"I want to meet them!"

He looked toward the limo and waved his hand.

"Kenzie! Come on! Let's all go meet—"

"No!" said Dayzee. "Kenzie, you, uh, better stay with the car. In case, um, maybe if—"

"Need a quick getaway," said Marilyn. "That could happen."

Dirk looked at each of them and ended up with Sophia.

She shrugged, gave him an exaggerated smirk, then said, "Booze runs, Dirk. What else could possibly happen?"

He grinned and pointed at her, saying, "Well, this is still Beverly Hills, right? Am I right?"

Sophia's eyes got big and stopped blinking, then she said, "No. You too?"

Dayzee laughed and said, "It sure as hell isn't North Holly—"

They froze at another roar and another scream, then watched more shrubs bouncing but only for a few seconds.

All around the grounds, prisoner yard guys and Dirk's new film crew stopped to look, too, but they gave up after a few seconds and got back to work.

"Sure looks like a healthy supply of young men working around here."

Dirk looked around and said, "Well, yeah. I guess."

Dayzee looked at Sophia, who was nodding and grinning at her.

She then looked at Marilyn, who was bouncing her eyebrows and holding up two fingers. She mouthed the word, "fountains."

"Oh, boy," Dayzee said with an eye roll. "Sure, Dirk. Let's go meet my parents."

"Great! Are they from out of town?"

"Ha!" Marilyn said before her sister elbowed her.

"Come on, Sis. Let's go meet Dayzee's parents," she said.

"Fine. Dirk? Girls? Let's go see the folks."

Dayzee accepted Dirk's hand, and the twins held hands as they began the short walk toward the porch. But a loud call from somewhere across the grounds brought them all to a stop.

"Boss! Hey!"

Everyone turned around to watch the young man carrying a tall stack of cardboard boxes, looking first around one side, then the other, as he approached them.

*  *  *

"Chang, right?" said Dirk. "All of you fellows are new, but soon you'll be—"

"Dead!" Marilyn whispered to her sister, earning her another elbow strike and a quick laugh too.

"—my veteran crew."

"Yes, Boss. I am Chang."

"What exactly is your specialty, Chang?"

He turned enough that Dirk and everyone else could see him without the stack of boxes in the way. With a big grin, he shrugged and said, "I do not know!"

"Just wonderful," Dayzee said softly enough for only the twins to hear, causing a giggle from Marilyn and a smirk from Sophia.

"Well, the agency sent you, so we'll figure it out," said Dirk. "Say, what's in the boxes?"

Still turned, holding the boxes out of the way, Chang nodded and said, "Boxes!"

"Yes, we can all see that. But what is inside the boxes?"

"Ah," he said, nodding. "More boxes!"

"Oh, boy," mumbled Dayzee.

Sophia whispered to Marilyn, "I know what will be in those boxes soon, Sis."

"Heads, Sissy?"

Dirk abandoned Chang and his boxes and strained to hear what the Kildare Killers were saying.

"Is that enough?" said Sophia. "I mean, to trade for that miracle potion?"

"Oh, I don't know, Sissy. I think the Collectors want to collect each head's cadaver."

"Wait, Sis. The cadavers belong to the heads? That's how it works?"

"No, Sissy, I think all of that belongs to the Collectors once they collect it."

"That makes sense. So, we can use those boxes to—"

"For the life of me," said Dirk, "I have zero clue what these splendid twins are talking about. I love it, though! You all just launch yourselves into the most endearing adlibs at the drop of a hat. When the cameras—"

"I liked my hat," Kenzie said from the other side of the limo. "Where's my hat? Damn lions!"

Dayzee, the twins, and Dirk stared at her for a few seconds. Chang broke the silence by stumbling, tipping the boxes around, then restoring their balance.

"Uh-oh," said Marilyn. "She's losing her mind, Sissy."

Sophia blew Kenzie a kiss, then said to her sister, "She's still damn hot, though."

"With or without her hat?"

"Yep. Can't say that about her head, though, Sis."

"Nope."

Their dialog ended, they looked at Dirk, who was staring back at them and scratching his head. He shook it quickly and turned to address Chang.

"Why don't you get those supplies into the larger of the guesthouses, alright? We have some out-of-state dignitaries that will—"

"State?" Dayzee said, shaking her head at Dirk. "Sure. Okay. Let's go with that."

Dirk continued.

"Well, just get that place ready, Chang. We'll figure out what to do with you soon."

"If he's still around," said Sophia.

"Oh, Sissy, he's like that burnt, headless, blind, diamond-toothed Colombian cowboy. Remember him?"

Chang had left for the guesthouse, and Dirk turned to hear Sophia's reply to her sister. She looked at Dirk with a grin when she spoke.

"No, Sis. But I remember his cadaver."

"Girls," said Dayzee, "we'll figure out the cadaver situation later. Right now, we have a family reunion to get to."

"Wait," said Sophia. "Hold up a second."

They watched Chang stumble with his awkward cargo around the limo, then stop near Kenzie.

"Hi. You drive them around?"

"Yeah, but I'm not really a driver. I'm an—"

Dayzee yelled, "She's an actress!"

The twins giggled. Dirk stared at each of them, then back at Chang and Kenzie.

"Okay. Good. If you take breaks, I can drive. I drive good."

Sophia smirked and said, softly to Marilyn, "He'll be lucky to live long enough to finish that conversation."

"Yes, Sissy. How true. He's already mostly a corpse."

"Girls," said Dayzee, "give him a chance. He just might—"

"How much potion to you think you might want, Dayzee?"

"Oh, Fia. I think a lot."

"So," said Marilyn, "let the cadavering begin!"

"Okay," Kenzie said to Chang, "sure. I'll let you know."

"Okay!"

He turned too quickly and struggled to keep it all stacked, then he left for the guesthouse.

"Are we finally ready to meet the family?" said Dirk. "I can't wait!"

"Oh, boy. Sure. Let's go," Dayzee said, and she led them up the steps and toward the front door.

# Chapter 4 – More Crazy Than Thrilling

"Dayzee," said Dirk, "this door will never do for the show. Oh, unless we can come up with a fun story on how it got that way. Is there one? What happened to it?"

The wooden front door was shattered and split and a large section of it was gone altogether. A slab of plywood had been sloppily nailed over it.

"Dirk, we did get a carpenter for that, but he, um, got distracted?"

"He was a slacker," said Sophia.

"Yes, Sissy, and then he was a cadaver."

"I kind of wish we had what was left of him now. We could trade that for—"

"Well," said Dirk, reaching for the knob, "these conversations just get more bizarre all the time. I absolutely love it, and so will the viewers. It's a weird thing but sometimes, it's better if they have no idea what's going on."

He shook the door and squealed it into the house.

"They'll love our show, then," said Dayzee. "After you, Dirk."

"Don't mind if I do!"

He walked in, Dayzee followed, and the twins followed her. Marilyn was the last one in, and she left the damaged door open.

When Dirk saw the door still open, he looked at Marilyn, and she shrugged and said, "Um, quick getaways, remember?"

He pointed at her and said, "Yes. For booze or who knows what?"

"We never know what," said Dayzee. "It's all a surprise to us too. Okay, up the stairs to—"

"Dayzee!"

Kenzie was in the yard, yelling while looking around the house.

"See?" Sophia said with a smirk. "There's always an emergency."

"Dayzee, your parents will have to be patient. First, let's go see what Kenzie—"

"Oh, no, Dirk. You stay inside. The girls and I will take a look."

She pinched his cheek and said, "Be right back."

* * *

All three girls walked over to Kenzie, then stopped and looked where she was pointing: toward the guesthouse which Chang had entered. The door was open, and two lions were slowly backing themselves out through the doorway.

"Did we call this, or what?" Dayzee said, allowing herself a few good laughs.

Both of the lions were chomping down on the collar of Chang's shirt, and probably him, too, and dragging him out of the guesthouse.

Sophia smirked and said, "I'm surprised he lasted this long."

Marilyn giggled, pointed at Kenzie, and said, "Oh, Kenzie, you know what to say. Say it!"

Kenzie grimaced, turned to watch the limp body being dragged toward the bushes, then faced the girls again.

"Damn lions," she said, still frowning.

"Oh, come on," said Dayzee. "A little enthusiasm, alright?"

Kenzie shook her head, and her frown softened.

"Damn lions."

Marilyn pushed up both corners of her mouth into a manufactured smile.

"Try it again, Kenzie. And smile!"

Kenzie gave up and laughed, then said, "Damn lions!"

"Yep," said Sophia. "That's just the way things go around here."

Dayzee nodded and said, "In Beverly Hills. Yeah. So, what do you think? Forget it being a guesthouse and call it a deathhouse?"

"I like that," said Sophia. "Good one."

"Thanks, Fia."

"Can we start calling the other guesthouse that, too, or do we have to wait?"

"Well, Mare, it might be more accurate to wait until—"

"None of you are really taking any of this seriously enough," Kenzie said.

"Ooh, look!" said Marilyn.

Two different female mountain lions, each holding one of Chang's boxes in her jaw, stood in the doorway and squinted as they studied the yard.

"Oh, boy," said Dayzee. "What now?"

"I bet there are heads in those boxes."

"I think Sissy's right. Those lady lions seem to be always prowling for head. They even packaged them up."

"Girls, no. Those boxes aren't big enough for human heads."

"See, Dayzee?" said Kenzie, frowning over the limo at her. "It's only getting worse. Yes, it's all kind of crazy and thrilling, but it's more crazy than thrilling."

"Eh," said Dayzee. "You take the thrills with a little crazy. So what?"

Sophia said, "I'll see your crazy and thrilling and raise you a few ripe cadavers."

"Ooh," said Marilyn, "yes! And I'll see all of that and raise you a batch or a ton of insane cosmic potion!"

"That's what you're calling it, Sis?"

Marilyn shrugged and said, "Well, why not, Sissy?"

"Huh. Okay."

"Girls, that's all fun, but we have lady lion issues right now."

Kenzie said, "None of you are taking this seriously. It's going to get worse. I can feel it."

"Oh, don't worry," said Sophia. "Until you're actually a member of the cadaver club, you—"

"I like that, Sissy. That's funny."

"—you don't need to—"

"All of you, look! They're on the move!" said Dayzee.

The lions held their boxes and began rushing back toward the front of the house, causing the girls to hurry behind the limo.

Dayzee watched them. The Kildare Killers watched them. All of the crew guys watched them.

The lions got to the front of the house, then leaped onto a trellis that spanned the full height of Dayzee's mansion. Their claws scraped and they growled as they climbed to the second floor, where they jumped into the room where the Collectors were waiting.

Keeping her eyes on the window, Dayzee said, "I think I'm starting to get what Dirk has been saying: I have no idea what in the hell is going on around here."

"See?" said Kenzie. "What the hell was that with those lions?"

"Oh, I know," said Sophia. "Those lions are delivering invitations to the club."

"What club?"

Marilyn nodded and offered a pleasant smile.

"Why, the cadaver club, Kenzie."

"You're all so—"

"Hot?" said Dayzee. "Thanks, so are—"

"No! I mean, yeah, but—"

"We'll figure it out later. Girls, let's go see what this is all about. Kenzie, can you guard the limo for a while?"

"Sure."

Dayzee took both Kildare Killers by their hands and aimed for the shattered front door.

*　*　*

"Hey!"

They all stopped.

"What now, Kenzie?"

"It won't be as easy in there as you think."

She pointed up and said, "Look."

Dayzee led the twins back to the limo, and they all looked up to the window where the lions had climbed in.

"Um, Dayzee, maybe Kenzie is kind of right," said Sophia.

"Yeah, Fia. Uh-huh."

"Those Collector things were already some kind of weirdos, Dayzee. They didn't need to start doing that kind of nonsense too."

"Uh, no. You're right, Mare."

Both Collectors stood in the window, and the girls could just make out the different colors of feathers in their fedoras—the only distinguishing difference between them—and knew that the female of the two was on the right.

And she was holding up her left hand, as if she were waving without moving it.

And it was burning like a perfect little torch.

"Uh, Dayzee?" said Sophia. "Maybe we should get the hell out of here."

"You might be right, Fia. That's . . . that's . . ."

"Kind of weird even for Beverly Hills," said Marilyn.

"Yeah, Mare. Uh-huh. But it's just her hand, and she—"

The female Collector crossed her hand over to her male counterpart, touched it against his head for just a second, and his head, just the top of it, became a larger, brighter torch.

"Oh, boy. Girls, we still have to go in there."

"Uh, to save Dirk?"

"No, Fia. Not for Dirk."

"To, um, save those poor little lions?"

"God, no, Mare. Uh-uh."

From behind them, they heard Kenzie say, "Because you're all crazy enough to join that club?"

None of them turned away from the sight of the Collector's head burning while his teeth chattered silently.

"No, dammit. None of that. Girls, and Kenzie, this is my goddamn mansion. No twisted, freaky—"

"Chattering."

"Yeah, Fia. No chattering—"

"Burning."

"Thanks, Mare. Yeah. No chattering, burning trash from some portal in my basement is—"

"It's not in your basement, Dayzee."

"I know, Fia. It's just too much trouble to give the proper directions to it. All I'm trying to say is that there's no way they're burning down my mansion. Let's go kick some Collector ass!"

Dayzee held a hand out to each of the Kildare Killers.

Sophia took one and said, "Huh. This should be fun."

Marilyn giggled and said, "Any excuse to hold your hand, Dayzee."

"You're both right. Finally, I think we're ready to—"

"Hey, wait!" Kenzie yelled behind them.

Without turning around, Dayzee said, "Maybe that girl needs to join the club you were talking about."

"Oh, Dayzee, no!" said Marilyn. "Who would drive us?"

Sophia leaned around Dayzee to see her sister and said, "Sis, she's more than just a driver."

"Oh, yes, Sissy. Especially all the times you were with her upstairs, almost always in one bed or another, and neither of you seemed to like to wear any—"

"Alright, Sis. We get it."

"So do you, Sissy."

"Girls, let's just see what that actress wants this time."

Sophia rolled her eyes and shook her head, and Marilyn said, "Besides Sissy, you mean?"

"Mare, if we play this right, maybe we can get Kozy back. How's that sound?"

Marilyn clapped her hands and said, "Yay, Kozy!"

# Chapter 5 – They Really Are on Fire

Dayzee and the twins turned to look back at Kenzie, who had moved to their side of the limo when the lions were roaming about and making their deliveries.

She'd called them over her shoulder and then resumed her study of the tall, thick hedges on each side of the entrance gate. From leaning over the hood, both palms flat on the clean metal, Kenzie's skirt had traveled up, revealing more generously her long, toned legs.

"Oh, my, Sissy. That's not acting. Those legs are real."

"Strong, too, Sis," said Sophia. "When she pinned me down upstairs, back when we were trying to kill that first assassin, I—"

Marilyn giggled and said, "That's a good word, Sissy: 'assassin.' Two asses, your and hers, and then the word 'in.' I could take some guesses what that all adds up to. Ask me. I dare you."

"Girls," said Dayzee, "Kenzie might be right about this all getting out of control. We can give some careful attention to all of our asses later."

To Kenzie, Dayzee called out, "What, Kenzie? More lions?"

She spoke over her shoulder again, still teasing with her long legs, and said, "I'm taking a break from guarding the limo. I want to see what's going on in the bushes."

Dayzee smirked and said, "Huh. At least I know she's not talking about any of us."

"Good one, Dayzee."

"Thanks, Fia. Hang on, Kenzie, we'll come with you."

"And just like that," said Marilyn, "we're back to that word about Kenzie's ass and Sissy's ass and—"

"Mare, let's get this done, then we have to stop those freak Collectors from burning down the mansion, alright?"

"Oh, fine."

Dayzee, still holding their hands, brought them to join Kenzie, and they all began a slow procession toward the shrubbery, stopping only occasionally to pry spiky heels out of the turf.

*　*　*

All four of them stopped alongside the tall wall of evergreen shrubs which bordered most of Dayzee's estate.

Kenzie pointed and said, "Here's where one of them got dragged in."

"Chang?"

"No, I don't think so, Dayzee. One of the other ones."

"Do they all even have names?" said Marilyn. "Wouldn't it be easier if they didn't?"

"Sis has a point. They're just going to lose their heads anyway."

"We don't know that, girls," said Dayzee. "Maybe they'll keep their heads this time."

Marilyn laughed and said, "That won't stop them from looking for more."

"Good one, Sis. Yep."

"Kenzie? You dragged us out here, and it wasn't easy with the pointy heels we're all wearing. Lead on."

"What? I never said I was going in there."

"You can't see anything from out here," said Dayzee.

Then, she leaned to look past Kenzie and said, "Wait. I thought I saw a flash of orange in there somewhere."

"A lion?"

"No, Mare. Prisoner."

"Prison lion food."

30

"That's funny, Sissy, but true too."

Dayzee turned to glance up at the Collectors, who still burned like candles in an upstairs bedroom window. She shook her head and looked again at the wall of bushes.

"You know we need cadavers, Dayzee."

"Yeah, Mare. Yeah, we do."

"For that nirvana potion. Lots of it."

"Yeah, Fia," said Dayzee. "Fine. I'll lead the search for the lion bait."

She parted the branches enough to walk through, and Kenzie and the twins followed, all complaining about getting scratched.

Through the thick foliage, they stood in a narrow alley between the dense growth and the high wrought iron fence. A mat of pine needles cushioned their steps, and only light traffic was passing in each direction on Dayzee's street.

"Well," she said, pointing, "that was easy enough."

"I see his head," said Marilyn. "He still has it."

They all took a few steps closer to the orange jumpsuited man lying flat on his back.

"Sheesh," said Sophia. "That's different."

"See?" Kenzie said with her voice rising. "This is getting out of control. What the hell is this about?"

"Kenzie, those lady lions took this gentleman's feet. That's not so weird."

"Um, Dayzee," Marilyn said while tugging on the sleeve of her blouse. "That is kind of weird. We've never seen that before."

"Special order," said Sophia. "Feet to go."

Kenzie's stare was locked on where the man's feet should have been, Marilyn waited with her eyebrows up high, and Dayzee's slowly shaking head evolved into a grin toward Sophia.

"Fia, that's brilliant. You Kildare Killers—I just love you! Yes, I think you're right."

"I don't get it."

"Mare, think about it. Those boxes that Dead Chang carried into—"

"That's what we're calling him now?" said Sophia. "We don't even know that he's dead."

"Yet, Fia. Let's get a jump on things. Okay, back to the boxes. They were too small for human heads, right?"

"Oh, I see," said Marilyn. "Human feet, though?"

"Yeah, Mare. The only question is why."

Kenzie pried her eyes away from the dead guy and said, "Uh, you know what?"

"I sure do," said Marilyn. "This one won't be dancing."

"Sis, they never were dancing. And besides, that assassin is—"

"Ass. Ass," she said with a giggle.

"—that assassin is long gone. Ordinary dead guys are no problem."

Kenzie groaned and said, "You know, to ordinary people, dead guys sure are some kind of problem."

She panted and looked at each of them in turn.

Marilyn giggled softly and worked the straps of her white dress down over her shoulders, then peeled the cloth down to reveal her breasts.

"Really, Sis? Why?"

"Why not is the question, Sissy. Oh, it's only because it'll cheer up Kenzie."

Kenzie had locked her eyes on Marilyn's bare breasts.

"See? It works."

"Huh," said Sophia. "Yeah, that always works. Me too."

She quickly unbuttoned her blouse, then snapped open the clasp of her bra, and pulled everything to the sides.

Kenzie's eyes got dragged to her breasts instead.

"I think I saw a smile," said Sophia.

Kenzie laughed once, kept smiling, and kept gazing at Sophia's breasts.

"Oh, what the hell," Dayzee said, and she bared hers too.

"Well," said Kenzie, "that's, um, that's way better than—"

A lion roared from one side of them, then another from the other side.

"Girls, I think lady lions are liking what they see too."

"How could they not?"

"Good point, Fia."

"Ha!"

"I wasn't even trying to be funny, Mare. Kenzie, you give us a fun view of yours too. Right now, quick, then we need to get back to—"

"Isn't there another dead guy back here somewhere?" said Kenzie.

"Eh," said Dayzee. "We haven't confirmed that he's dead yet. Besides, lions have to eat. Let's get—"

"I'm sure that he's footless," Sophia said with a smirk.

"And not dancing, Sissy."

"What about Chang?" Kenzie said while unbuttoning her blouse. "Shouldn't we try to find him, at least?"

"Oh, Kenzie, he's too dead for us to worry about."

"How can you be sure?"

Dayzee grinned while buttoning up.

"Easy. Because his name is Dead Chang."

*　*　*

Dayzee led the way back out onto the lawn, still buttoning up her blouse, and Marilyn and Sophia waited until they were free of the grabbing branches and thorns before bothering to begin.

When Dayzee stopped, so did the other three.

She pointed at each of the crew members outside and working, moving from left to right, and said, "Dead. Dead. Dead."

"Who's going to kill all of them?" Kenzie said in a strained voice. "Why do they all have to die?"

"It's kind of a barter system," Sophia said after she'd changed her mind and popped open the top button of her blouse.

"We'll need bigger boxes," Marilyn said with a shrug.

"No, we won't, Mare. We just need to deliver them to the Collectors, somehow, then we can—"

"Who or what are the Collectors?"

"Oh, Kenzie, see that pair of flaming freaks up there?"

She pointed to the candles in the window.

"Your parents? Oh my God, they really are on fire!"

"Relax, they'll be fine," said Dayzee.

Sophia said, "How can they just burn like that without burning up?"

"Oh, I know," said Marilyn. "They're like wax dummies or something."

"No, they're not. I can see their teeth chattering from here!"

"Well, Kenzie, maybe they're cold?"

"Sis, think about what you just said."

Marilyn looked down and kicked at the grass.

"Oh. You're right, Sissy. They're probably pretty toasty."

"That head and that hand anyway."

"Girls, let's just get up there and figure this out."

While walking and holding the twins' hands, Dayzee tipped her head and said, "Remind me to get a carpenter out here for that door."

"Dayzee, that's just silly," said Marilyn. "We've tried that before."

"Sis is right. How many carpenters have died, then come back to life, then had to be killed again?"

"I don't know the exact number, girls, but whatever it is, we'll have to add at least one."

"Yep. Call Dead Carpenter, Dayzee."

"That's funny, Sissy."

# Chapter 6 – Flames Are Flaming to Inflame

After taking two steps through the doorway, Dayzee said over her shoulder, "Kenzie, maybe you should just—"

"No way, Dayzee. With all those lions? I'm not staying out there alone!"

She stood in the open doorway with her back to the yard, her eyes pleading with Dayzee and the twins.

"They're just cats, Kenzie."

"Hungry cats," Sophia said with a quick smirk. "But they still prefer—"

"Prison lion bait."

"Sis is right. They—"

A loud scream behind Kenzie got cut off by a savage growl. Kenzie didn't turn to see. Only her eyes, twice their normal size, showed her reaction.

"Okay, fine," said Dayzee. "Come on in. First, we have to find Dirk. Then, I'm going upstairs to—"

Dayzee shivered and turned to look at the landing at the top of the formal, gently curving grand staircase to the second floor.

The Collectors, their small brown teeth still chattering silently, a head and a hand still on fire, stared down at them with eyes set in pale yellow faces.

Each wore a black pin-striped suit jacket over a black shirt, and their matching trousers fell without wrinkles down to their brown work boots and visible white socks.

The invader on the left lifted his hat, which was engulfed in flames and hid the single black feather that the girls had seen at the Prism when they'd first arrived.

His mate, on the right, held her hand up to keep the flames from her hat, which sported a single gray feather—the only way to tell them apart.

The Collector on the left chattered his teeth for a few seconds more, neat rows of them lined up in a gash that stretched across his face above his squared-off chin.

Then, his chattering stopped. Both Collectors stared down.

Dayzee, the twins, and Kenzie stared up.

"We chanced a chance on our chance to bed each other in a bedroom bed."

"Sheesh," said Sophia. "That stink will never wash out."

"Oh, Sissy, don't joke. They're too scary."

"Uh-huh," said Dayzee with her hands on her hips. "Our deal didn't say anything about you sneaking into my mansion for some Collector fornication. And what the hell? Put out the goddamn fires, alright?"

He lowered his blazing hat back onto his head, and his teeth resumed their rapid, silent chattering for a moment, then stopped.

"These flames are flaming to inflame our lust as we lust after—"

"Hey," said Dayzee. "Just put out the damn flaming flames. Now!"

Both of them continued to chatter without a sound, and their fires died out like some dial had been turned.

"Thank you. Now, what do—hey, can she talk?"

"Not only can she talk. She can talk about talking, sometimes without even talking."

"Well," Sophia said with a smirk, "that pretty little thing is the talk of the town."

"Sissy, shh! That sure is funny, though."

"Well, let's hear it, then," said Dayzee.

Her chattering stopped, and it sounded like she was clearing her throat, which caused a few bloody lumps to coast out over her thin bottom lip and drop onto the stairs.

"Sheesh, what the hell is that?"

Kenzie groaned and collapsed, and no one even looked.

"She's a pretty little thing, Sissy. You said so," Marilyn said, then giggled nervously.

The female Collector rubbed her lips together, then said, "Those flames were flaming to inflame our lust as—"

"Oh, just stop," said Dayzee. "Look, if you're just going to repeat The Collector's lines, you might as well—"

"Her name is also The Collector."

He began careful, robotic steps downward, and she matched him like a mirror image.

"Yeah," Sophia said under her breath, "come on down and party with us."

"Oh, Sissy, be nice. They have spectacular potion, remember?"

"Oh, you're right, Sis. Can't forget that."

"Girls, stop whispering back there. This is serious."

"We'll try, Dayzee."

"Okay," Dayzee said to the Collectors, "we need to fix this right now, before this operation goes any further. We need to give your 'sweetest sweet sweetness' a name of her own."

"I remember that," Sophia said to her sister. "That's how he described her at the Prism."

"Spitting bloody chunks on Dayzee's steps sure is—"

"Girls, hold up. Well, handsome, how about it?"

Marilyn whispered to her sister, "Dayzee called him that at the Prism, Sissy!"

"Sarcasm, Sis. She does have a good memory, though."

"Shh, girls."

The Collectors turned their beady, close-set eyes on each other for a second, then focused again on Dayzee.

"Well, very well," he said.

"He kind of slacked on that one, Sis."

"Sure, Sissy, but he still stuck some weirdness in there."

"Girls."

His jaw rested and when he began clearing his throat, Dayzee and the twins each took a step back.

But no bits of gore dribbled out.

"She is a beauty in her beautiful ways, more beauteous even than—"

"Beauty?" said Dayzee. "We're calling her Beauty?"

The Collector tipped his head, let his teeth fly for a second, then stopped them and straightened back up.

"No. Lola."

"Huh. Makes as much sense as anything else. What do you girls think?"

"As long as her potion checks out," said Sophia, "she can call herself any goddamn thing she wants. Sis?"

"Ha! I bet Betty would be a better name!"

"You betcha, Sis! Better believe it!"

"Girls, you have to stop! That's pretty funny, though, Mare. Okay, The Collector and . . . Lola. We need to move you out to—"

"We will first collect for our collection the cadaver which you have cadaverized for us."

He raised a long, bony finger with one more joint than a human's to point at Kenzie, lying unconscious behind Dayzee and the twins. Every one of his fingers sported large, bone-white rings.

"Huh?" said Dayzee. "Hell, no! You can't take—"

Sophia bumped her and said, "Potion, Dayzee. We're so close."

"She's not even really an actress," said her sister. "And barmaids are a dime a dozen."

"Girls! We can't let them take Kenzie!"

Marilyn sighed and said, "Ooh, for just a bit of that potion, maybe we could give them just part of her?"

"Sheesh, Sis."

Dayzee stared from one to the other, then Sophia leaned toward her sister.

"Uh, not her boobs, though. I kind of like those."

"Oh, Sissy, and remember the whole bit about the word 'assassin?'"

"No, not that part either. It would have to be—"

"Girls! Kildare Killers! We're not giving them Kenzie, not when there's an endless supply of corpses out there that—"

"Cadaver Collectors collect cadavers," he said, then froze in place with his teeth chattering silently.

"Yes, cadavers. We know."

Dayzee looked down, laughed a few times, and pointed at their shoes.

"Hey, didn't you two have gigantic hooves when you got here? What's with the work boots?"

"Two future cadavers didn't wait for the future to become cadavers. They parted with these parts so that we could partake of participation with normal walking particulars."

Marilyn sang, "And a partridge in a pear tree."

"Good one, Sis. All I had was, 'sounds like a fun party.'"

"You Collector things are exhausting," Dayzee said, staring at The Collector's beady eyes.

She pointed quickly at Lola and said, "You too, Lola."

Marilyn leaned forward to whisper in Dayzee's ear.

"Dayzee, didn't the lions get those feet? How did that happen?"

Dayzee nodded, cleared her throat, then said to both Collectors, "You, uh, kind of boss around mountain lions now?"

"For a fee, felines will suspend feelings and show fealty to—"

Dayzee held up a hand. He switched from talking to chattering.

"I'm done asking questions," said Dayzee. "You know what? I don't even care."

"Sissy," Marilyn whispered, "what kind of fee are they—"

"Hello! A little help?"

They all stopped at the sound of Dirk screaming from somewhere in the house.

"Oh, I forgot about him," said Dayzee.

"Squid boy."

"He's not a squid anymore, Sissy. That Moe guy's head that we put in a blender fixed him right up."

"We should check the pool later, Sis. I bet there's a giant squid splashing around and—"

"Girls, he was never a squid. We should check the pool, though. That's a good idea."

To the Collectors, she said, "Before we get you settled into your own personal residence, we—"

"The deathhouse," Sophia said, then snickered.

"So true, Sissy."

"—we need to check on an associate. So, seat yourselves in one of the seats in—"

"Seattle?"

"Close. But still funny, Sissy."

"—in the living room. It's right over there."

All three girls watched silently as the Cadaver Collectors walked past them mechanically and toward Dayzee's living room.

When they were at their closest point to the girls, the male Collector stopped walking, then stopped chattering, then took a deep breath.

"Whoa. No, mister. Uh-uh. We've had enough out of you for now."

He tipped his hat while getting his teeth busy again, then followed Lola to the living room.

"Well done."

"Thanks, Fia. Okay, so what about Kenzie?"

"We could undress her, Dayzee."

"Really, Mare? That's your best idea?"

Marilyn pouted while her sister said, "No. Let's take her upstairs and undress her."

"If we had time, girls. If we had time! But we need to fish that squid out of whatever trouble he's splashed himself into."

Sophia smirked and said, "Now, that's a good one, Dayzee."

# Chapter 7 – I'm Donating the Booze

"If she wasn't mostly unconscious, that would be pretty hot."

Sophia shook her head and said, "It's still pretty hot, Dayzee."

They'd managed to pick Kenzie up onto her spiky heels, but she was still wobbly, so the twins hugged her close from each side. Kenzie's arms were up and over their shoulders.

"Yeah, Fia."

"Just think if we did what I suggested," Marilyn said with a pout.

"Oh, even hotter. Yeah, undressed," said Dayzee. "We'll get to that later, girls."

"How about now, Dayzee?" said Sophia. "All that talk about exploding potions has got me—"

"It's exploding potions now?"

"Sure. Yeah, I bet. Anyway, I'm itchy as hell, and I—"

"Me too, Dayzee," said Marilyn. "Let's all go upstairs, get undressed, wake up Kenzie or leave her asleep, then—"

"Mare? We do have a few things going on, you know. Mountain lions. Prison lion chow and film crew chow. Even Dead Chang is out there—"

"Dancing!"

"No, Mare, and neither are those two that donated their particular parts to the Collector party."

"Good one, Dayzee."

"Thanks, Fia."

"Hello? I could really use some help!"

"Ugh, and there's that squid guy too," said Sophia.

"Fia, try to be more compassionate. He's filming us in our very own reality show, isn't he?"

"If he lives long enough," Marilyn said with a deep sigh.

"True. Either way, let's go see what his deal is."

*　*　*

Dayzee walked behind the twins as they supported Kenzie between them. She took sliding steps, sometimes stumbling and sometimes mumbling.

"Well, we're not moving fast," said Dayzee, "but it's a hell of a view from back here."

Marilyn giggled and said, "I'm sure it looks like there's an assassassin in your mansion!"

"Good one, Sis."

"That really was, Mare. I'm not arguing. Oh, look at that closet door. We should have remembered that those portal trash characters came—"

"The Collectors?" said Sophia.

"Uh-uh, Sissy. One of them is Lola."

"Yeah, those freaks," said Dayzee. "They came up through there because some kind of portal is down there in the basement."

"It's not in the basement, Dayzee," said Sophia. "Remember Bruno? He said 'stairs, door, tunnel, then portal.'"

"Either way. So, where is—"

"Oh, thank God!" Dirk said from somewhere in the darkness of the stairwell in a room beyond the torn-up drywall at the back of the closet. "This is wild down here. We'll need some good lights if we're going to film whatever the hell is going on down here."

"Uh, Dirk? How about if we just get you up out of there first?"

"Sure, Dayzee. That's a good plan. Then, we'll have a pleasant chat with your parents. Then, we can—"

"Wait, Dirk. Why are you down there in the dark?"

"Oh, these stairs are all beat to hell. I kind of twisted an ankle. If the stairs weren't destroyed, I could have—"

"They're destroyed?"

Sophia whispered to Dayzee, "Remember those hooves that those freaks used to have?"

"Before they got new parts?" added Marilyn.

"Oh, yeah. Okay. Hey, Dirk, we'll get you out. We'll need a flashlight. Maybe a drink or two first. Then, we can—"

"Dayzee, no drinks!" said Dirk. "Hey, did you hear that?"

"Nope. What?"

"It looks like an old wooden door, also beat to shit, and there are funny noises coming from the other side."

"Funny, how?"

"Uh, like blind horses?"

"Uh-oh," said Marilyn.

"Things with hooves," said Sophia. "In the dark."

"Not in Dirk. Just in dark, Dayzee."

"That's helpful, Mare."

"Dayzee? Can you girls get me out of here?"

"Sure. Hang on."

She leaned away and slammed the closet door, splintering it more.

Sophia grinned and said, "It would save time if you could just call a Dead Carpenter, Dayzee."

"Thanks, Fia. That's helpful too. Let's go find a flashlight."

"What about her?"

"Oh, just set her down, Mare."

"Then, undress her real quick?"

Dayzee watched Sophia grin back at her and bounce her eyebrows a few times.

"Well, I'm tempted, Fia. But a squid is about to get stampeded by corpse collecting—"

"Cadaver collecting, Dayzee."

"Right, cadaver collecting horses from some unknown portal at the bottom of one of three stairways—that we know of—in this giant house."

* * *

Dayzee aimed the beam through the drywall and followed it into the dim room housing a circular stairway. She looked up and chuckled at the skylight so high above.

Marilyn looked, too, and said, "Is that in the attic, Dayzee? Or is it somehow even higher?"

"Damn, this place has roofs that we don't even know about. We'll figure that out later."

"Dayzee," said Sophia, "point that light at the stairs for a second."

She did, and they saw that the old stones were cracked and chipped and crumbled.

"That's why I only wear stylish heels," Sophia said while nodding at the sight.

"And you sure wear them well, Fia. No horseshoes for you?"

"Maybe if Kenzie wanted to play rodeo with her, Dayzee."

"Chaps, sure, Sis. I don't know about horseshoes, though."

"Chaps would be sexy, Sissy. Oh, and a riding crop. You could sure teach her a few things. Ooh, or maybe she could—"

"Girls? Remember Dirk?"

"Vaguely."

"Wonderful, Fia. Even after he bankrolled you and your sister because he was such a big fan."

"He still is a fan, Dayzee. He wants to make us all even more famous with 'Kildare in the Hills.'"

"Only if we get him out of this mess, right, Mare?"

"Oh, I suppose so. Okay."

"Hey, Dirk! The twins are coming down there to help you up."

"We are? Says who?"

"Fia, you and your sister have been practicing toting living bodies around with Kenzie. You're perfect for the job."

"Fine. Come on, Sis."

She took Marilyn's hand, and they carefully placed their steps on the damaged stones, with a flashlight beam bouncing around to lead the way.

*   *   *

While the twins held Dirk, who was favoring his injured ankle and covered with dust, they all looked down on Kenzie, still not awake and lying near the closet.

"Girls, why don't you take him to the great room. I'll—"

"Stay here and undress Kenzie all for yourself?"

Dayzee stared for a second, then said, "Well, as tempting as that sounds, no. Dump him, then—"

"Uh, dump me?"

"On the couch? Okay? Then, come back here for Kenzie."

"And what exactly are you contributing to all this work?"

"Well, Fia, I'm donating the booze. I'll even mix it all up and serve it!"

*   *   *

"She sure does look like that Kozy fellow," Dirk said, seated on the couch with Kenzie leaning against his shoulder and snoring.

"Doesn't she, though? Way better boobs," said Sophia.

"Sissy's right. They're different, anyway."

"Here are your drinks, girls."

Dayzee handed cocktails to each of them.

"I'll be back with yours in a second, Dirk."

"It's been quite a day already, Dayzee. Why not bring the second, too, while you're at it?"

"Good idea."

Dayzee went back to the bar, and Sophia said, "Hey, Sis, talking about different boobs, what if we could split Kenzie in half? You know, half of each?"

Dirk stared at her until Marilyn spoke.

"Not up and down, though, Sissy. Maybe at the waist?"

"Oh, yeah, good point. It wouldn't make sense to split some things."

Dirk was again staring at Sophia, his head shaking slowly.

"Which one of them would be on the bottom, Sissy? And which one on top?"

"Well, both ways could be fun. Hey, remember when we wanted some kind of switch built into her?"

"Yeah, or a secret word or something."

"Yeah, Sis, like that. If we had either of those, we could change top and bottom back and forth as many times as—"

"Dirk," Dayzee said as she extended a large drink glass out to him, "here's your double. Hey, are you alright? Those eyeballs are about ready to pop out."

"It's just these remarkable twins, Dayzee. Whatever comedy routine they just practiced was gold. Absolute gold! I didn't understand a bit of it, but it was perfect for the show. The audience will never know what hit them."

Some thumping against the door to the garage, down at the end of a hallway, got all of them to look. Even Kenzie opened her eyes for a second, then slumped again into Dirk.

"Speaking of getting hit," said Dayzee. "What now?"

"I'll go see," said Sophia. "Be right back."

"The last time this happened, Sissy came running back and said a bunch of dead guys were getting into the house. Oh, and we were all mostly naked too. Oh, and the boss was tied to—"

"Tied to the idea of giving us all raises, Mare. Yeah, I remember."

Sophia set her drink down and got up. Before she began her walk to investigate, her sister said, "Let's see that strut, Sissy."

"It's all I know, Sis."

She began an exaggerated strut down the hallway, and all eyes were on her the entire time. Even Kenzie sat up, rubbed her eyes, and stared at the sight before fading out again.

* * *

When Sophia returned, she wasn't running, and she wasn't strutting either.

"Here we go again," she said and plopped down next to Kenzie, who sighed and slumped over onto her instead.

"Huh," said Dirk. "It was nice while it lasted. What's wrong with her?"

"Just too many thrills around here. She'll be fine. So, what's the story, Fia?"

Sophia leaned enough to look at Dirk first, then at Dayzee.

"Um, things and parts of things are being, uh, collected. Sort of."

Dayzee looked quickly toward the living room, then back to Sophia.

"But those Coll—my parents are—"

"Oh, no, not them. The, uh, neighborhood cats. Someone left a garage door open, and a sloppy little pile is—"

"How sloppy, Sissy?"

"Well? I'll just say that it's good that you have a sewer kind of thing in your garage floor, Dayzee."

Dayzee grinned and tipped her head, waiting.

"We're waiting, Sissy."

"Okay, fine. Sheesh."

"And there we go," said Dayzee. "Even without an assassin, we—"

"You still have your very own assassassin, Dayzee," Marilyn said with a giggle.

"Right. Yeah, I sure do. Um, Fia, were you sure to lock that door?"

"I tried, but it's still broken. Hey, maybe get a Dead Carpenter for each door? There's a lot of them that need fixing."

"What on Earth is going on in this house?" said Dirk.

Sophia scoffed and said, "Nothing much to do with Earth."

"Maybe a comet, Sissy."

"Yeah, or that place where Bruno got crushed down to size. Remember that?" said Dayzee. "Well, never mind that. Let's finish our drinks, maybe swill down a few more, then—"

"Meet your parents?" said Dirk. "Yes, I'm really eager to work out some plot points with—"

Dayzee was staring toward the living room and saw light flickering on the walls and coming from where she'd left the Collectors.

"Oh, boy. Hold up on that, Dirk."

She chugged her drink and slammed the tumbler onto the bar.

"Girls, maybe use that kitchen stairway and give Dirk another tour upstairs, alright?"

"How good of a tour, Dayzee?"

"Oh, Mare, he's injured, remember? Really show him a nice time."

"What about Kenzie?"

"I'll keep an eye on her, Fia. But first, I need to—"

"Undress her."

"Mare, if everything else checks out okay, hell yeah. I'm undressing her."

Dayzee hurried to pour more whiskey in her glass and downed it quickly.

"Shoo! Both of you! Dirk, you just hobble along as well as you can."

He glanced at Kenzie, then said, "I, uh, wouldn't mind watching when you undress—"

"Just go! All three of you!"

*   *   *

Dayzee watched the twins walking along with Dirk, each holding an arm, until they'd traveled up the kitchen stairway and out of sight.

She'd just picked up her drink when a crash, sounds of splintering wood, and eager growling stopped her cold. But only for a second. She finished the drink and set down the glass before looking along the hallway to the garage.

"Oh, this is getting so out of control."

A large female lion's tail appeared first, then the rest of her as she backed toward Dayzee's great room. In her jaw was clamped one arm of a headless guy in an orange jumpsuit, and she dragged him along one step at a time.

"Why with the heads all the time?"

She dropped down to kneel in front of Kenzie and said, "Kenzie, wake up. You really have to wake up."

Kenzie didn't wake up.

Dayzee gave the approaching lioness another glance.

"Kenzie, seriously, it's no time to tune out."

Kenzie stayed tuned out, so Dayzee rose up, then sat on her lap and held her face in both hands.

"Kenzie!"

She let go enough to slap each cheek.

"Kenzie, really, come on!"

She gave the lion another look, and the lion turned enough to look back, her face fur matted with blood.

"Oh, boy."

She gave each cheek another slap.

"Kenzie! This is serious!"

She wound up to strike again, and Kenzie opened her eyes, saw Dayzee's hand, and grinned.

"I sure have been bad, Dayzee. I've been a very bad—"

"No, it's not like that. I'm just trying to—"

"Take control? I can play that game with—"

"No, look!" she said and tipped her head toward the lion, who had dropped the cadaver and was sniffing in all directions.

"Oh my God," Kenzie said and hugged Dayzee close.

Dayzee said, "If ever there was a time to say it, Kenzie, this is it!"

Kenzie held Dayzee by both arms, leaned her back, and took a deep breath.

Then, to the bloody lion, she screamed, "Damn lions!"

# Chapter 8 – Stripped Together Upside Down

"Alright, Kenzie, we have to move!"

Dayzee tried to step back down from Kenzie's lap, but Kenzie didn't let her go. She only pulled her in closer again.

"Save me, Dayzee! Save me!"

She looked up at Dayzee, who shook her head while looking directly down at her.

"Damn," she said, "if we weren't about to get mauled by murdering lions and covered with headless dead lion bait, I'd—"

"Slap me again?"

"Kenzie, what's wrong with you?" Dayzee said as she wiggled her arms free, causing all kinds of bouncing.

Kenzie looked straight ahead and said, "Huh. That's a sight, you getting all jiggly like that. Anyway, Dayzee, I think I'm losing my mind."

Dayzee shifted around and stood close, looking down at Kenzie, and said, "We're both going to lose our heads if we don't run!"

She grabbed Kenzie's hand, forced her up onto her heels, and they ran, laughing hand in hand, away from the lion and toward the living room.

* * *

"I haven't seen this room yet," Marilyn said as she pushed in a bedroom door on the second floor. "Have you and Kenzie, Sissy?"

"That's funny, Sis. I could have seen it on my own, you know."

"This house is so gigantic," said Dirk. "Maybe no one in the universe, ever, has been in this room?"

"That's funny, Dirk. Someone brought the furniture in there."

They all stepped inside the extravagantly decorated room and stopped, with all eyes pointing toward the bed.

"Huh," said Sophia. "We did wonder if Dayzee had a room like this."

"Oh, Sissy, she really does have a trapeze!"

"Damn, Sis. Right over the bed and double-wide too. Unreal."

"Let's swing for Dirk, Sissy!"

"Sis, I'm not so sure that he—"

"Oh, no, girls. I insist. I only wish we had a camera up here to catch it for the show."

"Don't have to tell me twice," Marilyn said as she giggled and stood up on the bed.

"Watch a pro, Sissy."

She held the padded bar with both hands, dropped herself down to hang there, then slipped one leg at a time up and over the bar, never losing her heels.

"Uh-oh, Sissy," she said as she let go. "This sure is a short dress."

"Sis, you're incredible."

"We'd edit that for the show so that you'd said 'edible.'"

"Why, Dirk, you're a rascal. Very true, though. Come on, Sissy, get up here with me."

"Seriously, Sis?"

"Mm-hmm. I won't start stripping until you can strip with me."

"Gladly, Sis. Exercise like that makes me more graceful. After some gymnastics with you, I'll strut around like I own the place."

"Well said, Sissy!"

"You girls are unbelievable," said Dirk. "What a reality show!"

"We've never stripped together upside down, Sissy."

"Huh. You're right. I've thought about it, though."

"Me too!"

* * *

Dayzee and Kenzie rushed into the foyer, still holding hands, and came to an abrupt stop at the entry to the living room.

"Dayzee, this can't really be happening. Did someone drug me?"

"No, but all of us almost undressed you."

Kenzie looked away from the Collectors, each of whom were holding up a hand burning like a torch. She popped her eyebrows and held Dayzee's gaze.

"Several times. We probably will soon."

"You sure were playing rough too."

"Oh, yeah. That's in my repertoire. I just don't know which should come first: undressing you or showing you who's boss?"

"Oh my God, you're all insane. This house is insane."

Still, she smiled, then turned toward the Collectors again.

"What about those freaks, Dayzee?"

"Okay, listen close. Run out front, find a yard guy, then—"

"They're in orange prison jumpsuits, right? That's them?"

"Yep. There's no time so even if the first one you find doesn't have a head, you'll still have to—"

"Dayzee! No!"

"Okay, fine. Geez. Find one that has a head, and tell him to get his hose in here quick."

"That's kind of funny, Dayzee."

"Thanks, Kenzie. Now, go. Hurry!"

Kenzie sprinted to the front door, and Dayzee turned to face The Collector and Lola. She stared at their mirthless, chattering faces with both fists on her hips.

* * *


"We'll film a private edition, girls. The general public just couldn't handle this."

"Sissy and I sure can handle things," Marilyn said with a giggle, then she began nudging the straps over her shoulders and up along her arms.

"Well, that's a wild sight. Wild!"

"Lifting your dress up is different this time, Sis."

"Oh my, yes. Oh, and I can still drop it down too. Things are all mixed up, though."

"I'm unbuttoning," Sophia said as she held Dirk's gaze and began popping buttons, starting near her waist.

"Me too," said Dirk, and he started taking off his shirt.

Sophia pulled in a sharp breath and turned toward her sister, who turned to her, and they were so close that they could rub noses.

"Sis, um, wait a sec," she whispered.

"What, Sissy? Dayzee wanted us to—"

"I'm just about ready to climb right up there, girls."

"What about your broken ankle?"

"All better, Marilyn!"

"No, Sis, we can't," Sophia whispered. "Remember what happened to us last time with this joker?"

"Oh. Now I do. We got that squid infestation."

"Yep. And we don't have those clone inoculator guys anymore."

Marilyn looked toward Dirk and whispered to Sophia, "Oh my, he's sure ready to inoculate us, though."

"Yeah, Sis, and pack a bunch of squid babies into us. We need to get out of here."

"What are you two whispering about? You know, since you're so close to each other, don't be shy. If you both want to—"

A lion roared from somewhere on the first floor, a loud crack signaled the demolition of the trapeze, and Marilyn and Sophia fell to the bed.

"Saved by the lion, Sissy."

"Damn lions. We could still kiss, though, Sis."

"We could, Sissy."

"You should," said Dirk. "I mean, just for that special edition of the show. Not for my benefit, girls. Nope. Not for—oh my God, that's something to see."

Several quiet seconds passed, then another lion roar echoed up and down the second-floor hallway.

Marilyn giggled and said, "We should probably get up, Sissy."

"Yep. We should."

"Damn lions," Dirk said to himself. "Of all the times . . ."

*　*　*

"Just what the hell are you two celebrating?"

"We sometimes summon lions with something somewhat—"

"Whoa!"

His diatribe ceased, and his chattering teeth commenced.

"You're summoning those lions? That's why they're dragging bodies around? Why?"

The Collector said, "It's a timely time for a timepiece to—"

Lola held her hand, the one not burning, in front of The Collector's face, stopping his babbling. His teeth launched into a busy chatter while hers came to a sudden stop.

"He's losing his mind," she said, shaking her head and getting in some quick chatters. "It's way past his feeding time."

"Wait a second," said Dayzee. "You don't . . . I mean, he . . . he's—"

Lola wiggled her chin from side to side a few times, then said, "He's kind of a freak, talking like that all the time. I keep telling him to stop that nonsense, but does he listen? Nope."

"Oh, for the love of lions. Okay, fine. I'll talk to you, then. Why exactly do you collect corpses? They're just—"

She held up one finger, silencing Dayzee.

"Cadavers."

Dayzee rolled her eyes and said, "Okay, sure. Why?"

"You've noticed our teeth?"

Dayzee squinted and leaned in, trying to study the two rows of brown teeth lodged in her gash of a mouth as it vibrated open and shut rapidly and silently.

"Uh, sort of. They're always crazy busy with—"

"Pumping blood to keep us moving."

"Oh, I see. That crazy teeth business pumps your blood and—"

She pointed at Dayzee's face again, her teeth froze, and she laughed once, quickly, before rushing another burst of chattering, then stopping to speak.

"Not *our* blood."

"Uh . . . oh. Yuck. That's supremely disgusting. So, Lola, how about if we stop playing with fire, alright?"

"I am starving too. Perhaps you require motivation."

She touched her burning hand to the nearest upholstered chair, and the flames spread rapidly.

"Dammit, you're paying for that!"

* * *

Marilyn and Sophia were still straightening out their clothing, holding hands and walking down the hall toward the stairway. Dirk was close behind.

"Damn lions," he said again to himself, but the twins heard him.

"I'm telling Kenzie about that room, Sissy. And I'll make sure that no lions interrupt you."

"You probably want to watch, too, huh, Sis?"

"I do," said Dirk, causing Marilyn to giggle just as they began their descent. "And I'll get someone to fix that trapeze too. Damn trapeze."

* * *

Dayzee sped around the corner, found a fire extinguisher in another closet which didn't have a concealed portal, then raced back into the room.

"There," she said as she sprayed the burning chair. "That's about enough of that."

The Collector, chattering like mad, touched his hand to another chair, igniting it instantly.

"Hey, my furniture! Damn you guys!"

She doused it completely before it could fill the room with smoke.

"No! No, you'd better not!"

Just as Lola was reaching her torch for the coffee table, Dayzee snuffed it out. Then, she smothered The Collector's flaming hand too.

"What is with you two? We had a deal, right?"

Lola nodded, still chattering, then held them still.

"We need cadavers now. You want your potion?"

"I do!" yelled Marilyn.

"Oh, you bet I do," said Sophia.

A lion roared from somewhere near the living room.

"Just wonderful," said Dayzee. "One question, then we got to get you and your damn lions and your corpses out to—"

"Cadavers," said Lola.

"God, you're both annoying in your own ways. Here's the question: where the hell does that monster potion of—"

"We're not fond of the word 'monster.'"

"That's kind of understandable," Sophia said with a snicker.

"That's funny, Sissy."

"Fine!" said Dayzee. "Damn cadavers!"

"Huh," said Sophia. "That's a new one."

Lola started clearing her throat, and they all took a step back. But no gory bits slithered out of her slit of a mouth.

"The potion which will soon enthrall all of you when—"

"Even me?" said Dirk. "Hey, I'm game. How does that work?"

Dayzee and the twins shook with laughter.

"That I want to watch," said Marilyn.

"Me too, Sis. Even if I do vomit a little bit."

"Dirk, not now," said Dayzee. "Continue, Lola."

Her teeth came to a sudden stop, and she said, "When we process cadavers to sustain our corpse-like integrity, we—"

"Uh, you mean 'cadavers.'"

"I do not. The Collector and I are true corpses."

"Sheesh. Never thought I'd hear anyone say that."

"Well, Sissy, that's only because corpses don't always want to talk."

"Girls. Lola, go on."

"The potion is a powdery, granular waste product that we excrete after—"

"Oh, just stop!" said Dayzee. "Your crap is the potion? Really?"

"I'm sticking with the old stuff," said Sophia.

"Me too, Sissy. No crap for this girl."

"Okay, you two corpses, we're moving you out to the guesthouse. Then, we—"

"Deathhouse, Dayzee," Marilyn said with a pleasant smile.

"Yes. Yeah, that's right. So, Lola, let's get you and your hubby out there. The lions and their cadavers will follow us?"

The Collector stopped his chattering choppers and said, "They will trail us along the trail we—"

"Oh, just stop," Dayzee said and covered her face with both hands. "You two are exhausting."

She gave each of them a blast from the fire extinguisher, depositing enough to cover their faces. Only their rapidly biting teeth could be seen moving beneath the mess.

"That's funny, Dayzee."

"Crap for potion?" said Sophia. "That's what they deserve."

The lion roared from close by.

"Okay, girls, and Dirk. It's been fun, but we're going to end up as cadavers for these extinguished freaks, then they'll turn us into crappy potion."

"Sheesh. Now's the time, Dayzee."

"You're right, Fia. Damn, only in Beverly Hills."

# Chapter 9 – We Need Another Lion

Dayzee wiped the foam away from just their eyes, then stepped back. "That'll have to do for now. Let's just keep you all foamy."

"It's probably not the best time," said Dirk, "with so much camera-worthy stuff always going on around here. But maybe you should introduce me to your parents, Dayzee?"

"Oh, Dirk! Yeah, I did say that, didn't I? Um, they . . ."

"They're really tired from, um, traveling so far," said Marilyn.

Sophia said, "Yeah, and they, uh, still have on their Halloween costumes."

"Fia! Yes! That's exactly right! Ha!"

"And, what, Dayzee?" said Dirk. "You just want to make sure their heads don't burst into flames?"

"Actually, now that I know about their crap, I don't care if—"

"She doesn't care if they stay for a long time, Dirk."

"Thanks, Mare. Yes, exactly right. They can stay in that deathhouse just as long as—"

"Oh," said Dirk, "it really is haunted, isn't it? This is fantastic. We'll do a bit where your parents are costumed again, and—"

The lion roared from just around the corner. They all listened to the sounds of something bulky dragging along the floor, a short distance at a time.

He got out his phone and started typing a text message, muttering, "We need a goddamn camera in here. This is just too good."

"Dirk, we need to get them out to that house. You can see how tired they are. Go on. Help them find their way."

Marilyn covered a giggle with one hand, and Sophia rolled her eyes and scoffed loudly. Dirk tapped his phone, grinned, and put it back in his pocket.

"Well, um, okay. Sure, Dayzee. But can't it wait until—"

"No! Got to go now!"

"Anything for you and Kildare in the Hills."

He got himself between the Collectors and nudged them along toward the mansion's back door. The girls followed behind, elbowing each other and trying not to laugh too loudly.

Just as Dirk was reaching for the doorknob, it swung in, and Kenzie looked in with a prisoner yard guy dressed in orange and holding a dripping garden hose.

Kenzie's eyes locked onto the pair of Collectors, their faces pasted with foam except for their staring eyes and busy teeth.

"This," she said to Dayzee, while still staring at the Collectors, "is . . . hey,"—she elbowed him, whipping around drops of water—"what's your name again?"

He tipped his glasses low, looked at each of the Collectors, then raised them up and kept studying them.

"I'm, uh . . . Scared. Scared Shitless."

"He's kind of funny, Sissy."

"Hmm. Kind of hot, too, Sis."

"Wonderful," said Dayzee. "Well, Mr. Shitless, squeeze that nozzle and give these two a cleanup, alright?"

"Do what?"

Kenzie elbowed him again and said, "Hose them down, Scared."

"That's a silly name, Sissy," Marilyn said to Sophia as she leaned toward her.

Sophia scoffed and said, "How about Dead Scared? Is that better?"

"Oh, Sissy, I think it's inevitable."

"Good word, Sis. I'm impressed."

"Lady," said Dead Scared, "you want me to . . . what?"

"Oh, just give me your hose," Dayzee said as she reached for it.

Sophia snorted once and said, "How many times has that been said in this house?"

With the nozzle in her hand, Dayzee pointed it at the frothy faces of the Collectors.

"I'll show you how to squirt that thing of yours."

"She did it again, Sissy! That's our Dayzee!"

Dayzee scoffed at the twins, then sprayed water at the Collectors' faces, causing their eyes to blink at a blinding rate as their teeth clamped together.

"This is just too silly," said Marilyn. "I kind of wish Rake Bark was here to see it."

"Well, Sis, he kind of is. His ashes anyway."

"There," Dayzee said and handed the hose back to Dead Scared. "Dead Scared, they're all—"

"Hey, lady, I'm not dead."

Marilyn giggled, Sophia rolled her eyes and grinned, and Dayzee shook her head and pointed at him.

"Sure you are. First, though, while you still can, take my parents to—"

"Oh, not me. These are your parents? They look so . . . so—"

"Collectorish?" said Marilyn.

"Good one, Sis."

"What does that mean? No, they're just—"

His eyes bugged out at the sight of the lady lion backing her way around the corner and toward the back door. She was taking short, slipping steps and trying to dig in her claws as she dragged the headless body, leaving streaks on the floor.

"If there was time, I'd have you clean up that mess," said Dayzee.

"Oh, but he's almost out of time, Dayzee."

"Yeah, Mare. So, Dead Scared, chop chop. Take them to the deathhouse."

Kenzie finally managed to look at Dayzee instead.

"I know I should take all of this more seriously," she said. "So should you and Marilyn and Fifi."

"She's still calling you Fifi, Sissy!"

"Huh. Nothing wrong with that."

Dirk's phone rang, and he read the text.

"Good, a crew is hustling to the back door right now."

Outside, several lions roared and two men screamed. Then, everything quieted back down.

"Sure they are, Dirk," said Dayzee, grinning at him. "Uh-huh."

"Dead Cameraman didn't make it, Sissy."

"Nope. To the deathhouse with them."

"Good one," Marilyn said while clapping her hands.

"All of you," said Kenzie, "don't you see how out of control this is getting?"

"Kenzie," said Dayzee, "we've seen all of this before. It's fine."

"I . . . I don't want to go no deathhouse, lady!"

"It'll do you good," said Dayzee. "Toughen you up."

The Collectors both spun around and stared at her, faces dripping water while their teeth chattered like mad.

"Oh. Uh, not like turning you into gristle. Just, you know, like—"

"Tenderizing?" said Marilyn.

"Seasoning," said Sophia. "Seasoning is always good."

Dead Scared had been looking from one twin to the other, shaking his head. He raised his hands as if surrendering and walked backwards slowly, out onto the patio.

"Oh, fine, Dead Scared," said Dayzee. "Tell you what: instead, you can be Dead Bartender. What do you think, girls?"

"I am kind of working up a thirst," said Sophia.

"We really shouldn't have to mix our own drinks, Dayzee. Good plan," said Marilyn.

A gunshot cracked the sky above Dayzee's estate in the Beverly Hills Flats, and a neat, red hole appeared in Dead Bartender's forehead just before he crumpled and folded into a twitching pile.

"Damn sniper," said Dayzee. "He's gone, then he's back."

"Dayzee!" said Kenzie. "You really don't see how bad this is getting?"

"She does have a point," said Sophia, nodding her head.

"She's hot and smart, too, Dayzee."

"Oh, fine. Kenzie, call Mack. He's good at mixing drinks. Better yet, take the limo and pick him up."

Dayzee waited with her eyebrows up as Kenzie only stared at her. Until the lioness roared from closer to the back door. Dayzee lowered her brows and shook her head a few times.

"It's either that or the deathhouse," Dayzee said, then bounced her brows twice.

"Fine! I'll go pick up Mack!"

"Good girl."

Kenzie scoffed loudly, turned, and left through the front door.

"She's hot when she's pissed off, Sis."

"Oh, I think it's more often than that, Sissy."

"Dirk?" said Dayzee. "You're up to bat. How about escorting my very tired—"

"But hosed down, cleaned up, and looking damn good."

"That's funny, Sissy. True, though. Oh, maybe not that last thing."

"—parents to the, um, guesthouse."

"Sure, Dayzee," he said and stepped back between the Collectors, taking an arm of each. "On the way, I'll see what's holding up that camera crew."

He began walking out with the Collectors, and Dayzee said to the twins, "The she-lions. That's what's holding them up while they're getting dragged to the deathhouse."

"So true again, Dayzee. But what about Dead Bartender who used to be Dead Scared?"

"And Scared Shitless before that?" said Sophia.

"The sniper saved us from having to rename him again, girls."

The twins backed away to one side, and Dayzee moved to the other as the lion continued grunting and dragging the headless, orange-wearing dead yard guy past them, out into the yard, and ready for delivery to the Collectors.

"We need another lion. Never an extra lion around when you need one."

"Damn lions."

"That's kind of ordinary, now, but it's always a good one, Sissy."

# Chapter 10 – I've Come Back for You

"This is more work than I've done in forever," Sophia said with a frown. "I've earned a stiff drink."

"That's funny, Sissy. Would you like that drink to be a headless stiff one? If so, go have a chat with that lion."

"You're hilarious, Sis."

"Girls, hold up on the drinks for a second. I just realized that we still haven't checked the pool. Remember what happened out there?"

"No, none of us were here. We were at the Prism."

"Mare, I know, but something gruesome happened out there."

"Oh yeah, that strange Moe character. We liquefied his head and used that to—"

"He was a damn good drinking buddy before he took a crunchy spin in that blender."

"He was, Sissy. Oh, and upstairs in Dayzee's bedroom. Remember that?"

"I mostly remember how Dayzee got herself all hot looking for that head."

"She was looking for head!"

"Girls, we all remember that. Yes, he was quite the talented head."

"Horny, too, Dayzee."

"Yeah, Mare. Oh my God, yeah. But you know what we did with that liquid head of his, right?"

"Was it still a head?"

"Sis, that's a profound question. I'd say no, it wasn't."

"Or was it a puddle that was owned by a head?"

"Sis, you're astounding sometimes."

"Girls! The important thing is what we did with that head by the pool. Remember?"

"Well, sure, it desquidded Cliff," said Sophia. "Made him Dirk again. Hey, if he ever starts acting like a jerk, we'll have a fun name for him."

"We will, Sissy!"

"Girls, why don't you two go take a quick look at the pool and report back?"

"Uh, because your yard is full of Collectors and lions and things?"

"Well, yeah, Fia, but you two could—"

"Have a quick fountain. Yes, Dayzee, that's a good suggestion. Come on, Sissy."

"No, Mare, that's not what I—you're already getting undressed?"

Marilyn was grinning and working her straps down over her shoulders.

"That's my Sis. Can't keep that girl dressed for too long. She's right, though."

Sophia grinned at Dayzee and started unbuttoning her blouse.

"Well, I can't talk you out of it. So, I can only insist that you make some real progress with that stripping business before you go out there."

"Oh, that's smart," said Marilyn. "We might be dodging lions and Collectors and—"

"And the sniper," said Sophia. "He's still up in a tree somewhere, and he—"

"No, girls, none of that. I just need something to make me smile before Dead Carpenter gets here."

"Aw, Dayzee needs a smile," Marilyn said as she wiggled and slipped her dress down to her waist. "How about that?"

"Sis, you're stunning."

"So are you, Sissy. Don't keep Dayzee waiting."

She didn't.

"Oh my God, you Kildare Killers! You've earned your fountains. Oh, but check on the pool, too, alright?"

* * *

Dayzee watched the twins walking toward the front door, undressing further with every step.

"Wish I had time for a fountain. Oh, maybe I can use that carpenter guy."

After Sophia had closed the door, after leaving no doubt in Dayzee's mind which one of them did or did not bother with underwear, she turned and began a walk toward the great room and the bar.

Looking down at the bloody drag marks which were crusting up, she said, "Somebody's cleaning that up. Maybe those damn Collectors."

She barely gave a glance toward the closet door beyond which waited ripped up drywall, then a circular stone stairway, also horribly damaged, then . . . she realized that she hadn't seen any farther than that. But she'd been told of an old wooden door, then a tunnel, then a portal.

Focusing again on the bar, which was within sight, including an open bottle of whiskey, she worked on her strut. But she stopped suddenly at hearing her named called from inside that closet.

By a very familiar voice.

"No, it can't be. Not after all that burning from all of us."

She turned and took a few steps closer.

"Dayzee? Sophia? Marilyn, are you out there somewhere?"

"Boss?"

"Dayzee, I hear you! I found the right portal!"

He charged through what was left of the door, sending shards and splinters across the floor.

"Somebody's fixing that," Dayzee said, giving him a big smile. "Boss, what the hell? Are you real?"

"Yes, Dayzee. I'm real. But what you and the twins so delightfully barbed and burned was *not* real. It was only a hologram of a clone, which is something new the labs have been cooking up for a while."

Dayzee had only a few steps to take, but she gave them her best strut.

"Boss, that clone hologram enjoyed the hell out of what we gave him. It's kind of a shame you missed out on all that."

"Who says?"

"Huh?"

"That's part of the technology, Dayzee. I, this very body of mine standing before you, was not just telepathically connected to the clone hologram, but I—"

"Look, today's already been the longest three weeks of my life. I can't keep saying and hearing 'clone hologram.' Try something else."

He looked down and rubbed his chin with one hand. He furrowed his brow and stared, then kicked at the remains of the door scattered all around.

Then, a smile took over, and he looked back up at Dayzee.

"Simple. My double? How's that?"

She sighed and said, "Much better. Okay, the girls and I burned and barbed your double, and you . . . what, exactly?"

"Dayzee, I felt every bit of that. Every single tiny point, every increase in temperature. All that smooth Dayzee and Kildare Killer skin. I was in Heaven!"

"Then, we burned you up like you were in Hell," she said, chuckling.

"Well, my double. Who cares about a double?"

"Nobody. So, you came back? What the hell are you doing here?"

"To put it as simply and clearly as I can: I've come back for you."

# Chapter 11 – You're Being Promoted

Kenzie screeched the limo to a stop directly in front of the Prism on Sunset Boulevard. She started to get out, then realized that she hadn't yet put the vehicle in park, so she locked the transmission and then got out.

But she left the engine running.

Through the heavy wooden door she strutted, still dressed for an audition that had been replaced by the calamities at Dayzee's mansion, none of which had been caught on film.

She strode right to the bar, where Mack was grinning and wiping his hands in a washcloth.

"Looking good, Kenzie. How did the audition go?"

Kenzie froze her face in a grin, kept marching toward him without speaking but with her heels smacking the hardwood floor, then tipped a barstool left and right repeatedly before letting it rest.

Then, she took a seat.

"Not good, huh?"

She snorted out a laugh and said, "Not even close."

"Um, okay. Well—"

"Set us up, Mack. Full glass of whiskey for each of us."

"What? No, I can't. I'm working and—"

"And you're leaving with me as soon as we chug that down."

"We're chugging it?" he said as he watched her while reaching blindly behind himself for a bottle.

"There's no time to waste."

"Is this about your audition? You need me for that?"

"It's about swilling some whiskey then leaving. Me and you. In the limo."

Another patron entered, and Mack looked past Kenzie, through the open door, and saw the limo and heard it still running.

Looking into her eyes again, he said, "Uh, where to?"

"Where else? Think, Mack. Think."

Mack scratched at his chin while pouring two tumblers full of whiskey, then he slid one closer to Kenzie. She picked hers up, and they clinked them together.

He was about to taste his, but he stopped to watch Kenzie pour her entire glass, chugging every last drop.

"Uh, yeah. Sure."

He gave his drink a sip, and his eyes never left hers.

"Who has a mansion, huh?"

"Well, lots of folks have—"

"Who hangs around here all the time with two super-hot twins from Kildare?"

"Oh, that has to be—"

"Who has her parents visiting from God knows where? And they're some kind of collectors or something? And whose yard is crawling with mountain lions? Hmm? Who, Mack?"

"I thought you meant Dayzee because of the twins. That's Marilyn and Sophia, right?"

Kenzie grimaced, belched, and pushed her glass back toward him.

"They're from Kildare," he said while refilling her glass. "I think. But Dayzee has parents, and they collect stuff?"

"Lions."

"They collect lions?"

"Maybe, Mack. Who the hell knows? Whatever, there are tons of lions. Finish your drink."

"Uh, maybe you could explain what—"

"Finish your damn drink."

His glass shook as he raised it up, tipped it, and let it all pour.

"Good. You're almost ready."

"Uh, what else do I need?"

"Nothing. You'll never be ready. Come on."

She turned and gave him a good view of her hips swaying in her short skirt as she strutted toward the Prism's door.

Mack stared for a few seconds, then smiled and ran after her, yelling to the kitchen staff, "I'll be back quick!"

He skidded to a stop when he heard Kenzie only say, "Ha!"

* * *

"I'm not happy with those creepy Collector people, Sissy."

"Sis, I could put up with them and how they like to start fires if they could deliver that supernova potion like they promised. Creepy dead liars."

Marilyn took her sister's hand as they walked toward the pool from the sliding glass doors along the back of Dayzee's mansion.

"We don't know that they're dead. They sure look dead, though."

"Hell, they're corpses. They said so. I'll tell you who else is dead, Sis: Moe. That head guy."

"He was a funny, horny head."

"Oh, not again."

Sophia stopped and reached down to help pull her sharp heel up out of the turf.

"Damn grass."

"That's funny, Sissy. Maybe what's left of Moe's head is funny too?"

"What, like he's telling jokes?"

"Sissy, you're just too funny sometimes. Oh, I think I see something."

They'd just stepped onto the stone patio that encircled the pool, and Marilyn was pointing to a slick region of muck waving around on the surface.

"That's Moe?"

"Huh. Maybe, Sis. Wouldn't there have to be a dead squid around here somewhere too?"

"Unless it squidded itself back into Cliff. I mean, Dirk."

"His name depends on if he's got a squid inside or not. Let's get closer."

Still holding hands, the girls walked to the pool's edge.

"Sheesh. That's gross."

"Oh, Sissy, I think that gross thing winked at me! It has a face!"

"Moe?" Sophia said to the slimy mess. "Is that you?"

Moe's face was stretched out to ten times its size, and the eyes were just dark regions in the puddle. Something like a mouth opened but also bounced around with the light waves.

It wailed and moaned for a few seconds, then closed again.

"I think he said we're hot, Sis."

"That Moe character just never stops flirting."

"Oh, wait. What's that?"

Sophia pointed below the Moe face slime. Both girls leaned to look.

"The squid! Moe's a squid now!"

"That clown just can't—"

"No, Sissy, he was a clone."

"Right. That clone just can't catch a break. First, his head got ripped off, then it ended up in a blender, then—"

"Uh-uh, Sissy. Before the blender, he had a very nice date with Dayzee."

"Yeah, Sis. We kind of helped ourselves to some of that fun too."

"Mm-hmm. That was nice."

She pointed at the undulating tendrils dangling from the puddle face of Moe floating on the water.

"But that's not very nice. We have to go tell Dayzee."

They began getting dressed while studying the mess in the pool.

A young man behind them said, "Tell who what?"

The girls turned to see a yard guy wrapped in orange, standing close and leaning to look into the pool.

"Just what we need, Sis. Hey, what's your name?"

"Kline. You are?"

"Horny," said Marilyn.

"You got a partner?" said Sophia.

Another young man was walking toward them, and Kline tipped his head back and said, "Yeah, Morris."

Marilyn put an arm around her sister and whispered in her ear, "Morris. That's kind of like Moe. It's a sign, Sissy."

Kline said, "You want that mess dredged out of there? I guess the pool is kind of part of the yard."

Morris took off his ball cap and wiped at the sweat across his brow, which was glistening in beads on his very dark skin.

"I'll get the net," he said.

"Wait. Hold up," Sophia said as she reached for the last two buttons of her blouse. "The slime can wait."

Marilyn shook her head and reached for the straps on her shoulders. "But we can't."

Morris had taken a step toward the small pool house, but he froze with his eyes on Marilyn's chest.

"Morris is for me, Sissy. Morris? Are you for me?"

She popped the straps to the sides and wiggled and tugged until her dress had passed below her breasts.

Morris stared. And stuttered.

"I, uh, I mean . . . damn, those are—"

"Yes, Mr. Morris. Yes, they are. Sissy, show Kline."

"Gladly, Sis."

She opened the last button and pulled the blouse open, revealing a lacy black bra. She squeezed her breasts together much more than necessary when she used both hands to pop open the clasp.

Kline was staring. Morris was pointing at Marilyn's chest but his eyes turned to what Sophia was revealing.

Even Marilyn was watching while clapping her hands silently.

"I guess these,"—Sophia said as she pulled everything to the sides— "are for you, Kline."

"God," said Kline as he wiped at some drool on his lower lip, "you two are so, so—"

"Hot?" Marilyn said with a giggle.

She put her arm back around her sister's waist and leaned in to whisper.

"This is all going insane, Sissy. We have no reason not to burn them."

"You're right. If we don't, the lions will get them anyway."

"Damn lions," Marilyn said with a giggle, then kissed Sophia's cheek.

"Yeah, Sis. So, I say we barb the hell out of them, too, alright?"

Marilyn gave her sister's cheek another peck and said, "Damn barbs, Sissy!"

* * *

"You came back for me? Why?" said Dayzee.

"If you had an actual bartender, I'd order us a drink and explain it to you."

"We sent Kenzie to get Mack. That'll be his job. Come on, though, I'll be his stunt double until he gets here."

"Let's go," he said and held out his arm.

Dayzee took it, and he escorted her to the bar, where he selected a stool and she went around to get drinks.

She pushed a full glass toward him and said, "Please, don't tell me the Guild is sending another assassin. We had a hell of a time surviving those damn things."

"But you did survive, and the Guild sure noticed."

"Which means that they're going to dig even deeper into the vile stockpile of weird shit in their labs and send something even worse? Boss, I don't know if we'll make it. Not with Collectors sniffing around, lions running wild . . . all kinds of crazy shit."

"Dayzee, you don't get it. The Guild isn't sending anything else after you."

"Good. Damn. They'll just leave us alone already?"

"Well, no. Not you anyway."

"Huh?"

"Dayzee, I've been sent here for a specific reason: you're being promoted."

"The hell you say. What kind of promotion?"

"The Guild was intent on ending your project by killing you and those gorgeous twins. Yeah, they really were. But you surprised them. You didn't just survive—you kicked ass with style. They admire that."

He took a long drink, set the glass down, and held Dayzee's gaze.

"They want to make you a general."

Dayzee's eyes were big and didn't blink while she lifted her glass, sipped it until it was empty, then set it down.

"A general? Uh, a military general?"

"Well, not with the usual uniforms and stuff. That would only cramp your style. No, they want you to stay on Earth, keep making those film things, and continue to plaster your images and videos all over that dreadful mind scrubber that Earth people call the Internet."

"Okay. I can sure do all that. General of what?"

"Besides living your usual lifestyle, you'll be assembling your team—kind of like an army—and you'll lead them into battle when we invade this hell hole and chop up and ship out all of its resources."

"I can do that. I can sure do that."

"If all goes well, you'll be promoted again, after that, to oversee a major portion of this world—maybe an entire hemisphere."

"To do what, exactly?"

"I think the term is 'warden?' The top prison guard."

"I played a prison guard in a film! I can do that!"

"You'll have to be exquisitely sadistic too. Can you handle that?"

"You already forgot how I tortured you once, then called you back and barbed and burned you into dust?"

"Well, my double."

"Let's go upstairs, Boss. I'll show you who's boss."

"Uh, not all the way to dust, right?"

Dayzee leaned across the bar and studied each of his eyes, showing him a sly grin.

"Only if you're a good boy."

*  *  *

Outside an upstairs bedroom door, Dayzee poured something into the Boss's whiskey glass that he'd brought with him.

"Oh, really, Dayzee? You know I don't need that."

"Drink up, Boss. You'll be twice the Boss with this."

"Fine," he said, then finished off his drink with the potion mixed in.

"A regular dose should still be crazy because I'm not exhausted like last time. Remember that? I was half dead from being so far from the portal at the Prism."

"Yeah, you seem fine. Is that because that portal somewhere under the house is active now?"

"That must be it."

"This should be fun. Guess what: that was a monster dose again."

"Dayzee, no! Who knows how monstrous a monster dose will make me?"

Dayzee grinned and looked down at his trousers already stretching.

"We're about to find out, Boss."

# Chapter 12 – The Boss, Still Lassoed

"Guys," Sophia said while she peeled her blouse off of her shoulders, "we're even hotter when you're lying down."

"Sissy's right about that. You boys like things hot?"

Morris's eyes were again riveted to Marilyn's breasts, and he grinned foolishly while nodding.

Kline's eyes were traveling between Sophia's breasts, back and forth, and she giggled and shook them for him.

"Exercise for those eyes, huh? Lie down, boys. Sis and I need somewhere special to sit."

"Yeah. Okay!" Kline said and quickly laid himself on his back on the patio.

Morris tossed his cap into the pool, and no one saw that a tentacle snaked up and over it, then pulled it under with a cloud of bubbles. He lay on his back next to Kline.

Sophia leaned toward her sister and said, "It's just so easy here."

"I know. Earth!"

Marilyn began shifting her hips and sneaking her dress up high, leaving it tight around her waist.

"Just one tiny little thing," she said with a giggle.

Sophia tossed her blouse behind her and said, "I love watching my Sis get naked."

"Usually she helps me."

"Even if she doesn't want me to."

"Those are the best times, Sissy!"

Marilyn peeled off her underwear and tossed it toward Morris. It ended up draped over his face and when he started reaching for it, Marilyn said, "Oh, no, Morris. Leave that right there."

The twins both laughed when he opened his mouth, pulled some of the sheer cloth in, then clamped it shut and stayed still.

"Good boy. I can't offer you that, Kline," Sophia said with a smirk.

"She rarely can."

"Oh, but maybe this," she said and slipped off her bra. "If you like what you see, you can thank spaghetti."

"Sissy, that's funny. Good one, though, even though Morris can't see them."

Sophia threw the bra toward Kline, and his grin was still visible when a single lacy black cup covered his eyes. Both of them quickly undid their orange jumpsuit zippers enough to show the twins what to focus on next.

Marilyn said, "Sissy, they sure are ready."

"Almost, Sis. Lucky for us that I brought some potion out here."

Marilyn clapped and said, "Goody! It's time for our fountains!"

Sophia leaned over and poured some into Kline's mouth, then strained some through her sister's panties into Morris's mouth.

"That was something different, Sissy."

"Make a note. We should do that all the time."

"Okay. Oh, but you'd have to wear panties, too, then."

"Oh yeah," she said with a grin. "Never mind, then."

"Look, Sissy, they're even more ready. Please," she said in a suddenly serious and formal voice, "be seated."

"Sis, you're the best. Don't mind if I do."

Seconds later, both girls had found very comfortable seats atop the two hypnotized earthmen, and they began a comfortable gyration, each with an arm around the other's waist.

After just another few seconds, Marilyn squealed and said, "Sissy, I think Earth Morris man is—"

"Sis, that's a funny way to say it."

"I know, but he's ready to go. It's fountain time!"

"Mine too. Hey, let's fountain first, then barb and burn later."

"Oh, Sissy, that's a wonderful plan. Yes!"

"One more bounce, Sis. Just one more . . . quick, look at me."

Marilyn turned toward her sister, and they both gasped as their fountains erupted and dazzling white light shot from their eyes like search lights.

"Oh, Sissy," Marilyn whispered, "your eyes!"

"Yours, too, Sis. Oh, damn, I needed a fountain so bad."

"Mm-hmm. Me too."

With eyes still burning intensely, Marilyn looked past her sister and said, "Of course. Here come the lions."

"Damn lions," Sophia said as she and Marilyn kept bouncing, getting the most from their fountains. "I'm not stopping."

Marilyn rubbed her sister's nose each way with her own.

"Me neither, Sissy. No way."

* * *

Dayzee locked the bedroom door, then turned to the Boss, whose face was showing some level of agony.

"Boss, are you alright?"

"Oh my God, Dayzee. It feels like a fire hose that—"

"Hmm. Fire hose, huh?"

She pushed his chest, backing him toward the window.

"Let's see about setting that beast free, alright?"

He reached for his belt, and she grabbed both of his wrists.

"Allow me. Your sadistic general is now calling the shots."

He raised his hands up, smiling, and she spun him around to face the window.

"Keep those hands in the air, mister. We've received word that you're harboring a fugitive monster that needs to be tamed."

"Oh, I sure am. I'm guilty as hell."

Dayzee gave him a sharp spank, then said, "Bad monster boy! And keep those hands up."

He was looking up at the ceiling, taking quick breaths, and Dayzee reached both hands around him. She pulled him back half of a step to give the much-needed room between the monster and the window.

"Oh my, you're stretching your pants so much the zipper is jammed."

"That's bad too?"

"You kind of hope so, don't you?"

"Oh, yeah. I can help if—"

"Keep those hands up!"

Dayzee yanked at the zipper, shifted things around, then gasped.

"Talk about someone being a handful."

She let go with one hand, and he said, "Too much for one hand, probably?"

"I have to risk it. This blouse has to go."

She fought with it, changing hands once, and let it drop to the floor behind her.

"Ah, yeah, both hands are better."

"I like what you're squishing into my back, Dayzee."

"In just a second, I'll be smashing them into your face. I need to lay you down on the—"

"Hey," he said, "those delightful twins are putting on a light show."

Never letting go of him, Dayzee leaned to one side, saw the dazzling display, and said, "Those gorgeous twins are having another fountain of youth already? Damn, they were supposed to be checking on Dead Moe."

"He's there. Sort of. Close, anyway."

"Oh, I see him. Sheesh, as Fia would say."

The girls looked up, pointing their laser eyes at the upstairs window, and both waved.

Dayzee shook the Boss's monster up and down and said, "Hello, Mare! Hello, Fia!"

"I feel so used," he said.

"You haven't even begun to feel used. You're in the capable hands of a cruel commander that's about to—"

"Oh, terrific. Look at the shrubbery."

"Now, who's being silly, Boss? Those girls don't ever forget to—"

"No, uh, the evergreen kind. Look!"

Dayzee saw the two lions watching the fountanizing closely, crouching and getting a good grip with their claws.

*　*　*

"Sissy, you can see Dayzee waving back at us. Um, I think."

"Oh, such a sweet kid. Sis, that's the Boss. Part anyway"

"Oh, my goodness, Sissy. He's more of a boss than when you and Dayzee and I abused and burned him."

"Which brings up an obvious question, Sis. How the hell is the Boss up there, waving at us?"

Marilyn's eyes were still blazing and so were her sister's as they bounced, continuing with their fountains, and watched the scene in the upstairs bedroom.

"Maybe he's a clone?"

"Could be," said Sophia. "Damn, though, Dayzee sure gets lucky in that room. She was getting busy with Kozy up there too. Remember?"

"Oh yeah, Sissy. Well, good for Dayzee. Ooh, my barbs are starting all on their own. Oh, wow . . ."

"Hey, wait for me," Sophia said, and she got her points digging into her man too.

"I kind of like Dead Morris, Sissy."

"Dead Kline isn't so bad either."

*　*　*

"Boss, those damn lions. I don't know if my gorgeous twins even see them yet."

She let him go, and he still waved to the girls a couple more times.

"We have to get out there. This whole thing is spiraling out of control."

"You can't be serious. You potion the hell out of me, awaken a demanding monster, then just pack up your goodies and leave?"

He turned around and watched Dayzee pick up her blouse but not put it on.

She saw where his eyes were pointed, and something else pointing, too, and said, "I'm not packing these up."

After whipping her blouse into a rope, she tied a knot around something, then looked into the Boss's eyes.

"And that's as packed up as that monster's getting too."

He grinned, and Dayzee took a step back, then yanked on the leash.

"Who's the boss now?"

"Careful. You might get a surprise."

"After living in the Hills so long? Hardly."

"Ugh. Already, that knot feels tighter."

"We'd better move then."

She gave her blouse another quick pull, watching.

"Remind me to make a drinking game out of this later."

*   *   *

Dayzee, still topless, led the Boss, still lassoed, down the stairs toward the kitchen, but he stopped where he was, a few steps behind and above her near the top.

She stopped, too, and said, "We really have to go, Boss. Those lions are—"

"Not interested."

"What?"

"The lions, Dayzee. You had to have noticed. They don't like our kind."

She looked down from his eyes, focusing level at him. Mostly his monster.

"So, there's no big hurry, you mean?"

"Speaking of big," he said with a laugh. "Ooh, getting painful too."

"Aw, poor Boss," she said and started loosening the knot. "Why don't lions like us?"

He waited until she'd looked back up into his eyes.

"Something about the taste, Dayzee."

She grinned and said, "Oh, you're saying we leave a bad—"

"Now, wait. I never said 'bad.'"

"Oh."

She lowered her gaze.

"I never say that either. Still, maybe you should try to lie down."

"On the steps?"

"Mm-hmm. Go on. I mean, since the lions don't care about the twins."

"Well, alright."

He laid himself down on the stairs and held a baluster with one hand.

"Let's just get this leash out of the way."

"Oh, good because—"

She laughed and said, "For now. Only so that I can . . ."

With her skirt raised, she stepped across him, one heel on a step to each side of him, and wiggled herself into place.

"Ah," she said, "there we go."

"Oh, that's a tight fit. Maybe you should just stay—"

"Nonsense," she said and started a steady bouncing. "Hmm . . . I'm on the stairs, and I can't decide if I want to go up . . ."

He smiled up at her.

". . . or down. Or up . . ."

"Oh, damn, Dayzee. I've dreamed of this."

Never slowing, Dayzee said, "Mm, I kind of always did turn you on. You're alright, Boss."

He squinted up at her and said, "And you still burned me to dust along with those twins?"

She dropped down suddenly, causing him to snarl and laugh once.

"Eh. Heat of the moment."

She continued as he said, "Good one, Dayzee. That's—uh-oh, I'm starting to slide down the stairs."

"I can fix that faster than you can say, 'Ow!'"

"Oh, you must mean—"

"Barbs. Uh-huh. If you keep sliding, I won't lose you. What do you say?"

"I say, barb the hell out of me."

Dayzee grinned down at him while his face twisted up and his eyes opened wide as her sharp points plunged into him.

"Huh. I was always going to anyway."

"Damn barbs," he said and let his head clunk back against the stairs.

Dayzee's barbs held him tight, and she barely moved her hips as she said, "Give me back that damn potion, Boss."

He only grinned with his eyes still closed.

With a pained, raspy voice, he said, "I, uh, I can do something else that—"

"The potion, Boss. Give me that goddamn—oh, here we go! Good boy!"

*  *  *

At the back door, the Boss was able to wrestle his zipper back up, but Dayzee hadn't put back on her blouse.

"Perfect uniform for a general," he said after brushing her hair back over her shoulders.

"Hmm," she said. "A sadistic one. Don't forget that part."

"I hope you never let me."

"I won't," she said, then looked through the sliding glass at the twins still shining their dazzling fountain light around the grounds.

"We're going to test my theory, Dayzee."

"What theory?"

"About the lions not wanting us."

"What? It's only a theory?"

"I'm hoping for the best."

"Damn bosses."

* * *

"Oh, Sissy, barbs are the best. I feel each one of them."

"So does he, Sis. Even though he's dead."

"Potion is perfect. They just never quit."

The girls kept bouncing, and the dead guys still wore panties and a bra on their faces. But Dead Morris's big smile was obvious through the thin white cloth.

"Uh-oh, Sis. The lions are coming."

"That's funny, Sissy."

"No, I mean, they're approaching. Should we stop?"

"I'm not stopping for any silly lady lions. It just feels too good."

"Okay. Me neither."

The lions drew near, close enough to sniff around the dead heads of Dead Kline and Dead Morris. While staring up at Marilyn and Sophia, each opened their toothy mouths and gingerly grabbed those heads, which had wisps of smoke puffing out from the heat that the twins were delivering.

"Uh-oh, Sissy. Lady lions are hungry."

"Or they're working for the creeps."

"They're collecting for the Collectors. Yes, that must be it."

Both lions lowered themselves and started to pull, each giving their dead human a sharp snap.

"Oh, my, Sissy! My barbs are still in him!"

"Damn. Mine, too, Sis. We should do this all the time."

"We should keep lions around for when we barb earthmen?"

"It sounds kind of silly when you say it like that."

The lions jerked the bodies harder.

"Oh, my!"

"Don't let go, Sis. Make them work for it!"

"Best carnival ride ever, Sissy!"

The girls got dragged along with the dead yard guys as the lions kept nudging them closer to the deathhouse.

"Sissy, they're taking us to the deathhouse!"

"Uh, we might have to unbarb these guys."

"I don't want to," Marilyn said with a pout. "And I've never heard that word before."

"Have we ever been dragged along with two dead prisoner yard guys by lady lions delivering the cadavers to Collectors while we're barbing and burning them?"

Marilyn laughed and said, "Sissy, that's plain silly! Okay, I'm unbarbing right now."

Sophia sighed loudly and said, "Alright. Me too."

They stayed stooped down, next to each other, arms around each other, and watched the lions dragging the smoking bodies away for the Collectors.

"That's some special delivery for them, Sissy."

"Hot, fresh, and on-time."

"Good one!"

# Chapter 13 – I Kind of Love Lions Now

"Your theory was damn right," Dayzee said as she slid open the glass door. "I'd miss those gorgeous twins if lions ate them."

"When the time is right, you might want to recruit them for your army here on Earth. What do you think?"

They left the house to begin a walk toward the pool.

"They're deadly as can be, Boss, but I don't think anyone can ever control them."

"I've seen you try many times. The Guild has noticed too."

She stopped to pry a heel loose from her yard.

"Shouldn't those lawn guys be doing something with this?"

The Boss laughed and said, "Like what? Covering it with concrete?"

"Maybe. I think my first battle as a general will be with every lawn guy in this world. Just to prove a point."

"And what point is that?"

"That if I can't get good help around here, then no one, anywhere, will get good help."

"You're vicious, Dayzee. I like that."

"I'll pencil you in for some burning and barbing later. Right now, let's go interrupt those twins by the poolside."

"They're still hugging? That's normal for them?"

"Oh, all the time and for any reason. Come on."

*　*　*

Sophia reached up from Marilyn's back and fluffed her wavy blond hair.

"Thanks, Sissy. I try not to tangle that up when I'm burning and all that other fun stuff."

"It's still gorgeous, Sis. I just love when your eyes light up like that."

"We should always do our fountains together. That's the best."

"What's the best?" Dayzee said as she and the Boss took the last couple of steps to stand in front of them.

"Boss?" said Marilyn. "Aren't you just dust in a can somewhere?"

"Nah," he said. "That was just a holo—um, my double. I'm fine."

"We burned up a fake boss?" said Sophia. "Huh."

"Yes, and believe it or not, I enjoyed all of it too. Thanks."

Sophia lowered her gaze to just below his belt and said, "You or your double, anytime."

"Oh, Dayzee, did you see us wave?"

"Yeah, Mare. Did you see us?"

Sophia snickered and said, "We saw something waving. Something gigantic."

"Oh, well, Fia," said Dayzee, "a generous dose of potion can bring out the best in a Boss."

Both girls looked at the Boss just below his belt buckle, then they both laughed.

"Not quite as gigantic anymore?" said Marilyn. "Why exactly is that, Dayzee?"

Dayzee sent a silent snarl toward Marilyn.

"Well, Mare, it—"

"The potion wasn't the only thing that was a generous dose, was it, Dayzee?"

Dayzee lost the snarl as she pointed at Sophia.

"Fia. Like you wouldn't believe. But, as you can see, he's all better now."

"You seem a lot less agitated yourself, Dayzee."

"Yes, Mare, I think you're right. You girls had some kind of magnificent fountains, didn't you?"

"Dayzee," said Sophia, "we figured out the best way. We fountain the earth guys as quick as we can then right away, we barb and burn the hell out of them."

"That does sound good. I'm doing that next time too."

"It gets even better," Marilyn said, squeezing her sister closer. "When the barbs are all dug in nice and sweet, then you get lions to yank those dead earth guys away just a little at a time!"

"With the barbs in? Really, Fia?"

"Yeah, Dayzee. Oh my God, that's the best. I kind of love lions now."

"Damn lions that I love so much!"

"Okay, sign me up. I want a lion of my own."

Dayzee laughed, waved a hand in a circle over her head, and said, "Lions all around!"

* * *

"I guess we have to get up, Sissy."

"Probably. No reason to get dressed, though."

They helped each other up, and Dayzee retrieved their tossed clothes.

She grinned and said, "Damn, I hate how I have to do everything around here."

Marilyn giggled while Dayzee helped her step into her undergarments.

"Sissy needs help, too, Dayzee. We're both in a trance from teaching those yard guys a thing or two."

"Well, if you insist."

She held Sophia's blouse for her, then looked over her shoulder at the Boss while she reached around and buttoned it up.

The Boss stared, and Marilyn pointed and giggled at the sight of the massive dose of potion's persistent effects.

"Oh, my," Dayzee said while Sophia placed both hands over hers.

"Mm. Still feels too tight, Dayzee," she said and shook herself from side to side.

"Oh, Sissy. Shame on you."

"Fine," Dayzee said, and she slowly loosened the top button of Sophia's blouse.

Sophia offered a rare pout and said, "Better . . ."

"Oh, Fia. I should know better than to ever try dressing you."

She popped open the next lower button, then gave each side of the blouse a gentle pull away to the sides, improving the view. The Boss's eyes opened more, and his dose of potion got even busier.

"Dayzee," said Marilyn, "you'd better stop playing with Sissy!"

"Oh, alright. If you insist. No time for monsters right now."

The Boss looked past the girls and said, "Ha!"

Marilyn looked behind her at the deathhouse, where Dirk had started walking toward them and the two Collectors were standing outside the door with their teeth chattering silently.

"Hmm. Speaking of monsters."

"Oh, about them," said the Boss. "Uh, wait. Did you mean the Collectors? Or . . ."

"He lost his monster, Boss," said Sophia. "A weird clone named Moe gave him some head, and he—"

"Sissy!"

"Alright, we used Moe's head to cure him of the squid living in his guts."

"But now, the head *and* the squid are living in Dayzee's pool."

"Dammit," said Dayzee. "If I could just get a good yard crew."

Sophia snickered and said, "We'd just kill them too. Not a realistic dream, Dayzee."

"You girls."

"Okay, about the Collectors. You should know that—"

"We already know, Boss," said Dayzee. "We had this sweet deal lined up with them: they'd give us this dreamy sex potion as long as we supplied them with corpses."

"Cadavers, Dayzee."

"Thanks, Mare. But Boss, we found out just now that they suck up spleens and blood and junk, and that potion is what they crap out of them. Not very appealing!"

"I'm so disappointed," Marilyn said with a pout.

"Ooh, no, that doesn't sound good. Listen, girls, there's something else: those Collectors are like Earth cockroaches. If any of you got the Native Infestations download, you'd know that—"

"Dirk got that infestation, back when he was Cliff," Sophia said with a smirk.

"Sissy's right, and I bet it wasn't in that silly download."

"Well, no," said Dayzee, "because that squid thing came from some cursed comet or something, remember? Not Earth."

"Oh. Yeah, now I do. Go on, Boss."

"Thanks, Marilyn. Glad we cleared that up."

He cleared his throat and said, "So, the thing about Earth roaches is that if you see one, there are likely dozens more partying in the walls somewhere."

Dayzee looked back at her mansion, then again at the Boss.

"Yuck. Please, not my house. I'll get a Dead Exterminator out here just as—"

Marilyn said, "He's already dead?"

"Well, let's not get hung up on every little timing detail. The thing is, I'll make sure that my walls are—"

"Uh-uh," said the Boss. "Probably not the walls. Where did these first two come from?"

"Oh, right. That damn portal in the basement."

Sophia took a deep breath, ready to correct her about the portal's location, but Dayzee turned to her quickly and pointed.

Sophia scoffed and grinned instead.

"Besides, we need some earthmen that can survive the heat and barbs and still give us our fountains. That's the ideal thing."

"I have another surprise for you," said the Boss. "I got a new, advanced upgrade that—"

Marilyn rolled her eyes and said, "Not more sorsciencery. We're so past all that."

"Sis makes a good point. That was nothing but assassins and Bruno changing into all kinds of other animals and—"

"No, girls, listen. I can switch to earthman mode. I can function identically to an earthman for short periods."

"You mean . . ."

"Yes, Dayzee. It's selective, too, so I can be an Earth type of guy to give those fountains of youth, but I can still be myself, which means—"

"Burning and barbing!" Marilyn said, clapping her hands.

"My kind of guy," Sophia said.

The Boss got a huge smile and said, "I can be that kind of guy for all of you. Um, as long as you don't mind, Dayzee?"

She scoffed and said, "Damn, just get my name on that list, alright?"

*   *   *

"Where are the cameras?" Dirk said as he got near the group near the pool. "There should be cameras. Always. Always should be cameras."

"Dirk?" said Dayzee. "Are you okay?"

He looked all around, not meeting anyone's gaze.

"Reality. Cameras for reality. Show. Where. They?"

He got out his phone and started tapping.

"Oh, boy," Dayzee said, shaking her head. "I think someone had his brain collected."

"Dayzee, that's silly," said Marilyn. "The Collectors collect corpses not just brains."

"Sis, no. They like cadavers. Tasty, toasted cadavers."

"We sent them a couple. Yes, we did, Sissy."

"Girls, hold on a second. Dirk, how do you feel?"

He held the phone away, put his other hand on his belly, and belched loudly.

"This gets better all the time," Sophia said with a smirk.

"Fia, wait. Dirk, are you sick?"

Marilyn whispered, "Sick of squids from diseased comets, I bet."

"Sis, who said the comet was diseased?"

"Well, no one, Sissy, but it must be because—"

"Dirk, maybe you should relax in a lawn chair for a while, alright?"

His eyes drifted all around, and he said, "Sure, Dayzee. With a camera. Because cameras are, are needed for shows that, um . . . I think I'll sit."

He fell backwards as if there were a cushioned lawn chair behind him and ended up flat on his back, still tapping on his phone.

Sophia pointed across the lawn at a three-man crew approaching with a camera, some lights, and some recording equipment.

"Squid can still boss his crew around," Dayzee said, nodding. "Not bad."

"He's not really a squid, Dayzee. But that might be," Marilyn said, pointing to the slimy slop floating on the water.

"Sheesh," said Sophia. "Again."

"Somebody's cleaning that pool, dammit," said Dayzee. "That reminds me: we should get Jiff out here for our own personal videos."

"Even with all the lions and Collectors and things?"

"Eh. Sure, Mare, why the hell not? We've got things enough under control that—"

She felt Sophia tugging on the sleeve of her blouse, so she turned to see.

"What, Fia?"

Sophia pointed toward the film crew moving in their direction while behind them, three lions were treading softly, close enough to pounce.

"Um, Mare. Maybe distract Dirk and make sure he doesn't flip out even more?"

"How? What do I do?"

Dayzee laughed and said, "What do you always do?"

"Oh, okay."

She walked over to Dirk, stepped one heel across him and kept one close on his other side, and started pinching her straps and easing them off of her shoulders.

Dayzee said, "You too, Fia. I can feel this damn show crashing and burning if Dirk's brain turns to mush from all of this."

"Fine. I like undressing as much as Sis."

"I know you do, Fia. I just love you girls."

Sophia stood by her sister's side and started to unbutton. Dirk stared up at them with the insane grin of a man who's totally lost but still likes to see bare breasts.

A horn blasted over the mansion from the entrance gate as Kenzie pulled the limo as close to it as she could.

Dirk jumped to his feet, his eyes darting everywhere. The twins moved in close to hug him and block it all out.

"I hear you, Kenzie!" Dayzee said and reached for her phone to send the code.

Three lions roared just as Dayzee sent the signal, and the gate started creaking open.

Three soon-to-be-dead men screamed.

The Boss laughed at all of it, and Dirk got squirmy, jostling all around, and he pushed through between the twins and splashed into the pool.

The screaming stopped, and the three mountain lions began dragging away the crew.

"More takeout, Sissy."

Kenzie tooted the horn again, and Dayzee, laughing, hit the code to close the gate.

She looked at the Boss, and they shared a smile.

"Only in Beverly Hills, Boss."

"Um, Dayzee?"

Dayzee turned toward the pool and the twins.

"Yeah, Mare?"

"It's kind of like a reunion. I think."

"What is?"

"Well," Sophia said, barely able to stop laughing, "we got ourselves a Dirk getting tight with a squid, and that weird slime character Moe is about to give them both head."

Marilyn sighed and started to lift her dress back into place.

"We really do need that photo Jiffy guy, Dayzee."

"Oh, good thinking, Sis," Sophia said, then she began unbuttoning the buttons that she'd just closed.

"Isn't he in jail?" said Marilyn.

"Yeah, Fia, but this is Beverly Hills. Weird things happen."

Her phone chimed, and she gave it a glance then tapped it.

"See? He's on his way! Gotta love the Hills!"

# Chapter 14 – Squid Babies Flying Everywhere

"Girls, shouldn't Dirk be our first priority?"

"Yes, Dayzee," said Marilyn. "We need to finish the show before he goes squidding away somewhere again."

"Mare, he might be a lost cause. He might even be Cliff again."

Sophia smirked and said, "Let him turn into a squid. We'll just use that Jiff buddy of yours."

"Fia, you're onto something—he could film our show. Maybe we should still save Dirk if we can, though?"

The Boss was nearest the pool, looking into it, and said, "Um, I think it's too late."

The girls all huddled together along the pool's edge. Everyone stared for a few seconds, and Sophia said, "Sheesh."

Dirk was floating on his back, his face completely wrapped in tentacles, one of which was holding a dripping sheet of slime that looked like Moe, including a ripped and tangled bit of black braid.

And Dirk's belly was swelling up, growing larger with every passing second.

"Girls, maybe we should back up?"

"Okay, Dayzee, but I don't want to get dressed just because of the Cliffie Dirk thing in the pool."

"You don't have to, Mare. I just think that balloon belly of his could pop anytime."

"Yeah," said Sophia, smirking, "and send tiny squid babies flying everywhere."

"I didn't even think of that," said Dayzee. "Run!"

With the clatter of heels on the patio and laughter from the Boss, they all retreated farther into the yard.

"Yay," said Marilyn while clapping quietly, "he stopped growing!"

"Even that squid from a comet probably can't keep growing like that forever," said the Boss.

"Okay, good," said Dayzee, "but how do we save him?"

"Where's your harpoon?"

"That's funny, Sissy. Smart, too, though."

"Girls, no. That might kill him, too, not just his squid guts."

The tendril with Moe's grinning face began waving around.

"Moe's mocking us," said Sophia. "We could harpoon him."

"That would teach him, Sissy. I'm a good aim. I'll—"

"Girls, I don't have a harpoon."

"Are you sure, Dayzee? We found your trapeze."

"Yeah, Mare, I'm sure. But a—"

"And another stairway," said Sophia. "There are probably more too."

"Fia, I wouldn't be surprised, but that doesn't mean I have a harpoon somewhere in that mansion."

The Boss said, "Maybe it's in one of the guesthouses?"

"Oh, not you too. Look, I'm pretty sure that—"

A gunshot rang out across Dayzee's property, and the balloon that Dirk's belly had become began leaking squirming, tweeting squids into the water as it deflated.

"Huh. Never thought I'd see something like that," said the Boss.

Dayzee raised a fist and looked all around.

"You're still a lousy shot!"

"Oh, Dayzee," said Marilyn, "maybe he was just trying to help."

"Sis has a good point. He aimed right at the sleazy squid factory."

"Fia, is that all Dirk is to you now? A squid factory?"

She smirked and said, "Not anymore. That's done."

"Look!" Marilyn said while pointing at the pool.

Long snake-like arms were twisting around, wrapping up what was left of Dirk and pulling him under. All went quiet except for a small fountain of bubbling water, then that stopped too.

"Okay, good," said Dayzee. "Finally, things are getting back to normal. Just a quiet time in the Hills."

They spun around at loud lion roaring and watched two of them running toward the pool. They leaped high then splashed down under the water.

"That's different," Sophia said.

"Cats breathe underwater, Sissy?"

"No way, Sis. They're hunting."

"Fia, you mean—"

They surfaced, one clamping down on a squid appendage and the other with something resembling Dirk in her jaws.

"The lions are feeding on that junk? In your pool, Dayzee?"

"Oh, I don't know, Fia. Why the hell not?"

* * *

The glass door on the back of Dayzee's mansion squealed as Mack slid it open, and he and Kenzie started walking toward the pool.

"I thought the inside was bad enough," Mack said to Kenzie, "but even the outside is all trashed up? What the hell is going on?"

"Just accept that it's all insane. That's what I'm doing. Damn, these heels."

She stopped to pry one out of the yard.

"You're staying dressed like that? How come?"

"I give up, Mack. I think I'm some kind of unpaid apprentice in Dayzee's crew now. This is how we dress."

"Well, damn, it looks good. What's going on by the pool?"

"Who knows? You heard that gunshot, though. I'm glad none of them got hit."

Mack looked past the pool and saw the two gaunt Collectors standing just outside the open door of the deathhouse.

"Uh, Kenzie. What the hell?" he said as he pointed that way.

"Oh, them. Dayzee's parents."

"Well, why do . . . why do they look—"

"They're from out of town."

"And that's supposed to explain it? Damn."

* * *

"Oh, no," Dayzee said when she saw Kenzie and Mack approaching. "Kenzie kind of lost her mind already, but we should try to shield Mack from some of this nonsense."

"We do need a sane bartender," said Sophia.

"I'll help," said Marilyn. "Should we go burn him?"

"Sis, how's that supposed to help?"

Marilyn pouted and said, "Sounds good to me, Sissy."

"Me too, Sis, but—"

"Girls, don't burn Mack."

She turned and began quick short steps toward Mack and Kenzie, and Marilyn followed close behind.

"Good, glad you're here, Mack. We need you right behind the bar because—"

"Your parents, Dayzee? Those two?"

She gave the Collectors a quick glance, then smiled at Mack.

"They're tired and, um, from out of town. Never mind them. They just—"

The lions started splashing and dragging the single giant piece of slop, consisting of Dirk, the squid, and Moe toward the pool's steps, leaving hundreds of baby squids swimming and diving. Everyone stopped to watch.

After dumping it all on the patio, the lions shook, sending pool water out in a cloud, then got solid grips.

"Didn't see that coming," Sophia said as the lions dragged the mess toward the Collectors near the deathhouse.

"Well, Sissy, it is a deathhouse."

"So, Dayzee's parents had a taste for seafood?"
"Good one, Sissy. Yes."
Mack, staring at the sight, said, "Dayzee, what exactly is—"
She took his arm and said, "Our drink order? Glad you asked. Let's go inside and get started. God knows, we need them."

# Chapter 15 – About to Become Lion Bait

"I kind of feel like I'm at the Prism. Except for all the crazy stuff."

"Oh, Dayzee," said Marilyn, "the Prism had some questionable things going on too. Remember that head that kept winking at me?"

"And the footrest that had sex with you? That place kind of went nuts too."

Dayzee sat at the bar in her great room, with Sophia to her left and the Boss and Marilyn to her right. Kenzie and Mack were tending bar.

Kenzie stood with her hands on her hips, still wearing a short skirt and heels, looking from one to the other and shaking her head. Mack had found a washcloth and was wiping his hands.

"Our favorite bar isn't as damaged as my house, though, girls. God, my house . . ."

At the end of the hallway leading to the garage, there was a crash, the sound of boards splintering, and aggravated growling.

"Oh, I just remembered all the carpentry work that we need. That's probably another lion snooping around."

"Uh, sorry, Dayzee," said Kenzie. "I should have reminded you that the garage door is still open."

"Damn garage door," Sophia said with a smirk.

"Funny, Sissy. True too."

Mack's wringing of his hands and knotting of the washcloth intensified.

"What about all those bodies in the garage?" he said. "What the hell is that all about?"

"Um, it's kind of like, I don't know, a stockroom?"

"A what?"

Marilyn said, "A stockroom is a place where dead earthmen are stored until the lions can deliver them all to the Collectors."

"Sis, I'm impressed!"

"A what?" Mack said again, his voice rising.

Marilyn cleared her throat, then said, "A stockroom is a place where—"

"No, Marilyn. No! I heard you. Dayzee, what the hell?"

"Just try to ignore all of that, Mack. Focus on bar tasks. I'm more concerned about the carpentry around this place."

Mack stared. Kenzie grinned, and her head kind of flopped around lazily. The Boss chuckled and sipped his drink.

"I'll call a guy to fix all that."

"You were going to call carpenters for each door, Dayzee."

"Oh, that's right, Fia. I should call—"

"Not just carpenters," said Marilyn. "Dead Carpenters. Remember?"

"That would save some time and confusion, Mare. Alright, how many are we ordering?"

Sophia snorted and said, "Like ordering takeout off a menu? Ha!"

"A Dead Menu, Sissy," Marilyn said with a giggle.

"Look," said Dayzee, getting out her phone, "let's start with one. Maybe we should try ordering a live one and keeping him alive?"

"As long as he's not a slacker."

"Every carpenter that got killed here was a slacker, Sissy."

"Sure," said Dayzee, shaking her head. "After they got dead."

"No excuse."

The Boss set down his empty glass and said, "Mack? If you don't mind?"

"Sure," he said with a blank stare. "Focus on bar stuff."

He picked up the glass and turned to fill the order.

While waiting, the Boss said, "You have some furniture issues, too, Dayzee."

"Oh God, that's right. Those damn Corpse Collectors were getting nasty with—"

"Cadaver Collectors, Dayzee."

"That's right, Mare. What did I say? It doesn't matter. They were burning things up in the living room, so we'll need some furniture guys too."

She turned quickly and pointed at Sophia, causing a smirk. Then, she spun quickly toward Marilyn and pointed at her, making her giggle.

"I know. I know! Dead Furniture Guys."

She held her glass up in front of her, and the twins held theirs up close to it.

The Boss drummed his fingers on the bar, and Mack hustled to get a full glass to him, which he then held up with the girls.

"To Beverly Hills!"

* * *

A loud crash from along the hallway to the garage led to a bouncing and rattling as a doorknob came rolling into the great room.

"Oh, boy. That's just wonderful."

"You already knew the door was broken up," said Marilyn.

"I know, Mare. I just mean that at least one lion is probably on the way toward us."

Sophia snapped her fingers and said, "Mack, another round."

"Are you crazy?" he said. "A lion is coming to get all of us, and you—"

Marilyn gave him a pleasant smile and said, "Well, not all of us, Mack. Just the ones that—"

"Are working the bar," Dayzee said quickly, then she pointed at Mack and Kenzie.

"Why us?" he said.

"Because you're local?" said Sophia.

"Huh?"

"Me too, Dayzee?" said Kenzie. "I don't want to get mauled by a wild animal!"

Sophia snickered and said, "Says the scantily-clad girl who was about to go to an audition."

"Good one, Sissy. Yes. Wild animals."

"I mean lions!" she yelled. "I'm not sticking around for that!"

She hurried around the bar, taking quick steps on her heels, and ran toward the stairway.

"Huh," said Dayzee. "That's a sight."

"She's just going to get lost up there," Sophia said while watching every move that Kenzie made as she rushed up the stairs.

"Oh," said Marilyn, "we were going to make a map. Remember that?"

"Impossible. The house is just too big, Mare. Alright, let's go find our escaping barmaid."

Sophia smirked and said, "Oh no, Dayzee. Escaping actress."

They finished their drinks to the sound of approaching growling and claws scraping on the wood floor.

"Uh, I think I want to run too," said Mack.

"Sure," said Dayzee. "You won't look as good as her, though."

"I don't care! I'm going!"

He hurried around the bar, started running for the stairs, then stopped and turned back toward the four calm individuals still seated at the bar.

"You really aren't worried about that lion?"

Marilyn nodded and said, "Might be more than one, Mack."

"Might be a whole flock of them," said Sophia.

Then, when everyone stared at her, she said, "So I didn't get that Earth indigenous stuff download. It might be a flock, though."

"Whatever it's called, I think it's heading this way," said Dayzee.

"They're still looking for head too."

"Good one, Sis."

"Alright," Dayzee said with a deep sigh. "Let's all get upstairs."

They pushed themselves back from the bar and its line of empty glasses, then began a walk toward the stairway. Kenzie had vanished somewhere on the second floor, and Mack waited halfway up.

"Will you hurry? Damn!"

"He's hot when he's about to become lion bait," said Sophia.

"Oh, Sissy, he's hot all the time."

All four were on the stairway, and Mack had just turned to lead the way when Dayzee said, "Oh, Mack. One more thing. Can you run real quick and get a full whiskey bottle? We might be hiding up here a while."

"Are you serious?"

"Well, yeah. I don't think vodka would be the best in a situation like this."

"I'm always okay with beer," said the Boss. "But that might be too much to carry."

"I'm starting to get hungry," Marilyn said with a pout. "Lunch sounds good. Maybe make some sandwiches, too, Mack?"

"No, Sis, hot food is always better because—"

"God," said Mack, "it's all of you! Fine. I'll get the damn whiskey."

He elbowed his way through them, and Sophia said, "You don't have to swear about it."

"He didn't mean it, Sissy. He just gets cranky sometimes."

They waited and watched as Mack ran behind the bar, got a hand on a full bottle, then got pounced on by a lion. They both fell to the floor behind the bar.

"Huh. So much for that bartender."

"Oh, Dayzee, he might be Dead Bartender now."

"We don't know that, Sis. He might—"

From behind the bar, the lion appeared with Mack in her jaws. She dragged him around the corner and into the hallway to the garage.

"Out to the stockroom he goes," Dayzee said while shaking her head.

"This is kind of getting out of control," said Sophia. "I liked Mack."

"You still have Kenzie, Sissy. Remember her? She might need to get tucked in after all this scary stuff."

"Girls, we should all see about tucking her in. She's the last bartender we have."

"She's an actress, Dayzee."

"Yeah, Mare. So we've heard."

# Chapter 16 – A Sexy Wardrobe Change

At the top of the stairs from the kitchen, the Boss stopped and looked along the hallways leading in each direction.

"My God, Dayzee, just how big is this house?"

"Huh. No one knows for sure. We could have taken the elevator if I could remember where one is."

"One?"

"Yes, Boss," said Marilyn. "We just found her third stairway a little while ago. How many more are there?"

"The question is," said Sophia, "where's Kenzie hiding?"

"Ooh, hide and seek, Sissy."

"We'll find her soon, Fia, as long as we—"

"Oh, um, maybe you three," said Sophia, "should just, I don't know, pick a room and get comfortable, and then—"

"Uh-oh. Sissy's getting itchy. She wants Kenzie all to herself."

"Well, Sis, I'm always itchy. Aren't you, Dayzee?"

"Damn. Like you wouldn't believe. All the time."

"We just burned two dead yard guys, Sissy and I, and it didn't help."

"We saw you and the Boss up in the window," said Sophia. "That didn't help?"

"Oh, no, Fia. With all the emergencies, we had to—"

The Boss grinned and said, "I liked the stairway. That's a good place to stop for a while."

Marilyn said, "Dayzee, on the stairs? Really?"

Dayzee chuckled and said, "I really dosed him up. He never would have survived with that kind of pressure."

"Good job, Dayzee. Nice."

"Thanks, Fia."

"And we're getting cheated out of that nightmare potion, Dayzee! That's not fair. Not fair!"

"I know, Mare. We sure are supplying the corpses, too, and we—"

"Cadavers."

"Right, Fia. So, we're doing our part."

"And you were doing the Boss's part too."

"Thanks, Mare. Yeah. And we're sure not done."

"I'm going to find Kenzie," said Sophia.

"And then, what? Sissy, you might need help. I'll help."

"Alright, Sis. We'll see if she's as good of an actor as she says."

"Hey," said Dayzee, "I want in on that. I'm at least as itchy as you gorgeous twins."

"I'm itchier, Dayzee."

"No, you're not, Mare. No way."

"I'm the absolute itchiest," said Sophia. "I'll prove it when I finally find that barmaid slash actress."

"Sissy, I think I'm the one that—"

"Oh, God, enough!" said the Boss. "You three sort it out. I'll be downstairs."

He began his hike down the stairs.

"Oh, that's right," said Dayzee. "Mack never did bring that whiskey up here for us."

"Such a slacker," Sophia said with smirk.

"Dead Slacker, Sissy."

"Girls, are we sure he's dead? I mean, do we know for sure?"

"Oh," said Marilyn. "I don't know, Dayzee."

"I say we call him Mack Slacker. How's that?"

"Oh, Fia, that's brilliant."

"Good one, Sissy!"

*  *  *

The three girls had picked a direction, and they took off with slow strutting toward the first bedroom door. Marilyn reached for the doorknob, but Dayzee stopped her.

"No, wait, Mare. You know, we're kind of having rotten luck with that rip-off potion, Mack becoming Mack Slacker . . . even that squidtastrophe out by the—"

"Oh, good one, Dayzee."

"Thanks, Mare. It's just that—"

"And the doors are all broken, a lot of the furniture is burned, and there's a portal with weirdos coming through."

"Yeah, Fia. All of that too. I'm just saying that we're due for some good luck. Come on."

She took each by a hand and led them farther down the hall.

"Where to, Dayzee?"

"Fia, let's go right to a luxurious bedroom just ahead."

"Aren't they all?"

"Well, yeah, Mare, but this one has a giant walk-in closet. You remember mine? Like that."

"So?"

"Fia, we should dress ourselves up a bit. Jiff is coming, remember?"

"Oh, you're right. We're finally going to get going on Kildare in the Hills. That Dirk squid guy turned out to be a slacker too."

"Yeah, Mare. Moe's still kind of hot, though."

"Ew," Sophia said, wrinkling her nose. "He's just a puddle of slime that—"

"I'm joking, Fia. Slime isn't my type."

"And just how did you become such a famous film star? Hmm?"

"That's funny, Mare. Good point, though. It took some acting."

"Bet you burned more than a few."

"Oh, hell yeah, Fia."

* * *

Dayzee held a finger to her lips, and the twins waited quietly, both watching her swing in the bedroom door. All three stood close together and looked into the room.

Kenzie was covered in a quilt in a plush chair in the sitting area, looking straight at them.

"Huh," she said. "Took you long enough."

They walked in, and Dayzee said, "We thought you'd be hiding somewhere. Like under a bed."

Marilyn whispered to her sister, "Like that headless dead guy she had sex with!"

"Sis, shh!"

"Oh, Dayzee, I don't know what's going on with me. I think I left my brain downstairs somewhere."

"With that lion?"

"Yeah, Marilyn. Why not?"

"Oh," said Sophia. "We think we have bad news about Mack."

"He changed his name," said Marilyn.

"No, Sis, he really didn't. We kind of changed it."

"To what?"

"Mack Slacker," said Dayzee. "We thought it was a nice touch to keep part of his original name to remember him by when—"

"What are you talking about? Since when is he a slacker?"

"Since he got dead?" said Sophia.

"Oh, Fifi, Mack is dead?"

Marilyn shrugged and said, "We'd have to ask the lion that bit him to know for sure."

"Oh, damn. Even Mack," said Kenzie, but she didn't seem upset.

"That's why they call it the deathhouse," Dayzee said, shaking her head.

"Who calls what, what?"

"Oh, Kenzie, I just mean the guesthouse. Things have gone kind of bad out there."

"Lions," said Marilyn.

"Squids too," said Sophia.

"It's just a mess. We came up here to get away from it for a while."

"And for a sexy wardrobe change."

"That's right, Mare. Kenzie, we called my photo guy, Jiff. He's on his way. We're finally going to start shooting for Kildare in the Hills."

"It's about time," she said and kicked the blanket to the floor. "I dressed for that audition, so I'm ready."

Dayzee studied her for a few seconds, then looked at Sophia's short skirt and tight blouse and Marilyn's short and tight white dress.

"This is all very nice, but it's time for an upgrade. And that closet,"— she pointed toward a closed door—"has just what all of us need."

"And what's that, Dayzee?"

"Why, Mare . . . lingerie, of course!"

*　*　*

They all walked into the closet, which was almost as big as the bedroom. When Dayzee flipped the switch, it lit up like a lounge, revealing walls full of drawers and cabinets, and a line of velvet benches divided it all in two. Full-height mirrors were everywhere.

"Oh, my goodness," said Marilyn. "Where to begin?"

"Sis is right, Dayzee. It could take months to pick something out of here."

"Nonsense, girls. These two cabinets,"—she pointed to the right—"have all we need."

"What's that?"

"Well, Kenzie, I can answer that with two little words: baby dolls."

"I think that might be one word."

"Is it, Fia? Huh. Alright. The point is, we should all wear those for the opening scene to our reality show."

"So," said Marilyn, "the big question is what colors we all pick?"

Kenzie said, "My favorite would be—"

"Hold it," said Sophia. "I just thought of something. Dayzee, you're wearing white."

Marilyn clapped silently and said, "Yay! That's hot, Dayzee!"

"Sure, Fia. Why, though?"

"Moe."

"Who's Moe?" said Kenzie.

"Oh, I know what Sissy's talking about. Yes, Dayzee, you have to wear white."

Dayzee started to grin, pointing first at Marilyn, then at Sophia.

"Okay. I'll wear white. Just like that other time."

"What other time?" said Kenzie.

"Oh, Kenzie doesn't know about that," said Marilyn.

Sophia snickered and said, "Nope. But we're going to show her."

*  *  *

"Oh my God, that's a sight," Kenzie said from her seat not far from the bed.

She wore red to match her heels. Sophia wore black to match hers. And Marilyn wore pink since Dayzee was the star that was wearing white.

"It happened like that?"

Marilyn was seated on the bed with her legs stretched out and slightly apart.

"Yes, like this. I had to hold—"

"Had to?" said Sophia.

"Yes, Sissy, it was necessary. I had to hold Moe's horny head still, so I sat with my legs spread just like,"—she rubbed inside her thighs with both hands, pushing them farther out—"this. There we go."

Dayzee crawled up, saying, "And I got in just the right position,"— she set one knee on each side of Marilyn's legs, facing away from her— "just about like this."

Marilyn giggled and said, "Oh, no, Dayzee. You were closer."

"Oh, was I?"

She backed herself closer to Marilyn.

"A little bit more."

Dayzee laughed once and said, "There's hardly any room left!"

"Mm. Not much at all."

Kenzie said, "And Moe's head, it was—"

Marilyn giggled and said, "I held it nice and snug between my legs."

Sophia snickered and said, "That head was close to your knees, Sis?"

Marilyn, giggling softly, said, "Oh, no, Sissy. I had to keep that head very nice and close."

"I remember," said Sophia. "He was in there tight."

"Yes, he was. So, I had to be right here like this, and Dayzee had to almost sit on my lap. Show her, Dayzee."

"I sure will, Mare. I'm imagining that horny clone head right there too."

Dayzee leaned back slowly until she rested on Marilyn's lap.

Marilyn tipped her head to hold Kenzie's gaze.

"I had to hold that head tight, Kenzie. It was squeezed in between my thighs and couldn't possibly get away."

"You, uh, you—"

"I think I played with your hair, didn't I, Dayzee?"

Marilyn reached up and started brushing around Dayzee's hair while still looking at Kenzie.

"Damn, I don't remember, Mare," Dayzee said while looking up, arching her back, and holding in a deep breath.

Marilyn said, "Well, I'm going to now."

"Damn," said Kenzie. "And Fifi, you were where?"

"Good time for her to call you Fifi, Sissy."

Sophia nodded to her sister and said, "Dayzee was kind of tipping from that head getting busy, so I had to—"

"Had to, Sissy?"

"Well, yeah, Sis. I had to join in just to help Dayzee keep her balance."

"Can you show me? Where exactly?"

"Sure, Kenzie."

Sophia took her time climbing up onto the high bed. She shuffled in close until she was kneeling between Marilyn's legs, right in front of Dayzee, who was seated on Marilyn's lap.

Dayzee looked up into her eyes and said, "Fia, I'm sure you were closer."

"Was I?"

Marilyn giggled softly while Sophia moved in closer, and Dayzee began tugging the bottom hem of Sophia's babydoll, then smoothing it down everywhere.

"Can't get much closer, can I?"

"Hmm," said Dayzee. "Maybe."

"I don't remember you fussing with my babydoll quite that much, though, Dayzee."

"I could stop."

"Hmm," said Marilyn. "You'd better not."

"Then," said Sophia, "I had to hold Dayzee like this,"—she reached out to place a hand on each side of Dayzee and held her thick mane with both hands—"and not let go. No matter what happened to her."

"Wow," said Kenzie. "She, uh, she could have, um, I mean, you were kneeling right in front of her like that."

Dayzee turned toward Kenzie and said, "Who says I didn't?"

Marilyn giggled.

Kenzie said, "My God," then stood and kept staring while stretching her arms out, raising her lingerie.

She relaxed and was about to begin the short walk to the bed when Marilyn said, "Oh, stop right there."

Kenzie stopped.

Sophia grinned and said, "You should probably stretch more, just to be sure."

Kenzie held her arms out.

"And . . . hold it," said Dayzee.

Marilyn said, "To whoever invented high heels, we owe him a lot for a sight like that!"

"Sis, you set that up, didn't you? To use that line?"

"Well, sure, Sissy," Marilyn said with a soft giggle.

"Alright," Sophia said and tipped her head for Kenzie to resume her walk to the bed.

She soon stood near with her bare thighs pressed against it.

"Damn that Moe," she said.

None of the girls stopped or looked toward her, but Marilyn said, "Why are you damning horny Moe, Kenzie?"

"Because . . . because I'm jealous of that damn head."

"Aw," Marilyn said gently, "Kenzie's itchy too."

"Poor Kenzie, Sis."

Sophia kept kneeling and playing with Dayzee's hair, pulling her closer, and they all turned enough to see Kenzie staring from one to the other.

Dayzee waited until Kenzie again looked at her, then she said, "Well, wherever could these gorgeous twins and I find an actress talented enough to play Moe?"

# Chapter 17 – Can't Let Go Now

Standing by the window overlooking the backyard, all four girls looked out at a scene of chaos and destruction. The window was small, so they were mostly hugging while pressed together, all of them still dressed in lingerie.

"That's some real trouble out there," said Marilyn.

"Yeah, Mare. We probably should have checked on that when we first heard the screaming."

"Nah," said Sophia. "Why stop? Something's always screaming around here."

"I couldn't stop," said Kenzie, grinning even at the sight of lions chasing yard guys and film guys around. "I couldn't even get myself free of that, um, demonstration of how Marilyn kept Moe focused."

"Oh, you sure stayed focused," said Marilyn.

"We had to stick to the script, Kenzie. There was no—"

"Had to, Dayzee?" Marilyn said with a giggle.

"Damn right, Sis."

"I was just saying that there was no way for Moe to escape either. When someone volunteers for that, they have to see it through."

Kenzie laughed and said, "Like when severed heads volunteer, you mean?"

"Actresses, too, Kenzie."

"Oh, you're so right, Fifi. So, what's next?"

Still looking out the window, Dayzee said, "That mess out there isn't going anywhere anytime soon. And that criminal Jiff isn't here yet. So, variations on a theme, anyone?"

"I'm in!"

"You're in for anything, Sis. Me too, though."

"Kenzie?"

"Well, Dayzee, in order for me to understand completely what transpired at that fateful event with the severed head of Mr. Moe, it would be only wise for me to experience it all from a variety of perspectives."

Sophia smirked and said, "I think she means—"

"Yes," said Kenzie. "Kenzie means yes."

*   *   *

The bedroom door was flung open, and the Boss stood there with a drink in his hand.

"Well, look at you all. What's the celebration?"

"Mostly," said Dayzee, "girls just want to have fun."

Marilyn said, "And we got dressed up for our reality show. Jiff will be here soon."

"And we were telling Kenzie about how Dayzee got cured of her squids by a head named Moe."

The Boss had been looking at each of them, then he focused on Kenzie and waited.

"I'm Moe."

"Huh?"

"Only this time," said Dayzee. "We're going to need a few more times through the scene."

"Well, okay. Fine by me. Hey, I just wondered if you saw what dragged itself out of the guesthouse."

"Oh, that damn deathhouse," said Dayzee. "What now?"

They turned back around and squeezed in closer to look out the window again. Standing near the deathhouse was something in the shape of a man, with about that many legs, some of which were more like parts of an octopus. It wore some of Dirk's clothes and had the face of Moe.

"Sheesh."

"True, Sissy. Very much."

"What the hell is that?" said Dayzee. "All that slop got stuck together somehow?"

"I'm still Moe, right?" said Kenzie. "You're not going back to that guy, are you?"

Marilyn said, "She called it a 'guy!'"

"If she does," said Sophia, "I'll sign you on as my personal Moe."

"Me too, Sissy. I need a Moe too."

"Girls, no one's trading Kenzie for that walking nightmare pile of slop."

"That's funny, Dayzee. Like that could ever really be a choice."

"Thanks, Mare. I wanted that to be funny."

"Sure," said Sophia, "but that thing isn't all that funny. What are we supposed to do with that? Even the Collectors didn't want it."

Dayzee mumbled to herself, "Well . . . it's not moving too fast . . . and the gates are closed . . ."

She spun herself back around and said, "Boss, go downstairs and have another drink."

He stared at her.

"Shoo! We'll be down in a second or two. Or an hour. Go on!"

He shrugged and walked out.

"Oh, and close the door. Yeah. Good. Thanks."

Dayzee looked at each of the Kildare Killers, then at Kenzie.

"Don't even try to argue with me, girls. I'm Moe next."

"Who's Dayzee, then?"

Dayzee thought for a few seconds, then said, "Well, good actresses—which we all are—should be able to play every part. Right?"

"Very true, Dayzee. Mm-hmm."

"I agree, Sis. Oh, yeah."

Kenzie said, "Do we have to change colors every time?"

Dayzee looked at the twins, chuckled, and said, "Such a sweet kid."

Sophia snickered and said, "Wait a second. I like her idea."

*   *   *

"I wanted to keep my babydoll," Marilyn said sometime later as they all traveled down the stairs and toward the great room.

"Sis, you're pouting again. We probably need these more normal clothes for the show. We can't be driving our audience crazy."

"Mare, we'll get back to that Moe scene someday soon. Right now, we have a Dirk squid to catch or kill."

"Or both," said Sophia.

"Dead Dirk Squid," said Marilyn.

"I'm Moe. I like being Moe."

"You've really lost your mind, haven't you, Kenzie?"

"If I didn't before, I did just now upstairs."

"Happy to help," Sophia said with a snicker.

"More like helping yourself, Sissy."

"It was only in memory of Moe."

"Funny, Sissy."

"Girls, we have to focus on—oh, what the hell is this?"

Dayzee spread her arms to her sides and stopped Marilyn, Sophia, and Kenzie behind her on the stairs.

"Oh, boy. This is just wonderful."

*   *   *

"Uh-oh, Dayzee," Marilyn said softly. "The dead are walking again?"

Sophia scoffed and said, "Serving drinks, too, Sis."

"Oh, but that's good," Marilyn said, pointing. "At least he's not looking for head."

"Want to bet?"

"Girls, hold on. I think our lives just got even more interesting."

The Boss was seated at the bar, and Mack Slacker was holding a washcloth in one hand, standing behind the bar and not moving at all. His blank eyes stared across the room. His face had been gnawed on.

"Yeah, that's interesting," said Kenzie. "But it would be hard to beat me being Moe upstairs."

Dayzee turned and squinted at her.

"Oh, Kenzie," said Marilyn, "we never abused that Moe character."

"Kozy sure did," Sophia said, shaking her head at Marilyn. "I'm not sure he liked it either."

Dayzee began grinning while watching Sophia speak.

"We did kind of abuse him, Sissy. Spinning someone's head in a blender might be considered abuse."

Dayzee shook her head at Marilyn.

"Girls, maybe *this* Moe is trying to tell us something?"

Marilyn giggled and said, "Somebody, quick: write abuse into the script."

"I'm all for ad-libbing," Sophia said, turning her smile toward Kenzie. "How about it, Moe?"

Kenzie nodded and said, "It's all for the reality show, right? Yeah, that might be a good—"

"Alright, girls, settle down. We'll figure that out later. Right now, we got a chewed-up bartender to figure out. Come on."

She led them all toward the bar, where the Boss spun around and smiled at each of them.

"He's not much for conversation, but he certainly knows his job."

Dayzee pointed and said, "Mack Slacker? How?"

The Boss said, "I think it's that portal in your basement, Dayzee."

Marilyn said, "Oh, no. It's not in—"

Dayzee elbowed her and said, "Yeah, Mare. We know. So, Boss, you're saying more Guild garbage is—"

"Guild garbage," Sophia said while shaking her head.

"That's kind of silly, Sissy. Perplexing, too, though."

"Another good word, Sis. Keep them coming."

"Only until I get hot enough, Sissy, then they have to stop that because—"

"Girls! Oh, you're still worked up, aren't you?"

Kenzie said, "Moe too."

"Oh, boy. So, Boss, it's something like that assassin thing, and it came back to get Mack Slacker back to work?"

"Back to dancing," Marilyn said with a giggle.

"Sis, he's not dancing."

"Not yet, Sissy. Just wait until—"

"Girls, please! Is he going to try to kill us, Boss?"

"No, I don't think you have to worry about that. Whatever got Mack dancing again seems—"

"Oh, it's you, too, isn't it?"

The Boss grinned and shrugged.

"It's kind of fun. Anyway, I think whatever they shot through that portal is more of a trickster. A prankster. I think this corpse will—"

"Cadaver," Dayzee said. "The Collectors like to call—"

"Aw, Dayzee," said Marilyn, "we're feeding Mack Slacker to those creeps?"

Sophia scoffed and said, "He can teach them to dance."

"That's funny, Sissy. Maybe they already know how, though?"

Dayzee held the Boss's gaze and shook her head, saying, "Those gorgeous twins, huh?"

"No one knows they're not from Earth? Or you, either, Dayzee?"

Dayzee's eyes popped open wide, and she tipped her head quickly toward Kenzie, who was calmly looking at each of them in turn.

Then, she turned to Dayzee and said, "I don't even care anymore, Dayzee. Because I'm Moe. And Moe doesn't care."

"Well, there you have it," Dayzee said. "We're good. So, Boss, you keep drinking whatever the dead bartender brings you. The girls and I have to go out and see about some kind of dead Dirk squid mess that made even the Collectors gag."

"I bet you have a joke for that Sissy."

"You know it. It's about Dirk and his biggest flipper and how he—"

"Okay, Fia. We don't need all the details. Are you three ready to go?"

"Upstairs for more?" said Kenzie. "Moe is. Yep."

She turned and started walking toward the stairs, and Marilyn and Sophia each grabbed at her arms. But all they got was the blouse sleeves and since Kenzie had been unbuttoning, the blouse began to peel back and off of her shoulders.

"You simply can't let go now, girls," Dayzee said with a chuckle.

"I'm not about to."

"Me neither, Sis."

A second later, Kenzie couldn't walk any farther. Both arms were angled back, and the blouse had trapped her around her wrists.

"Together, Sis. Ready?"

"Uh-huh."

"Okay . . . now!"

Together, they yanked at the blouse, releasing Kenzie who turned around to show them what they'd done.

"Topless is a good look on you," Dayzee said.

"Oh, yeah. Very nice, Kenzie. I mean, Moe."

"Sis, I just thought of something: we've been surrounded by topless dead guys, right? It just makes sense that we should be topless most of the time too."

"Sissy, you're brilliant."

She started pulling down her straps and walking away with Kenzie.

"Girls, no! Moe, try to cover up a little, alright? We have work to do."

Marilyn pouted and pulled her straps back up.

"Hey," said the Boss. "Here's an idea: you three go out and wrestle with squids, and Kenzie, I mean, Moe, can be my drinking buddy till you get back."

"Oh, I see," said Dayzee. "She can probably just stay headless too?"

Marilyn whispered, "I think she meant topless, Sissy."

"Uh, no, Sis. I think she wants Kenzie to stay headless when she's alone with the Boss. As in, without any head."

"Oh. Yes, that's probably right."

"Are we finally ready to deal with squid guts?"

"Oh, okay, Dayzee. Sure."

"Thanks, Mare. Fia?"

"Sure. Why not?"

Kenzie began buttoning up and walking toward the bar.

Mack Slacker stared across the room, motionless.

"Just scream if you need us," said the Boss, before taking a sip.

Dayzee said, "Just wonderful," before following the Kildare Killers out into the bedlam of the backyard.

"Oh, and Dayzee?"

"Yeah, Boss?"

"If you decide to try that mega potion of theirs, even if it's their crap, look me up. I'll schedule all of you."

Dayzee tipped her head toward Kenzie and said, "What about the earthgirl?"

"Oh, for sure. Uh, if you're alright with that."

"Sure, what the hell. I'm kind of curious what that might do to her."

"Dayzee, you want to watch? Is that what you're saying?"

"Damn, Boss, we all do."

# Chapter 18 – Reliable Prisoner Cadaver Help

Dayzee closed the sliding glass door behind them, then hurried a few steps to catch up with the Kildare Killers.

"Oh, look over there," said Sophia. "Some creepy parents you have there, Dayzee."

The Collectors were standing near the open door to the deathhouse and even from that distance, they all saw their teeth chattering like crazy.

"Huh. They look pretty content here. They must be happy with the supply of . . ."

She pointed toward Marilyn as they hiked across the grass.

"Cadavers!"

"Right, Sis. All except for that one," Sophia said, then pointed toward the pool.

The slimy, tentacled creature that used to be Dirk, and Cliff before that, was ambling slowly down the steps into the water.

"Sheesh. Not exactly a rocking Beverly Hills party, Dayzee."

"No, Fia. Not even close. So, girls, what's first? Have a chat with those creeps or slither over to—"

"She said 'slither,' Sissy."

"—to the pool and slap around that squid thing that should be producing our reality show?"

They all stopped and considered their choices, then turned to look toward the mansion at the sound of the sliding glass door squealing open.

Two new Collectors shuffled out, one closed the door, and they began the trek to the deathhouse.

"Will you look at that?" said Dayzee. "It's a Collector free-for-all."

"Are they all coming through that portal?"

"Yeah, Mare, I think so. Oh, and look at their feet."

Sophia busted out a loud laugh and said, "Those creepy things can't be for real. Hooves?"

"They won't be dancing with those heavy shoes, Sissy."

"Well, Sis, they're going to lop off some guy's feet and—"

"Some headless guy, Sissy?"

"Maybe. Sure. The point is that—"

"Girls, let's save that for later. We have work to do."

Marilyn pouted and said, "I want our reality show. That Jiffy guy better figure something out."

"Mare, he figured out how to sneak out of jail. He'll figure out our show too."

"When's he going to get here?"

"Soon, I hope, Fia. Maybe we should try to tidy up the yard before he shows up."

Marilyn laughed and said, "No one ever has used the word 'tidy' when dealing with Collector creeps and squiddy Dirk guys."

"Lions, too, Sis."

"Oh. Them, too, Sissy."

"Girls, let's go strangle that squid first. At least then we can maybe do a few quick shoots around the pool with Jiff."

"Okay, Dayzee, but I might never go in that water again."

"I'm with Sis. Slime like that doesn't ever come clean."

"Even though it kind of looks like Moe?" said Dayzee.

"Huh. I like the kind of Moe we met upstairs way better."

"She's a very good actress, Sissy. She even acted as if she liked it!"

* * *

"Alright, so what's your story?" Dayzee said to the squid man, stopping it halfway down the steps into the pool.

It turned, with a face reminiscent of Moe, only stretched and slimier. With a low wail, its mouth groaned open to allow a long tendril to begin snaking out and waving around.

"Sheesh," said Sophia. "That still looks like Moe, but there's some of Cliff mixed up in it too."

Marilyn pointed at the twitching, wailing humanoid slop and said, "Sweetie, you got two faces there, but neither one of them is very pretty."

"Sis, you amaze me sometimes. Well done."

"Thanks, Sissy. I've been saving that one."

Sophia turned toward Dayzee and said, "Imagine that Moe Cliff head working on your squid babies, Dayzee."

"Oh, Fia, that's disgusting! But, um, you think that would have worked?"

"Dayzee," said Marilyn, "a Moe like this could have cured you of all kinds of things."

"Ugh. Well, we'll figure that out next time."

Sophia smirked and said, "Next time we have a squid pool guest that looks like Moe and you have a squid in your oven that needs some fixing? That kind of next time?"

"Fia, you make a good point. Still, look at how that tongue of his—"

"She said 'tongue!'" said Marilyn. "And 'his!'"

"Well, Mare, we have to accept people as they—"

"She said 'people!'"

"Sis is making some good points, Dayzee."

"Okay. Yeah, she is, Fia. Um, I don't even remember what I was saying."

"Hey," she said to the squid, "what are we supposed to do with you?"

The tongue coiled itself back inside like a retractable power cord. With a voice somewhat like Moe, the thing said, "We can offer you a unique opportunity. Don't pass it up."

"We, who? Moe, is that you?"

"Yes, it's me. Well, sort of. Cliff is here too. And—"

"Not Dirk?" said Marilyn.

"Sis, he's been squiddified again. He's back to being Cliff."

"Oh, you're right, Sissy."

"And your favorite squid is here too. We're kind of a team."

"And what exactly is this golden opportunity of which you speak?"

Marilyn whispered, "Sissy, I love it when Dayzee gets all sarcastic."

"She sure put that squid slash Cliff slash clone head in its place, Sis."

"That's a lot of places."

"Girls, let him answer."

"She said 'him!'" Marilyn whispered to her sister.

Moe's face cleared slime from its throat and said, "Simple. I can impregnate you with squidlets, then deliver the inoculation you'll be begging for, and since the entity known at one time as Dirk has been completely dissolved and digested—and it was yummy—I can also—"

"Film the whole thing?" Sophia said, shaking her head at the quivering creature.

A slender tendril pointed her way, and Moe said, "Exactly. Really, Dayzee, who else could make you this offer?"

"Um, probably . . . I mean . . ."

"Let's take a little romp upstairs, alright?" said the mess.

"You'd have to, I mean . . . we'd need a wet sponge to keep you—"

Marilyn cackled and said, "Dayzee, you can't really be considering that!"

"Oh, Sis," said Sophia, "Dayzee must always be way more itchy than she lets on. Even that escapade with the fake Moe upstairs didn't—"

The Moe face of the squid snapped toward Sophia, sending pool water drops out toward the girls.

"Sheesh."

"Who is this fake Moe?" said Moe.

"Somebody that looks quite nice in a barely-there babydoll," said Marilyn.

"Sis is right. Think you could ever squirm all of that into some lingerie?"

The face's eyes turned down, and its dripping body sighed.

"No. No, I don't think so."

"So," said Sophia, "we'll just go ahead and put you out of your—"

"Fia, wait. I'm still thinking that maybe, even if Moe can't rock a babydoll like Kenzie, then—"

"Dayzee, no!" screamed Marilyn. "Don't you dare!"

"But—"

Sophia bumped her to the side and pushed the slithery mess into the water with the pool net, sending a plume of bubbling water to the surface.

"Sissy," Marilyn said, chuckling. "Really? I think that Moe thing kind of likes the water now."

"Oh. Right, Sis. We'll have to—"

With loud roars, two mountain lions launched themselves from the grass and splashed into the pool, diving under for the squid that twisted and squirmed near the bottom.

"Well, what the hell," said Dayzee.

They surfaced, dragged it out of the water, and backed away with it in their jaws. The girls watched as they dumped it in a sunny part of Dayzee's lawn and began chomping on it.

"No delivery to those nasty Collectors this time," said Marilyn.

"Seafood in the sun. Good girls, lions," said Sophia.

"Just how many times," said Dayzee, "has that slop been dragged around by lions? This reminds me of that dead, headless, blind Colombian cowboy, The Kid. They just kept dragging him away too."

"They did bring him back, though, Dayzee," said Sophia.

"Damn lions," said Marilyn.

They turned at the sound of Moe screaming while lions growled and ripped at the squid.

"Moe, we're sorry!" said Dayzee.

"Don't be!"

"Huh? Why not?"

"Who do you think is eating whom? Hmm?"

"Sheesh, Sis. I liked that head better when he was on a book on the bar, drinking with us."

"It's a head that went bad, Sissy. I've never heard of bad head before either."

"Girls. So, Moe, why are you screaming, then?"

The lions paused their feasting, and Moe's eyes locked onto the girls.

"Because I'm acting! I'm an actor!"

"Just wonderful. Another one," said Dayzee.

*   *   *

Dayzee was still shaking her head at the sight of vibrating, rubbery pieces of the Cliff squid thing getting chewed and swallowed on her lawn. The Moe head part of it split its time between howling in mock pain and laughing insanely at the sky.

"Go ahead and say it, Dayzee."

"Well, now would sure be a good time, Fia."

"You really should, Dayzee. This is almost too much."

"Okay, Mare. Yeah."

She reached for the sky and yelled straight up, "Only in Beverly Hills!"

Marilyn clapped, and Sophia nodded as Dayzee lowered her arms and scoffed at the madness all around them.

"I do feel better for saying it, girls. Oh, what do we have here?"

She pointed toward two yard guys in prison orange carefully navigating toward them, tiptoeing with their eyes on the feeding lions. Or feeding squid.

"Ma'am," said one, "uh, I think we quit."

"Yeah. Yeah," said the other, "send me back. Put me back in a goddamn cage."

Dayzee pointed at the lions feasting on a squid.

"You'll let a little challenge like that scare you off? Tsk, tsk."

"They're just kitty cats," said Marilyn.

"Uh, hungry, though," said Sophia. "We'll need some solid help around here to clean up whatever they leave behind."

Both men watched the cats for a few seconds.

"Uh, you're all really hot and all, and we like looking at you, you know, but um . . ."

"Really, lady, we just want to go. Can I use your phone?"

"Is it a local call?" said Dayzee.

"There she goes again, Sissy."

"She's kind of funny, Sis."

"Uh, yeah. Sure. One call to the warden, and he'll send the wagon for us."

"Well, boys," said Dayzee, "you've done a wonderful job with the grounds. I'll give you a good reference."

She turned enough to point toward the deathhouse.

"You'll find what you need right there in that, um, guesthouse."

"Uh, who the hell are they?"

"They're her parents," Marilyn said with a giggle.

"They live in a house on a toxic dump," Sophia said, shaking her head and grinning.

All of them watched the Collectors standing near the doorway, their rows of tiny brown teeth chattering silently.

"Um, they look kind of, uh . . ."

"Eager to help?" said Dayzee. "Yes, they are. They're very—"

All heads turned at the sound of the sliding glass door sliding open again. Two more Collectors stepped outside, one closed the door, and they proceeded toward the deathhouse.

"They're very polite, Dayzee."

"Yeah, Mare. I like how they keep the doors closed. Air conditioning isn't cheap."

"Wait," said the first guy. "Who are those two?"

Sophia snickered and said, "Aunt and uncle?"

"Oh, Sissy," said Marilyn, "you're just being silly. You know that's Dayzee's parents' dogs."

"Huh? What kind of dogs are those?"

Dayzee nodded and said, "Toxic dump, remember?"

"What? Yeah, okay, toxic is bad, but those two things—"

"No need to be impolite," said Marilyn. "You'll hurt their feelings."

They all watched the newest pair of Collectors clomping on their hooves toward the guesthouse.

The second yard guy had been mostly shaking quietly, but he said, "Hey, uh, Rufus, I think maybe—"

"Really?" said Sophia. "That's a real name? Damn."

"Yeah, lady. Yeah, he's Rufus. Uh, Rufus, I'm just going to run for the fence and hope I make it."

"I'm with you, brother. Something just isn't right here."

They turned and began a quick trot toward the line of shrubs and the tall wrought iron fence beyond it.

Dayzee and the twins watched them until they heard horses stampeding up from behind them.

They whipped around and saw the two fresh Collectors galloping at a high speed toward the escaping prisoners.

"Oh, will you look at that," said Dayzee.

"They're really hoofin' it."

"Very nicely said, Sissy."

Just as the two men were about to reach the wall of bushes, the Collectors leaped onto them, and they all tumbled in and out of sight.

"Never thought I'd see something like that," said Dayzee.

"Just can't get good, reliable prisoner cadaver help these days."

"No, Sissy. Not in Beverly Hills anyway."

"Right, girls. Maybe in other places."

They watched until the waving branches had settled, and the only sounds were lions biting into squid bones and the occasional alternating screams and maniacal laughter from the remains of a head named Moe.

# Chapter 19 – No Flocks of Collectors!

"Uh, Dayzee? Are we sure that those bad lady lions don't want us because we're not from Earth?"

"Well, that's probably true, Mare. Why?"

Sophia pointed behind Dayzee and said, "Lady lions are coming to get us. Lots of them."

Dayzee turned to look and said, "Wonderful. I don't want to take that chance, so we should get back in the house."

Sophia looked toward the glass doors and said, "Uh-oh. More lions are blocking the door."

"Can't we just throw some yard guys to them?"

"You want to just stay out here, Mare, and feed the lions? My yard is like an Earth zoo now?"

She shrugged and said, "Um, kind of. Except for the squid with the Moe head. No real Earth zoo has that, I bet."

"Never mind the squid, Sis. Let's make a run for the garage."

"Okay," said Dayzee. "But it won't be easy getting all the way around the house with these heels."

"Damn lawn."

"Another good one, Sissy."

"Not damn heels?"

"No, Dayzee," said Marilyn. "Never."

They hiked around the house and were about to hurry in where a door was opened up, but Dayzee stopped them.

"One second first."

She took out her phone, and Sophia scoffed.

"Yeah, you should give Dead Carpenter another call."

"Being dead is no excuse for being a slacker, Sissy."

"Girls, no, I'm trying to open the gate. Maybe some of this nonsense will run out for the rest of the neighbors to enjoy."

"Good plan."

"Except that it's not working, Fia," Dayzee said as she tapped the phone repeatedly and watched the massive iron gate not responding.

"Dammit, it's always something. Come on. Let's see what that Boss has been doing."

"Or who he's been doing," Sophia said with a smirk.

"Oh, you think, Fia?"

"I would," said Marilyn. "So would Sissy. We all would. Again!"

*　*　*

Dayzee and the twins were about to step inside the garage and at the same time, one of Dirk's cameramen, holding a camera, ran up to them.

"Please, don't let them get me! I'm just a temp, and I don't—"

"Dead Temp, Sissy," Marilyn whispered.

"Huh? What's that?"

"Nothing," said Dayzee. "Sure, come on inside. Does that camera work?"

"Uh, yeah. You want me to film this crazy stuff?"

Dayzee looked around at the front yard, where lions were growling and roaring and dragging men into the shrubbery, two lions were trying to scale the light pole where two men had sought refuge, and light traffic passed by like any other day.

"Well, maybe not this stuff. Inside is where the real action is probably happening."

"Oh, Dayzee," said Marilyn, "you think Kenzie and the Boss?"

Sophia scoffed and said, "Sis, she's probably Moe-ing him by now."

Marilyn stared at her sister, then Sophia said, "Okay, maybe not the exact same way. Still, though. Similar."

"Girls, let's not alarm this fine young bait, I mean, camera guy. Let's get inside before we test that immune from lions theory."

Sophia grabbed the shaking camera guy's hand, and they all hurried into the garage, where they had to file around a stack of fresh bodies, all of which still had their heads.

Dayzee stopped them all and pointed.

"Shouldn't the lions have delivered these by now?"

"These cadavers are certainly ready for the Collectors," said Marilyn.

"Do I have to be the one that says it?"

"I guess so, Fia," said Dayzee. "We want to hear it."

"Can't get good lion help these days."

"Good one, Sissy."

"Tell you what," Dayzee said to the camera crewman. "We'll hold onto that camera for a while, and you can start dragging these—"

"What? No way! I should be running for my life! I don't even know why I'm still here!"

"I do," Marilyn said as she started slipping her straps down over her shoulders.

She folded the dress down, gave him a pleasant smile, and said, "Here are two reasons."

The man stared from one to the other, sometimes looked up into her bright blue eyes, then returned for more.

"He needs more reasons, Sissy."

Sophia reached for the top button of her blouse, and the man said, "Uh, that's real nice, but I, um . . . I don't know if—"

"Hold on, Fia," said Dayzee. "Maybe you need a little help with that."

Dayzee stepped behind her, got really close, then reached around and started unbuttoning Sophia's blouse. Sophia locked her blue eyes on the soon-to-be dead cadaver delivery boy and reached high up with both hands to fluff around Dayzee's wild mane.

"That's . . . I mean," he said, "that's something, but I—"

"Usually when this happens," said Marilyn, "I sneak in real close and give Sissy a kiss. We're twins, you know."

While the man's eyes were darting around, trying to see it all at once, Marilyn giggled and stood near Dayzee and Sophia. She put her arm around Dayzee, pulling all three of them together, then turned her eyes again to the man.

"It starts with just a little kiss," she said, then gave her sister's cheek a quick kiss.

"Then," he said, "then . . . you, uh . . . you—"

"Then," said Marilyn, "I have to give Sissy a real kiss. She's so demanding sometimes! All you have to do is deliver these gentlemen to the, uh, guesthouse for us."

Dayzee had just opened the last button, and she slowly pulled open Sophia's blouse.

"Uh-oh," she said after exposing Sophia's lacy black bra. "Well, that's just not right."

Marilyn leaned in closer to her sister but kept her eyes on the camera guy.

"No, that's not right," said Sophia. "Not when—"

Dayzee popped open Sophia's bra and exposed her breasts completely.

Marilyn finished for her sister, saying, "Not when Sissy's getting undressed. Oh, no, she expects so much more than just a silly kiss on the cheek."

"I'll do it!" he yelled. "I'll deliver all of them. Don't move, none of you!"

He set his bulky camera on the hood of the limo and grabbed the top body. Still trying to watch the stripped girls all in a bunch, all three ready to do so much more, he grunted and began dragging the top dead guy out of the garage.

"I'll be back! I'll be right back!"

"Doubtful," said Dayzee.

"Earth," said Sophia. "It's almost too easy sometimes."

Dayzee hadn't let go, and neither had Marilyn. Sophia was still playing with Dayzee's hair with both hands.

Dayzee whispered in Sophia's ear, "I'm even itchier around all these dead guys."

Marilyn cooed to her sister, "Mm-hmm. Me too, Sissy. Everything is just making me itchier."

Sophia snickered softly, then in a more serious voice, said, "Who am I to argue? I'm just so demanding sometimes."

*  *  *

"Well," said Dayzee, "we should probably get inside. That Cadaver Yard Guy never came back for the second one."

"Slacker," said Sophia.

"They're turning him into superhero potion, Sissy."

"Ugh. If it wasn't actually their crap, I'd be more excited."

"Still, girls, we're honoring our bargain with those creepy toothy things. Soon, we'll go collect our potion and then, who knows?"

"Dayzee, maybe we'll dazzle all over. Not just our eyes."

"Oh, you know, Mare, you might be onto something."

"I'm wearing sunglasses just in case," Sophia said with a snicker.

"Smart girl, Fia. We all will."

She yanked open the door to the house and led the way inside. They heard music playing in the great room but no conversation.

"Huh," said Dayzee. "Any guesses?"

"Oh, maybe Kenzie is acting like Moe when Moe was just a head on a book on the bar. Remember that?"

"How's she going to do that, Sis? No, I think Kenzie is hiding somewhere, and the Boss is swilling all your booze and listening to some tunes."

"Oh. Yes, Sissy. That's more likely."

They rounded the corner and stopped to stare first at Kenzie dancing and swinging her blouse around, then at the Boss, who had a glass in one hand, a whiskey bottle in the other, and a gigantic smile.

"No, don't stop," said Dayzee. "What you two are doing is helping immensely with the lions and Collectors and cadavers and stuff."

Marilyn said softly, "Good one, Dayzee."

"Somebody's got to drink your booze," said the Boss.

"And do a striptease?" said Sophia, shaking her head.

Then, after watching for a few seconds, she smiled and said, "And a damn nice one too. No, don't stop, Kenzie."

"Or are you Moe?"

"Mare, no, she's only Moe when someone—"

"Is looking for head," Marilyn said while clapping quickly.

"Sis, you're still itchy?"

"Oh, Sissy, all the time. More than ever. I think all the Earth thrills are making me crazy."

"There's a theory about that, girls," said the Boss. "You've all been conditioned to survive here, but that's mostly physically. Your minds and emotions, though? They kind of get jerked around after a while."

"Uh," said Dayzee, "about how much of a while?"

He looked at his watch.

"No, you have to be joking."

"Dayzee, yes, I'm joking. Your horniness is all your own doing. If it's getting worse, it's probably—Kenzie, you could probably take a break."

"No, she can't," said Sophia.

"Uh-uh," Marilyn said, watching Kenzie gyrate.

Dayzee shrugged and said, "These girls. So, Boss. Yeah, it's getting worse."

"I think it's because you're all fantasizing about that voodoo potion."

"It's voodoo now?"

He laughed and said, "I think maybe it'll feel that way. Yep."

"Any day now for that potion," Dayzee said and hooked a thumb toward the deathhouse through the glass doors. "We're providing cadavers like you wouldn't believe. Those weirdos even had a chance for some fresh seafood."

"Did they like it?"

"No," said Marilyn, and she patted the barstool next to her for Kenzie to take. "They sent that seafood packing."

"To the pool," said Sophia. "God, what a mess that was."

"Then, some lions got it," said Dayzee. "That squid slop has been dragged around almost as much The Kid, that slacker blind Colombian cowboy."

"Okay, so you seem to have things under—"

He stopped, and all heads turned toward the closet and the sound of hooves clopping up the stone steps.

Marilyn said softly, "Oh no, that can't be more—"

"Well, Sis, do you think that maybe those are just—"

Two more Collectors crashed through the jagged edges of the door and stepped out where everyone in the great room could see them."

"—horses?"

"That's funny, Sissy. Not really, though."

"Oh, boy. Just wonderful. See what we're dealing with, Boss?"

"Like cockroaches, didn't I say?"

"Only bigger," said Kenzie, and everyone turned to look at her.

She wore a silly grin and was snapping her blouse like a whip.

At seeing nothing but staring eyes, she stopped and said, "What?"

"Nothing, Moe," Sophia said with a smile.

"I'm an actress, too, Fifi."

"She remembers your special name, Sissy."

"Girls, that's all cute and fun, but we have to figure out this Collector nonsense."

The clopping resumed, heavy iron horseshoes striking Dayzee's mansion's polished wood floors.

"You're paying to refinish that!"

"Dayzee, they'll never stop. Your guesthouse will—"

"Deathhouse," said Marilyn.

The Boss pointed at her and continued.

"—will only contain so many of those things. They'll break down your fence and obliterate the Flats too."

"All of Beverly Hills, Dayzee," Marilyn said with a pout. "Oh, and the Prism. Oh, that's not good."

"Sis, relax. We'll figure something out."

"It's that portal, Dayzee. As long as that's functional, those damn things will keep flocking in here."

"Dammit, no! No flocks of Collectors! What can we do?"

"There might be a way to destroy it. Let's go take a look."

"Uh, you want me to go too? Can't you just, I don't know, take a short walk and—"

"It's your mansion, Dayzee, so it's your portal. Come on. It'll be fun."

Dayzee sighed and said, "Girls, I guess you can just wait here. Drink with Moe."

"I'm Moe."

Dayzee sighed again.

"Yes. Yeah, Kenzie. You might have found your true calling in life."

"We'll find a way to keep her busy," said Sophia.

"No, Fia, you—"

"I'm going up to that closet. I want red this time."

"Sis, you can't have red because—"

"Girls! Oh, all of us are so damn itchy! Just sit still, let Mack Slacker—hey, what happened to Mack Slacker?"

"Oh," said the Boss, then he coughed into his hand. "He, um, he had to use the restroom."

Dayzee only stared at him, her face twisting into a scowl as her eyebrows climbed way up.

"Ew," said Marilyn. "I'm never using that room again, Dayzee."

Everyone looked at Sophia and waited.

She finally smiled and said, "Sheesh?"

# Chapter 20 – We Need a Bomb

"How old are these steps, Boss? Any idea?"

"Older than your mansion. Someone knew about this and built your house right above it."

They were taking careful steps on the broken stones, and Dayzee said, "Yeah, it was that Silvio. And he said somebody, maybe you, instructed him to conceal it and never tell me. Was that you?"

"Wasn't me. Maybe a clone of me."

"I guess it doesn't matter. He got what he deserved."

"Which is?"

"Lion chow. Two starving she-lions dragged him right down my street."

She looked up and pointed at the skylight so high up that it was just a postage stamp of light.

"I don't even know where that is. How many attics does this place have?"

"More importantly: how many Collectors? Have you been keeping count?"

"Nope. We tried that with dead bodies a few times, and we always lost track."

"Oh, look at that. A big old wooden door."

"Yeah, and smashed to hell. Alright, it's through there."

She waited. He waited.

"Well?"

"I'm not leading the way," said Dayzee. "You're the Boss. It's your job."

"Fine."

He took her hand, and they crunched their way over shattered slivers of old wood, leaning to get through. Before them waited the tunnel.

"Oh, great. I thought maybe Bruno made up that thing about a tunnel."

"I suppose not, Dayzee. You ready?"

"Sure. Let's go."

They hunched down and got through the tunnel as well as they could and entered into a small, dark room, where they stood and brushed dust and dirt off of themselves and each other.

Dayzee squinted in the dark, looking around at the walls.

"Bruno said there was some kind of ladder in this room."

The Boss looked around, too, then bent to pick something up, a piece of rusty, twisted metal.

"Like this?"

"Oh, it was here, like he said."

She searched more, then pointed and said, "Those freaks destroyed it. There are just pieces of it now."

"Well," said the Boss, "with massive hooves and heavy horseshoes, what do you expect?"

"Horseshit."

"That's funny, Dayzee."

"Thanks. Well, okay, the portal's in here somewhere. Go ahead and destroy it."

The Boss began scanning in every direction, then Dayzee said, "It's kind of chilly down here."

He put his arm around her.

"There. Hope that helps."

"It does. Thanks. So, what do you think?"

"I think I like hugging you."

"Aw, that's sweet. But I meant about the portal. Any ideas?"

He looked all around again and said, "I don't even know where it is. There's nothing here until someone or something opens it, just like by that statue at the Prism."

"Well, how the hell did you get here?"

"I'm not sure, Dayzee. I think I landed at the Prism portal, then two of those Collector clowns jumped to this one, and I kind of tagged along after them. But I don't know how to operate this one."

"So, there's no off switch, huh?"

"Nope, afraid not. Oh, we need a bomb. We'll blow all of this up. What do you think?"

"Sure, let's blow the place up. Can we save the mansion?"

"Oh, yeah, for sure. Probably. But I don't have a bomb."

"Boss! Dammit! Who does?"

"The labs, of course. We'll have to use the portal at the Prism to get there, though."

"Wonderful. You know, this is kind of peaceful down here, away from all that crazy stuff. Maybe you and I could—"

One corner of the round room started shimmering, making a low wailing sound.

"And . . . here we go."

Their heads appeared first: two Collectors, faces yellow even in the gloom, rows of tiny brown teeth chattering silently.

"I'm starting to kind of dislike those things."

"You're funny, Dayzee. What do you say we do some running?"

"Yeah, Boss. Run like hell!"

* * *

The Boss took Dayzee's hand and led her through the tunnel, then through the splintered old wooden door, then up the crumbling stone steps. But she stopped him halfway up and pointed.

"That damn skylight. That bothers me. Do we have time? I want to—"

The splintered door crunched and pieces scattered across the dusty floor as the two Collectors rammed their way through.

"Oh, those freaks."

"They're never going to stop, Dayzee. Come on. It'll take a while to get back here with a bomb."

"No quickie with barbs on these steps. I sure would like the creepiness of that in this dark, scary place where—"

The first heavy iron hoof hit the lowest step.

"Dayzee, we have to move. Come on!"

He pulled her arm, forcing her to follow, and they ran, sometimes laughing, up to the closet, then out into the house.

*　*　*

As they approached the great room, Dayzee said, "Boss, I hear music, but I bet Kenzie buried herself under blankets and pillows on the couch. This has to be too much for a regular earthgirl."

"I'll take that bet. She's not so regular anymore. She likes to play being the head of someone named Moe?"

"Oh, uh, yeah. That's not so regular. And she does play a damn good Moe's head."

"You'll have to tell me all about that sometime."

"You barged in on the tail end of it."

He pointed with a grin and said, "Oh, I did. Good choice of words. More than one tail too."

"Pull up a chair next time. It won't be long before those gorgeous twins and I get Kenzie to—"

They rounded a corner and saw Marilyn and Sophia seated at the bar, drinks in their hands, laughing and pointing at Kenzie, who was dancing in the middle of the room. She'd tossed most of her clothes around the room, all except for her panties and heels.

"Hey!" said Dayzee. "We're risking our lives down there, trying to figure out how to stop that damn Collector infestation, and—"

"Maybe you should call an exterminator, Dayzee," said Marilyn.

Sophia scoffed, never stopped watching Kenzie, and said, "Yeah, a Dead Exterminator."

"Could that work, Boss?"

"Dayzee, there's no way. He or she would be a Cadaver Exterminator in no time at all, and they'd just keep doing their collecting."

Dayzee pointed past the twins and said, "Looks like Mack Slacker finished his business."

"Yes, Dayzee, but he went back for more."

"More what? Hey, Mack Slacker. What's your story?"

His head turned slowly, and his blank eyes locked on Dayzee.

"Geez. Sorry I asked. Carry on back there."

"Maybe he doesn't like being teased."

"Oh, Mare, you might be right. What are you suggesting?"

Sophia said, "Let's get him back to just Dead Mack."

"Well, sure. Okay. That's not nearly as judgmental."

"So," said Sophia, "did you plug up that leak down there?"

"Oh, Fia, no. We need a bomb."

"Call your bomb guy, Dayzee," Marilyn said calmly while watching Kenzie dance. "I'm sure you have a guy for that too."

"It's Beverly Hills, Sis. Of course, she does."

Dayzee took a barstool on one side of the twins, and the Boss took one on the other side. All watched Kenzie dancing.

"No, I sure don't know a bomb guy."

"You had a guy to get the headless, burned body out from under the bed, remember?"

"Yeah, Mare. Carlos. But you girls burned him to dust."

Marilyn giggled and said, "Oh, we did. Yes."

"Didn't you have a guy to get a dead body out of a stuck elevator too?"

"Yeah, Fia. I wish it were only that easy this time. There are dozens of guys I could call for that. But a bomb? Huh."

"Girls," said the Boss, "the only way is to go back to one of the labs and bring a bomb here to Dayzee's mansion."

Grinning at Kenzie leaning enough to place both hands around an ankle, then caress her leg slowly as the straightened up, keeping her eyes on Sophia's, Sophia said, "Uh . . . have a nice trip."

Dayzee leaned forward to look at the Boss, who also leaned forward, and she shook her head. He only shrugged.

"I think we should all go."

"Dayzee, that's just silly. It takes only one, or at the most, two people to—"

A line of earthmen appeared at the glass doors, pounding and screaming to come inside.

"You were saying, Mare?"

"Well, that's not a big deal, is it, Sissy?"

"No, Sis, and we can't let in everyone that's scared about—"

A lion pounced on one of the men, silencing him as it chomped and chewed and removed his head.

"Yeah, Fia? Go on. Tell us all how it's not a big deal."

"Um, Dayzee," said Marilyn, "maybe I will tag along if—"

Another lion pounced, and a headless body in an orange jumpsuit quivered, started to fall, then straightened back up.

"Ha," said the Boss. "That thing, that assassin kind of thing, jumped right in there. That dead guy didn't have time to hit the ground."

"That could be another drinking game," said Dayzee. "No, look. All of you. We need to go."

Marilyn pouted and said, "But Kenzie is such a good dancer. We can't leave her without an audience."

"Sis is right. I volunteer to stay. And since the headless guys and lions will be in here soon, she'd be safer if she did her little dance upstairs where we could lock the—"

"Fia, no. We'd better bring her along, too, at least to the Prism."

Sophia looked at Kenzie and said, "Do you want to get dressed, Kenzie?"

She stopped dancing long enough to shake her head and say, "Uh-uh. Not me, Fifi."

"She's still calling you Fifi, Sissy."

"Damn," said Sophia, "and she's dancing naked for me, and she—"

"She's dancing for me, too, Sissy."

"What about me and the Boss? We like it too. Oh, but really, girls, we have to go. One of you, grab her clothes. Somehow, we can try to get her dressed in the limo."

"You get her clothes, Sis, and I'll get Kenzie."

"Oh no, Sissy. I'll get Kenzie and you can—"

The newest Collectors had reached the closet, and their heavy hooves were stomping the floor as they swatted at the shredded door.

"Girls! Both of you have fun grabbing Kenzie, and I'll get her damn clothes!"

"I'm Moe."

"Oh, boy. Gets better all the time."

Marilyn and Sophia quickly moved in to hug Kenzie from each side, and she put her arms up over their shoulders. Dayzee and the Boss gathered up the few garments that Kenzie had dropped around the room, and they were finally ready to go.

But the freshest Collectors were standing side by side, blocking the hallway to the garage. Their small eyes wandered around the room, each tracing its own path, then all four eyeballs focused on Kenzie and the twins.

"What now?" said Dayzee. "Girls, try burning those freaks. We should have tried that a long time ago."

"What about the potion, Dayzee? I want that potion."

"Me too, Sis. We're not killing any of these things."

The three girls had walked over and were facing the faces with rapidly chomping teeth which made no sound at all. Dayzee and the Boss were right behind them.

"I don't know," said Dayzee, "maybe just heat them up enough to move them aside?"

"Like a cattle prod," said the Boss, and all four girls stopped to look at him.

"What?" he said. "I'm just glad I got the Animal Husbandry download. Who knew it would become so useful?"

Dayzee scoffed and said, "Girls, prod the hell out of those two. And why the hell are they blocking us like that?"

"Oh," said Marilyn, "I think I know."

"Yeah, Sis. They heard the word 'bomb,' and they don't like it."

Dayzee got up close behind the three girls, put her arms around them, and looked up at the ghastly faces from between Sophia and Kenzie.

"Hey, you two. Don't make me call a Dead Exterminator. They probably have some kind of bug juice that would melt you down to sticky puddles."

The one on the left stopped chattering and said, "Your dead ex would never find the right spray to—"

"Hey, wait a minute," said Dayzee. "I don't have a dead ex. I said Dead—"

"If your ex is an ex-exterminator, for example, we could execute him and—"

Dayzee reached a hand between Kenzie and Marilyn, snapped her fingers, and pointed at the talking Collector.

"Enough. Geez, you guys."

She angled her finger toward the Collector on the right.

"You," she said, "it's your turn. Look, will you just get out of our way? And don't give me that jabbering nonsense that this one was."

"Yes," said the Collector with a single gray feather poking up from her fedora, "he does tend to go on like that."

Dayzee pointed at the feather, and Marilyn said, "A girl Collector. Yay!"

Sophia said, "Sis said 'girl.' Ha!"

"Oh, I did. Well, sissy, kind of a girl."

"Wait, girls, let her talk. So, can we get past?"

"You plan to destroy our means of escape from this hellish world?"

"Uh, yeah," said Sophia. "Just to keep millions more of you from camping in the walls."

"A million would be a lot," Marilyn said, nodding. "That was funny, though."

"Girls. Look," Dayzee said to the female Collector, "the yard and deathhouse are full of dead bodies for you."

They turned at the sound of a yard guy near the glass doors screaming. The screaming stopped when a lion snagged his head and pried it loose. The body started to fall but never dropped all the way before returning to full upright position.

The Boss raised a fist and said, "The assassin thing again. Nice work!"

The newly-dead yard guy saluted as if it still possessed its head.

"It's got a sense of humor too!"

"Wonderful, Boss."

Dayzee continued.

"And there are more cadavers for all of you every second, it seems. So, how about it? Plenty of gory stuff for you to suck up."

She tipped her head, chattered for a few seconds, then let her teeth rest.

"And after they've been consumed?"

Dayzee scoffed loudly and said, "Hey, it's Beverly Hills. You'll never run out."

"Good one, Dayzee."

"Thanks, Fia."

"Very well," said the Collector. "We have a need to consume until we are full."

"Well," said Dayzee, hugging the three girls squeezed together in a tight line, "this yard will always need a yard crew."

"And we tend to burn through them."

"Good one, Sissy. Very true too."

"Fine," said the Collector, and they both left for the sliding glass doors.

"Finally," said Dayzee. "Can we get going already?"

# Chapter 21 – The Dead Man Strut

"Fia? You might have to let go of Kenzie. Just for a second or two."

"I'm Moe."

"Sure you are," said Dayzee.

"Oh, alright," said Sophia.

While the Boss held open the limo's back door in the garage, Sophia stopped hugging Kenzie long enough to start climbing into the back seat.

"I'll hug her twice as much, then," Marilyn said with a giggle.

"Uh, no, Mare. Let Kenzie get in there too."

"Oh, okay."

She let go, and Kenzie sat then shifted right up against Sophia. Marilyn followed quickly and made an extra effort to squeeze Kenzie tight between them.

"How cozy," said the Boss. "Uh, Dayzee? About that bomb?"

"Right, we have to go. I could probably drive, or . . ."

He stared at her for a second, then coughed and said, "Oh, hey, why don't you let me?"

"Well, if you insist," Dayzee said with a smile, then hurried around to the passenger side.

They slammed the front doors and looked at each other for a moment, listening to the whispering and giggling in the backseat.

Then, they turned enough to look at the entry door to the mansion, where the two most recent Cadaver Collectors were standing in the open doorway and waving.

Dayzee waited until the Boss looked her way, then said, "Just another day in the Hills, Boss."

"It's always like this?"

"Uh, no. This is crazy. It's all getting way out of control."

"You still want that bomb, though, right?"

"Better than calling a dead ex," she said, giving him a smile. "Because I'd have to marry him then ex him then dead him, and we don't have that kind of time."

He nodded, started the limo, and began backing out of the garage.

* * *

An angry lion jumped up onto the rolling car then back down and trotted into the garage, where she began nosing around the stack of bodies.

The Boss locked the brakes when the rear bumper impacted a headless guy in an orange jumpsuit, which caused the backseat passengers to turn to look.

Marilyn glanced at her sister and said, "He's looking for head, Sissy. He can't have Moe's head."

"I'm a head. I'm Moe."

Sophia snickered and said, "No, Kenzie. He'll have to find his own."

"Boss, we really don't have time for this nonsense," said Dayzee. "How about getting this heap moving?"

"Sure. I mean, he's dead already, right?"

Dayzee shrugged and said, "We're not really sure. Probably."

"Close enough," he said, gave it some gas, and rolled the limo backwards to the sounds of squishing and crunching of bones.

"Somebody's cleaning that up, dammit," Dayzee said with a laugh.

"Yes, Dayzee. One of the Collectors will suck it all up."

"That's kind of all they do, Sis. Think about that: all day long, just sucking things up."

"That would be good, Sissy, except for the things they like to suck up."

The Boss had backed far enough that they could see the twitching body parts, dressed in orange, flopping around in a sloppy red pool.

"Oh, my driveway . . ."

"Look," said the Boss, pointing into the garage. "Those two are coming out through the garage. They'll clean it up."

"Okay, good. Let's get to the Prism. I need a drink or ten. How about you girls back there?"

No one answered, and Dayzee waited a while, then turned to look. She grinned, then looked at the Boss.

"Oh, those girls. No matter what they do, they just get itchier and—oh, there's Dead Mack, up by the porch."

"He's hitchhiking?"

"Yeah, Boss. Dead hitchhiking. Well, I guess he still feels like he belongs at the Prism. Let's give him a lift."

The Boss rolled the limo up to the hitchhiking dead bartender and hit the brakes. Dayzee popped open the door, then shimmied over up against the Boss.

"Come on, Dead Mack. You probably want to get back to the Prism too."

He stood still for a second, a washcloth hanging from one hand.

Over her shoulder, Dayzee said, "He still looks good, though, doesn't he, girls?"

She waited, but no one answered.

"I'm not even looking. God, those girls. Mack, we don't have—"

"Dead Mack," Marilyn said with a giggle.

"He might be self-conscious about that name, too, Sis. I think I would be."

"Oh, okay. Yes. Carry on, Dayzee."

"You too, Mare," Dayzee said with a loud scoff.

Dead Mack began moving clumsily until he was close enough to turn and sit on the seat.

"God, he never used to be this slow."

"Well, Dayzee," said the Boss, "he's dead now. That makes a difference."

He lifted his legs one at a time and rested his boots on the passenger side floor.

"And just like that, we're ready to go. Let's rock and roll."

The Boss squealed the tires before looking out through the windshield, and the limo plowed through a dead or dying film crew guy, right after the lion that was about to eat his head screamed and lunged off to the side.

His body splattered and rolled over the hood, up the windshield, and back down the other side, leaving a gory trail.

Sophia leaned forward and said, "That just seems right. Our limos always have gross stuff all over them."

"Sissy, we should make the Collectors detail our limo."

"There's no time, Mare. Do you remember why we're going to the Prism?"

"Um . . . oh, yeah. To get a bomb."

"Not quite, Sis. Pretty good try, though. We're going there to use the portal."

"Oh, it's like saying Dayzee's new portal is in her basement."

"That's right," said Dayzee. "It was actually through the closet, down the stairs, through the wooden door, then down the tunnel. So, we're—"

Kenzie said, "Prism, portal, lab, bomb, portal, Prism, mansion, closet, stairs, door, tunnel . . ."

The twins had frozen, staring at her, and Dayzee and the Boss had turned around, also staring. Everyone waited as the seconds ticked by.

"Then . . ." said Kenzie.

No one blinked. More seconds crawled past.

"Kaboom!"

"Moe's funny, Sissy."

"Yep. She's a good head."

"Can't argue with you, girls. Alright, Boss, how about if we crash the Prism? I think it's bring your own bartender day."

"Dayzee's funny, too, Sissy."

"Sure thing, Dayzee," said the Boss.

He got the limo to slow roll toward the exit gate while Dayzee tapped her phone to open it. But it didn't open.

"Dammit, I think these lousy gates are still the fault of The Kid. They were his job."

"Sure, Dayzee, but he got dragged away a long time ago."

"I know, Fia, but still. There's no way I'm giving him a good reference. He'll never work in this town again."

Marilyn leaned to look past Kenzie at her sister and tried to stifle a giggle.

Sophia only rolled her eyes and said, "We'll see about that."

"Another good one, Sissy. Dayzee would hire him again."

The Boss brought the limo to a stop near the gate, and two lions jumped onto the hood. From the shrubbery on each side, a Collector emerged and walked rigidly toward the car.

"Oh, boy," said Dayzee. "Alright, the lions don't want us, but maybe those chattering fools do."

"I don't think so, Dayzee," said the Boss. "They're kind of running a business here: corpses for potion, remember?"

"Cadavers," said Sophia.

"Corpses for cadavers, Sissy? How does that—"

A loud clunk accompanied the appearance of a hole in the limo's hood, shaking the car before they heard the gunshot.

"Oh, that guy still? Dammit, where the hell is he?"

"Who is he?" said Marilyn. "That might be the question."

"Very astute, Sis."

"Why, thank you."

"Alright, Dead Mack," said Dayzee, "you're up to bat because you're already dead. Get out there and open that gate."

He didn't move.

"We're seriously calling him that again?" said Sophia.

"Well, it's accurate."

"Um, he's dead, Dayzee."

"I know, Mare, but he has to pitch in too."

"Dead Mack!" she said while snapping her fingers in front of his glazed eyes. "Chop, chop!"

The dead bartender sighed, pulled the door handle and swung the door open, then tipped and fell in slow motion onto the driveway.

Marilyn giggled and said, "Hey, Dead Mack, just because you fall once doesn't mean you're going to fall all the time."

"Uh, Sis? I think that's supposed to be 'fail.'"

"Oh, I think you're right, Sissy. Either way, we just can't get—"

"Reliable dead bartender help?" said Sophia.

"Yeah, Fia," said Dayzee. "Exactly. Oh, wait. He's getting up."

Sophia leaned over from the driver's side, tipping Kenzie into Marilyn, and the twins kept her squeezed in tight, her face trapped between two pairs of breasts.

"Kenzie," Marilyn said, giggling, "can you still breathe in there?"

She nodded, didn't try to free herself, and said, "Comfy."

"Another good place for Moe's head," Sophia said with a smirk.

Even the Boss had leaned over to get a better view of Dead Mack.

Dead Mack had risen up to his hands and knees, the washcloth still in one hand, and a second later, a bullet thumped into his back.

Another second later, Dead Mack shook his head slowly and said, "Not my best day."

"He can talk!" said Dayzee. "This is amazing!"

"That lab," said the Boss. "They're always coming up with new stuff."

"Come on, Dead Mack," said Sophia. "Get your lazy ass up!"

Dead Mack rose to his feet and struggled to keep his balance, then he began shuffling toward the gate.

"Hey, Dead Mack, let's see some strutting!" said Marilyn.

He began swinging his arms in an odd rhythm, and his steps got longer.

"Huh," said Sophia, "the Dead Man Strut. Like a new dance."

"Yes, Sissy. Uh-huh. Um, do you still have to smoosh Kenzie between us like that?"

"Nope. No, I don't have to, Sis."

"Okay."

Dead Mack was walking backwards, one hand grasping part of the gate and opening it wide for them to drive out. He started walking back toward the car but stopped when Dayzee yelled at him.

"No, Dead Mack! We need you to close the gate again, alright? Geez, do I have to explain every little detail to you?"

"He can talk, Sissy, but maybe he can't think."

"He still has his head, Sis. That's something."

"Head," Kenzie said while squeezed in tightly between soft Kildare Killer pillows. "Moe's head."

"Boss," said Dayzee, "are you sure you can't build a bomb in my kitchen or something? Even this is out of control."

"Nope. Sorry, Dayzee."

"Sissy, you could probably lean back now and let Kenzie breathe."

"I could. But I think she likes it there. And I like her there."

# Chapter 22 – Thrown Out of the Flats

"Oh, look at that," Dayzee said as the Boss cruised the limo along the curb, nearing the Prism on Sunset Boulevard. "Our usual place is open."

"Well, Dayzee, they know it's us."

"How, Mare? Sunset gets limos trolling up and down it all day long."

Sophia smirked and said, "Covered in blood and guts?"

"Oh, good point. Probably not as often."

"Here's good?"

"Yeah, Boss," said Dayzee. "Damn, it seems like months since we've been here."

Marilyn laughed and said, "Oh, but it was only today. We've been busy."

She turned her head and said, "Kenzie's still busy. Sissy, we need to go inside."

"Kenzie," said Sophia, "do you want us to stop squeezing you in like this?"

She shook her head slowly, many times.

"Oh, Sissy, I like when she answers like that. Dayzee, watch."

Dayzee spun around on the front seat and the Boss did too.

"Kenzie," said Marilyn, "is your name . . . Bob?"

Kenzie turned her head from side to side as much as she could manage, held securely where the twins wanted her to stay.

"Try something for 'yes,'" said Dayzee. "See what that's like."

"Kenzie," said Sophia, "are you really Moe's head?"

She stared at Dayzee while she rubbed her cheeks against them up and down. Many times.

"As fun as that probably is," said Dayzee, "didn't you girls forget something?"

Both twins grinned at her and shook their heads slowly, while Kenzie continued to nod slowly.

"Oh, this is making me dizzy. Girls, you forgot to get Kenzie's clothes back on her."

"No, we didn't," Marilyn said with a giggle.

"Nope," said Sophia. "Didn't forget."

"But she's still . . ."

All three nodded in perfect time.

Dayzee looked at the Boss, waited for him to acknowledge her, he didn't, and she slapped his arm.

"Huh? Oh, I was just—"

"I don't blame you. I just wanted to comment about that, and those three are all too itchy and distracted to pay attention."

"Sure. What's that?"

Dayzee gave him a big smile for a second, then said, "Only in Beverly Hills."

"Uh, well, I got that Geographical Database download, and it—"

"I know, I know! Fine. Also in North Hollywood. Let's all get inside."

Dead Mack, to Dayzee's right, got bumped and tipped and clunked his head on the window.

"See? Dead Mack's eager too."

*　*　*

The Boss pulled the Prism's heavy wooden door shut after all of them had walked inside.

"Girls, maybe hold up Dead Mack, alright? I think Kenzie can stand on her own."

"She didn't want to get dressed on her own."

"No, Sis, she liked us dressing her."

"Kenzie," said Dayzee, "do you recognize any of this?"

Kenzie stared around the room while soft classic rock played from the jukebox.

"The Prism? Hey, I work here."

The twins looked at each other and both shrugged.

"Well, so much for Moe. Kenzie's back."

"It was fun while it lasted, Sissy."

The Boss said, "Change of plans. You can all wait right here, I bet. I'll get the bomb and be back before you know it."

They all looked toward the tall statue wearing a western hat.

"I'm still picking up some unusual vibe from that guy."

"Sure it's not just the portal?"

"No, Dayzee, I'm pretty sure it's that guy. Maybe his hat. Anyway, I'll be right back."

He took a brisk walk over to the silent statue and promptly vanished.

"Kenzie, do you feel like getting back behind the bar?"

"Uh, sure, Dayzee. Um, where have I been? I have just weird bits and pieces of memories: weird guys, lions, lingerie, and—"

"What kind of lingerie?" said Marilyn. "Do you remember?"

"Uh, just that it was all lacy."

"Close enough," Sophia said with a grin.

"Huh?"

"Nothing, Kenzie," said Dayzee. "Why don't you take Dead . . . I mean, Mack with you and get us some drinks?"

"Make them doubles."

"Yes. Sissy and I like to double up. We're twins."

"Okay. Come on, Mack."

She took his arm and matched his slow pace toward the bar, sometimes looking back at the girls with her eyebrows popped up high.

* * *

At the bar, Sophia sat to Dayzee's left and Marilyn to her right. They'd finished half of their drinks, and they watched Kenzie glance down at the washcloth in Dead Mack's hand, then back at them.

"He's usually wiping his hands with that," she said.

"He, uh, he's probably too tired," said Dayzee.

"What happened to his face? He's all torn up from something."

"Um, playing with a cat?" Sophia said, causing Marilyn to giggle.

"Sure. Yeah, that could be. He's not talking much either."

"No, Kenzie, but that could be because he's just focusing on his work."

"Yeah, Marilyn, I guess. But I'm getting tired of picking him up."

"His balance really is kind of shot to hell," Sophia said while nodding.

"We should have been counting how many times, Sissy."

"That never works, Sis."

"Well, whatever," said Kenzie. "Ready for refills, girls?"

Dayzee downed the last of hers, set the glass on the bar, and said, "Yeah, set us up."

At that, Dead Mack started to turn slowly, snagged a bottle, and turned back toward the bar. All of them watched as he uncapped it, then poured into Dayzee's glass.

He filled it to the top.

And he kept pouring.

"Uh, Mack," Kenzie said as she gently took the bottle from his hand. "We don't want Dayzee to get too drunk, do we?"

"I do," Marilyn said then winked at Dayzee.

"Me too," said Sophia, "and maybe you, too, Kenzie."

"Or Moe," Marilyn whispered.

"Or who, Marilyn?"

She pointed at Dayzee's glass and said, "I only said, 'No mo.' You know, for Dayzee."

Someone farther down along the bar called Dead Mack, and he turned and began a hobbled hike in that direction.

"Oh, boy," said Dayzee. "The things that happen in this place."

They watched Dead Mack stop in front of a young couple and take their orders. He was about to get their drinks, but they kept talking, so he stayed. The girls watched his mouth moving and the couple nodding. They appeared to be sharing a pleasant conversation.

"This is just weird," said Dayzee. "Nobody knows the difference."

"Difference with what?" said Kenzie.

"Nothing. You said you remember lingerie?" said Sophia. "What color?"

Kenzie got a silly grin, nodded, and said, "Red. It was definitely red."

"Huh," said Dayzee. "Like your heels?"

Kenzie looked down, then back up, and said, "Yeah. Ooh, I feel kind of funny."

"You've been through a lot," Marilyn said, nodding calmly.

"I have?"

"Lots of acting," said Sophia. "I mean, really good acting too."

"I remember calling you Fifi. That's always fun."

"No reason to stop that," said Dayzee. "Oh look, the Boss is back."

"Where did he go?"

The Boss was walking toward them with a compact briefcase.

"Uh, just to, um, talk to that statue guy."

"Huh?"

"Nothing, Kenzie. But we have to get going. I think you should come with us."

"That should trigger some memories," Sophia said with a smirk.

Kenzie stared at her, squinting.

"For us, too, Sissy. It might take lots and lots of read-throughs, though."

"I have no idea what you're talking about but if you're talking about Dayzee's mansion, I don't know exactly why, but I really want to go back."

"I know why," Marilyn said with a soft giggle.

"Sure, Sis, but we'll have to remind her anyway."

"Girls, we might not have time. We have a fuse to light up."

She clunked down her empty glass, the twins did the same, and they all spun around to leave for the limo.

* * *

The Boss cruised west on Sunset, and Dayzee looked over the seat at Kenzie tucked in between Marilyn and Sophia.

"I'm not sure we should have left—um, Mack there, girls."

"He's covering my shift, Dayzee," said Kenzie. "I have to go back soon and let him get on with his life."

Marilyn laughed loudly, and Dayzee frowned at her.

"What's so funny about that?"

"Nothing, Kenzie. Do you remember that you were coming to my house to be in that reality show?"

"Uh, vaguely. Yeah. That's why I dressed in a short skirt, right?"

"Yep," said Sophia. "Well, we're not so sure about that show anymore."

"No, Sissy, it's not looking good. We can have a drink at Dayzee's bar, though."

The Boss took the sweep to the left, then, after a couple of blocks, another left.

"Lots of nice houses in the Flats, Dayzee."

"Yeah, Boss, it's alright."

"Must be some interesting neighbors?"

"Sure. They're alright."

She turned to look at the twins to finish: "As long as they keep their damn cats out of my yard."

"Damn cats," Marilyn said, then sighed.

"I bet, um, Mack would agree."

"That's funny, Sissy."

"Mack doesn't like cats?"

"Well, Kenzie," said Dayzee, "it's just that—"

They all heard sirens in different directions but saw no flashing lights.

"Huh. Something's going on."

The Boss rolled the limo to a stop several houses from the entrance gate to Dayzee's estate. Across from Dayzee's house, there was a small group of people talking and pointing toward her house.

"Oh, boy. Now what?"

The Boss idled up to them and when Dayzee powered down her window, they recognized her.

"Well," said an older man, "if it isn't the famous Dayzee Dazzle."

"I don't have time for autographs. Sorry. We need to—"

A woman holding a poodle said, "Nobody wants your autographs, Ms. Movie Star."

"Oh, um, okay. Nice poodle you got there. That—"

"I used to have three! I only found the skeletons of the other two."

Dayzee looked at the Boss, but he only shrugged, so she turned again toward the neighbor.

"Well, there have been reports of mountain lions that like to—"

"Damn lions!" Marilyn yelled from the backseat.

The woman leaned and frowned toward the backseat, and Kenzie said to her, "I think I remember people calling me Moe. Was that you?"

"What? Why, I never. Ms. Dazzle, we've all gotten together and signed a petition to have you thrown out of the Flats."

"What? Why?"

She pointed across the street at Dayzee's wrought iron fence, where a motionless, ragged man in an orange jumpsuit held the bars and stared out.

"Things like that. Why do you abuse your staff like that? You obviously work them to the bone, and you—"

"Hey," said Sophia, "at least he still has a head."

The woman leaned and stared again. The poodle in her arms stared too.

"But if he didn't," Marilyn said with a giggle, "he'd sure be looking for it."

"What are you—"

She snapped her head to face Dayzee again.

"A lot of us have influential friends in politics around here, and your days are numbered, lady."

Marilyn leaned to look toward the woman over Dayzee's shoulder and said, "We tried counting all kinds of things, and we never could."

"Yeah," Sophia said with a snicker, "like—"

"Girls. Hold on just a—"

"I remember enjoying being Moe. What was that all about?"

"Look, neighbor," said Dayzee, "we're just trying to work out some business deals with some visitors from, um, out of town. And we've somehow let things get just a little out of control."

Every head turned at a scream and a roar, but all they saw through Dayzee's fence was a few waving shrubs that came to a rest quickly.

"Stuff like that!" said the neighbor. "What just happened to that poor man?"

"Off to the Collectors!" said Marilyn.

"Yeah, Sis, and off with his—"

"His paycheck if he doesn't clean everything up before leaving," said Dayzee. "It's so hard to get good help around here."

"Not for us," said the neighbor. "We have the most delightful youngsters that take care of everything."

"Send them over," Sophia said with a snicker.

Marilyn leaned forward and nodded while saying, "Sissy and I just get so itchy. Kenzie too. And Dayzee. We all get—"

"There's, um, some poison ivy all around the house," said Dayzee.

She tipped her head back toward her fence and said, "That fellow probably ran off for some lotion or something."

"Well, why did he roar?"

"Uh, he, um . . ."

She whispered to the Boss, "Drive! Start driving!"

To the neighbor, she said, "Indigestion!"

The car began to roll, and the small crowd started walking with it.

"Yeah, that must be it! Look, gotta go! It was nice to see you all!"

"You're getting thrown out of the Flats!" faded behind the limo, and Dayzee watched more than a few of them shaking their fists in the air.

"Dammit, maybe we should get those people collected."

"Yes, Dayzee. It would only be fair if they were turned into potion to give us all monster orgasms."

"What?" said Kenzie. "I don't know what you're talking about, but sign me up!"

"Kenzie, dear," Dayzee said while tapping her phone, then laughing at the gate opening, "you're already signed to a very important role."

"More like an *under* study," Sophia said with a big grin.

"And you're just going to have to practice and practice until you get it right!"

"I can't even stop you two anymore," said Dayzee. "Home, Boss."

# Chapter 23 – It's Only Getting Worse

The Boss zipped the limo just past the gate and onto the driveway, and Dayzee gave her phone a few more taps, then turned to look.

"Damn gate."

It hadn't closed and while she was watching, the band of neighbors screamed and scattered when a pack of lions rushed past them, then through the gate.

"Oh, boy. It just keeps getting—"

"Dayzee!" called someone from the outside, and she leaned out to look.

"Jiff? What are you doing up there?"

He sat atop one of the tall stone towers on each side of the massive iron gate.

"I thought you knew I was coming. I couldn't get in, so I climbed up to take a look."

"Well, get down from there. We have a reality show to film."

"Dayzee, no way! I'm not coming down there with all those lions running around."

"Dayzee," said the Boss, "uh, did you leave the toaster going or something?"

"Hang on, Jiff."

She pulled herself back inside and looked out through the windshield.

Plumes of smoke were billowing up above the top of the house.

"Those damn Collectors! They're burning the guesthouse!"

"It's a deathhouse, Dayzee. Big difference."

"Thanks, Mare. That's helpful."

"What's the plan?"

"Oh, Boss, I don't even know anymore."

A lion jumped onto the hood, holding a snarling head in her mouth.

"You all saw that, didn't you?" said Marilyn. "He winked at me!"

"Yeah, Sis, even when dead, ripped off of its body by—"

"Here we go again," said Marilyn. "We never did settle that. Does the body belong to the head? Or the other way around?"

"Oh," Kenzie said, holding her belly, "I don't feel so good."

Marilyn looked up at the limo's ceiling and said, "Please send Kozy back. If not Kozy, then Moe."

"Even just Kenzie is pretty hot," Dayzee said, looking back at them. "But never mind that. Boss, give it some gas, maybe chase that she-lion and her head away, then—"

"Oh, okay," said Marilyn. "The head belongs to the lion. That makes sense."

Dayzee stared back at Marilyn for a second before finishing.

"Chase her away, then pull into the garage. We need to get inside for—"

"Whiskey," said the Boss.

"Kenzie dancing," said Marilyn.

Sophia scoffed and said "Kenzie acting."

Dayzee let out a gigantic sigh, then said, "How about this: let's see what's burning. Could that be kind of a reasonable idea too?"

*   *   *

The garage door was open, and the Boss whipped the long car in, chasing lions out, each holding a body part.

"Sheesh."

"Oh, Fia, they're just trying to help."

Dayzee looked past Sophia and said, "Just wonderful. Now, the gate closes, which means these lions aren't going anywhere."

"Oh, sure they are. They're going to the deathhouse."

"Thanks, Mare. Yeah, you're probably right."

They all looked everywhere, saw that no lions were lurking, then every car door opened, then slammed, and they all hurried into Dayzee's mansion.

After Dayzee had closed the damaged door as well as she could, she said, "Damn Dead Carpenters."

"They're all slackers, Dayzee."

"You know who wasn't a slacker?" said Marilyn. "Moe. Hey, he's kind of still around, in a way."

"Moe?" said Kenzie. "Oh, I feel—"

"Funny."

"No, Fifi. More like . . . horny."

"Like maybe 'Moe' is a trigger word?"

"Oh, yeah, I felt that."

"When I said, 'Moe?'"

"Sissy said, 'Moe!'"

"I did say—"

"Girls! We can all trigger her later."

Marilyn clapped silently, and Sophia nodded and grinned, but Dayzee shook her head, grabbed the Boss's arm, and led the parade down the hall and into the great room.

* * *

Dayzee tried to pull the Boss along with her to look through the glass doors at her backyard, but he yanked his arm free and aimed for the bar.

"Fine, Boss, the twins and I will—"

The twins plopped down on stools at the bar.

"Alright, Kenzie and I—"

Sophia snagged Kenzie's blouse sleeve and kept her close, then nudged her to sit between her and Marilyn.

"Just me? Okay, I'll report back when—"

"Make mine a double, Boss," said Marilyn.

Sophia scoffed and said, "And try to be a little snappier than that dead guy that we had to fire."

Dayzee attached her hands to her hips, her mouth still open, her sentence unfinished as she watched the scene.

"Sissy, we didn't fire him. Not really. We kind of loaned him out to the Prism."

"You think he's coming back, Sis? How long would it take for him to hike here?"

"I bet he could drive. He still has his head."

"Yeah, Sis, but he's still looking for more."

"Just like a guy, Sissy."

Dayzee coughed loudly, causing them all to look her way, then she frowned and continued toward the back of the house.

"Oh, that's just wonderful," she said to herself at the sight of the smaller of the two guesthouses burning and sending up clouds of smoke.

A few lions and Collectors stood nearby, watching and sometimes throwing body parts inside.

"Sheesh, as Fia would say."

She backed away from the glass, then turned and strutted toward the bar.

"Girls. Boss. Kenzie. Those damn—"

"Kenzie might be Moe again."

"Well, Mare, we should ask her. Kenzie, are you in the mood to play the part of Moe again?"

Seated between Marilyn and Sophia, Kenzie finished her drink, reached it over her shoulder, and the Boss took it for a refill.

"Here's the thing, Dayzee. I remember all of it. All the lingerie, taking turns acting like a Moe head . . . all of that. But I'm not Moe. How the hell could I be Moe?"

Sophia leaned forward and grinned at her, saying, "Do you need to be Moe?"

"Mm, Fifi, no, I do not. Being in this house is just making me itchier than I've ever been."

Dayzee said, "That's so good to hear! We'll have to make some time to—"

She turned at the sound of one prisoner yard guy and one temp film crew guy pounding on the glass doors.

"Hey, don't break that! Take yourselves to the deathhouse!"

She pointed past them, and they turned to look. A second later, lions dragged them both to the sides and out of sight.

"This isn't normal stuff," Kenzie said as she reached near her shoulder for the full glass that the Boss was handing her. "I'm horny as hell, but maybe that's because I'm completely insane."

"It's driving me crazy too," Marilyn said. "Like those two slackers that should have politely taken themselves to the deathhouse. Sissy, they could have cut out the middleman."

"Uh, maybe middle lions, Sis?"

"Yes, that's more correct."

"Girls. Kenzie, you'll get over it," said Dayzee. "We just have a few things to—"

She stopped, and they all turned their heads around, listening to the sirens getting louder.

"Is Jiffy going to film those Dead Fire Men driving in here, Dayzee?"

"Sis, they're not dead yet."

"Oh, really? What if Dead Mack got—"

"Even more dead," said Dayzee.

"No, Dayzee, that's just silly. I mean, maybe Dead Mack got tired of the Prism, and he applied for a job with them. What then?"

"Can't argue with that. Alright, they're dead, but is Jiff—"

"Fia, they can't all be dead."

"Not yet!" said the Boss.

Dayzee shook her head and pointed at him.

"You're catching on, Boss. So, Fia, yeah, I think Jiff will be filming all of it. None of that will be good for the show, though."

"Look," said Kenzie, "I'm way past caring, but I gotta say that none of you are taking this seriously. Can't you see that it's only getting worse?"

"Eh," said Dayzee, "nothing we can't handle. A little fire."

"Creepy Collectors, too, Dayzee."

"Yeah, Mare, and lions. Lots of lions."

"Don't forget the super squid flopping around on your yard."

"Is he still flopping, Fia? Are we sure?"

"One more thing. Perhaps the most serious of all," the Boss said, causing them all to turn his way.

He held an empty whiskey bottle over a glass, shaking it lightly to get out the last few drops.

Marilyn said, "Does Dead Fireman Mack make deliveries, still?"

"He'd better bring back that washcloth," said Dayzee. "Another common criminal, like Jiff."

"Is Jiff dead yet?"

"Fia? Really?"

Sophia shrugged and waited.

"Alright, he might be. Those Collectors are some greedy little creeps. They're probably sucking up every little bit of blood and slime, and maybe they're not even waiting until a guy has a natural death and—"

Kenzie laughed hysterically and said, "Who the hell around this mansion has ever had a natural death?"

Marilyn nodded to Dayzee and said, "She does have a point."

"We can't concern ourselves with that right now, Mare. A better question might be who has had the most unnatural death?"

"Good one, Dayzee."

"Thanks, Fia. I think it's a fair question."

"Certainly not the real headless clone Moe guy," said Marilyn.

"Sis, he's still kind of around, I bet. Whatever slop is being chewed up on Dayzee's lawn probably still has part of his face."

"True, Sissy. How about The Kid?"

"Girls, are we even sure that he's completely finished? I keep waiting for him to—"

"Ask you on another date?" Marilyn said with a loud giggle.

"Oh, Mare, that was—"

Horse hooves were clomping up the stone steps.

Dayzee looked at the Boss, who tipped his eyes down to the briefcase bomb.

"Oh, it's so easy to forget with all the thrills."

"Thrills?" said Kenzie.

"Well, kind of. So, Boss, we should probably get down there with the bomb."

"Unless you want those weirdos tackling us, we need to time it just right."

"Smart, Boss. Yep."

He hustled around the bar with the briefcase and met Dayzee near the wrecked closet door just as the first gigantic hoof jutted out and stomped on the floor.

"Hey, easy on the—"

The Boss hugged Dayzee with a hand over her mouth, getting a giggle out of her, and they stayed unnoticed as the two freshest freak Collectors trod heavily toward the back doors.

The Boss had gone into the closet, still holding Dayzee's hand. She turned to survey the scene one final time and saw the twins pushing Kenzie out toward an empty floor space.

"Oh, those two. More dancing?"

"Something wrong, Dayzee?" the Boss said from inside the closet.

"Yeah. I want to watch too."

He yanked her arm, and she laughed as he led her toward the portal to set the bomb.

# Chapter 24 – A Telepathic Bomb Ticking

"That bothers you, doesn't it?"

Dayzee had stopped them both halfway down the old stone steps, and she was looking up at the skylight high above them in the darkness.

"Where the hell is that?" she said. "I need to take some time and, I don't know, count rooms or something."

"Maybe make a map?"

"Mare keeps bugging me about that. Yeah, we should try."

"Not now, though. Portals to bomb."

"Caravans of Collectors to stop," she said.

"Dancing Kenzie to watch?"

She laughed and said, "Yeah, Boss. She's truly losing her mind, but she's—"

"Still hot?"

Dayzee kissed him quickly on the lips, then said, "Yep. Come on. Let's bomb the hell out of that portal in my basement."

He was about to speak, but she pointed at him until he only laughed.

* * *

"Just how far underground are we?" Dayzee said as she stood up after traversing the tunnel to the portal room.

"Who knows, Dayzee? Deep."

She looked around, but it was too dark to see even how big the room was.

"I should have brought a flashlight."

"No need, Dayzee. Let's just set the bomb right here. It's powerful enough to wipe out that portal, even if it's set back somewhere."

"It can't be dynamite, can it?"

"From our labs? Not a chance. It's a mix of sorcery crystals and brain cells that have been charged up with telepathic energy waves. It—"

"Those lab boys are truly mad. Not just fun mad, like Kenzie."

"She is kind of a fun mad, isn't she? Anyway, this thing ignites some kind of storm that chops up space and time and reality, then mushes it all into a glob that sets like concrete. At least, it's supposed to fill the void with concrete. I don't think it's ever been tested."

"So, the house will be okay?"

"Should be. But we might want to get ourselves back to the Prism when things get blown."

"Oh, I don't believe it. Even at a time like this, you're looking for—"

"Always, Dayzee. Especially after that mega dose of regular potion. I can't even imagine what that fully-refined from blood and guts super crap potion would do."

"It doesn't sound nearly as fun when you say it like that."

"I'm kidding. I bet it's the best. We'll see. Right now, though . . ."

He stooped down and popped open the case to reveal a screen with images of Collectors and lions and Kenzie dancing naked.

The Boss laughed and said, "See? Telepathic. The Collectors and lions are mine. You?"

"Oh, yeah, I was just, um, remembering how, you know, when—"

"Another second and you would have seen my view from on the stairs. Wow, that was nice. So . . ."

He started tapping at the moving images, causing the Collectors to begin chattering, the lions to start snapping and growling, and Kenzie held her bare breasts and blew them both a kiss.

"Aw, that was nice," said Dayzee. "Telepathy is fun. Such a sweet kid."

"Huh. You would know. Alright, it's set for enough time to allow us to escape."

"We have to do more than escape, Boss. We really should try to fix all that nonsense going on up there."

The Boss held Dayzee by her shoulders in the dimly lit underground chamber with a ticking bomb at their feet.

"Eventually, Dayzee—soon—this thing is going to blow. Damn, it's going to blow."

She tipped her head and grinned at him.

"I kind of don't mind you calling me a thing. You are, aren't you?"

"Damn potion," he said, laughing.

"Aw, poor Boss man," she said and grabbed him.

"Lucky for you, I'm itchy as hell. I'll defuse this damn bomb of yours."

* * *

Kenzie was dancing slowly to the classic rock, swaying her hips with her hands high above. She'd unbuttoned her blouse, and it seemed to open and close in time with the music.

But she stopped the next time around, when she was facing the bar.

"Oh, Marilyn and Sophia."

She lowered one hand to point but kept moving her hips.

"Your drinks."

"Oh, Kenzie," said Marilyn. "I don't know. You're more of a dancer than anything."

"And a head," said Sophia. "You give a damn good performance as Moe's head."

"Well, thanks to you both. But I'm not just a dancer and an actress— I'm still a bartender too. Let me refill those for you."

She started dancing toward Dayzee's bar while reaching for the buttons of her blouse.

"Whoa," said Sophia. "Uh-uh. New job title."

Marilyn giggled and said, "Topless Bartender."

"I can do that. Not Dead Bartender, though, please."

"Oh, no, never," said Marilyn.

"So, Sis said topless."

Kenzie grinned and said, "That she did," then peeled off the blouse and threw it toward the twins.

She'd just gotten behind the bar and grabbed a bottle when Dayzee's phone rattled and chimed on the bar.

"Uh-oh, Sissy. Dayzee didn't take her phone downstairs."

"You make it sound like a nice, comfy basement, Sis."

Kenzie picked it up, tapped it to turn on the speaker, then laid it on the bar.

"Uh, hello? You called for a carpenter?"

Marilyn whispered, "No. Dead Carpenter? Yes."

"Sis, hush."

Sophia cleared her throat and said, "The lady of the mansion is unavailable at the moment. We are aware that she summoned someone who works with wood, though."

"That's funny, Sissy."

"Huh? Look, I'm outside the gate, and some fire trucks just pulled up."

"Well, duh," said Kenzie. "Look at the sky, carpet man. See the—"

"That's 'carpenter man,'" Marilyn said, shaking her head and giggling.

"Yeah," he said, "I'm the carpenter man."

"Sarcastic, too," Sophia said softly with a smirk.

She leaned toward the phone and said, "Can you climb that fence?"

"What? No! That thing's too high! Oh, wait, there's some dude trapped up there. Hey! Are you alright?"

"It's Dead Jiffy!" Marilyn said and clapped a few times. "Our new show is going to start now, Sissy."

"Sis, look around. Don't we have a few things to clean up first?"

Kenzie set a drink in front of each and said, "We'll need a wardrobe change too."

Sophia pointed at her and said, "Red?"

"Uh-huh. Yep."

"Can't wait, but we really do have to—"

"You still there, lady?" the carpenter said through the phone. "I ain't climbing the fence. Can you just open the gate?"

"Hang on. I need the code."

Sophia put a hand over the phone and said, "If he was dead, like he soon will be, he could just pry that gate open."

"How, Sissy?"

"Remember Dead Mack? He managed."

"Oh, that's right. So, if he gets his head bit off, then he can open the gate and come inside to fix everything?"

Sophia was grinning long before her sister finished, then she turned to Kenzie and said, "Such a sweet kid!"

"She is," Kenzie said, then grabbed the phone and tapped it a few times, saying, "I've seen Dayzee boss those gates around enough. Maybe this will work."

They waited a second or two, then the carpenter said, "Good. It's opening. Thanks. I'll see you in a minute."

Kenzie tapped to end the call and said, "Uh, we kind of doubt it."

"She's catching on quite nicely, Sissy."

"She's topless too."

* * *

"Oh my, Boss, I've never been so . . . anchored."

She'd shoved him to the dusty ground, where he lay on his back, the only sound in that subterranean chamber being the steady ticking of the bomb that they'd set.

She gave him another slow bounce, then a grind, then said, "Hey, how is a telepathic bomb ticking?"

"Make it fun for me. Hit me with some barbs. Wrap me in some burning heat. See if I can answer you with all that attacking me."

"You're such a sporting kind of a Boss."

She looked up at the ceiling, kept her hips moving with her hands flat on his chest, and hummed a classic rock melody.

"Uh, any time now," he said.

She looked down and said, "No, I don't think you want all that. Oh no, you'd never like that."

Then, she continued humming to the darkness above them.

"Please, Dayzee. I need to be savaged with all you got."

She ignored him and kept humming and bouncing, sometimes needing more force to overcome the tight fit.

"Dayzee, please! Just a barb or two, alright? Can you just turn up even a little bit of—"

She hit him with everything: the temperature flew up to its highest, and the barbs dug in to their deepest.

He tipped his head back in a silent scream, and Dayzee slowed, barely moving, but smiling as each point hung up and got pulled each way, over and over.

"Cat got your tongue?" she said. "Maybe a nasty she-lion, Boss?"

"Ah . . ."

"You asked for it. Now, take it!"

She tried to raise herself up, and that lifted the Boss too.

"Oh, dammit!" he said.

"So, tell me, Boss. Answer the goddamn question now."

"What . . . what question?"

"How the hell is a telepathic bomb ticking?"

He forced in and out several raspy breaths, laughed with his face knotted in a tight grimace, and said, "It's not. We just think we hear it!"

"Will we hear the explosion?"

He let out a miserable laugh and said, "Which one?"

"Ha! Scream all you want, Boss. No one will hear you in this basement."

"It's not a—"

Dayzee found a few more barbs. Quickly.

"Ah!"

* * *

A voice called from down the hallway that led to the garage.

"I'm here! I see the problem. This door, right?"

Marilyn said, "How did he get past all the lions and Collectors and things?"

Sophia smirked and said, "Maybe he really is dead, Sis. Dayzee had that good plan of calling guys that were already dead."

"Oh, yes. Cut out the middle . . . lions," she said, then giggled.

"Look, I'm having fun and horny as hell," said Kenzie, holding a drink up to her lips. "But really, you two, this is way crazier than it's ever been. You can see that, right?"

Sophia turned to Kenzie for just a second, saying, "Eh. We can handle it."

Then, she turned to her sister and said, "Sis, we don't know when Dayzee and the Boss will get back. Why don't we take Topless Kenzie and that—"

"I like that name," Kenzie said, smiling and holding both breasts.

Marilyn didn't look her in the eye and said, "That should always be your name, okay?"

Kenzie nodded, then Marilyn turned back to her sister.

"As I was saying, let's take her and that Dead Carpenter fellow upstairs and have some fun."

"Fountains, Sis? We should do fountains again."

"Yes, and barbs and burning and—"

"What about me?" Kenzie said.

Sophia pointed and said, "You could be Moe again."

"Okay! I can do that!"

"Sissy, maybe we should let Topless Kutie Kenzie have a chance to—"

"That's what we're calling her now?"

Marilyn shrugged and said, "Sure. Why not? But let's see if she can get a fountain, too, like we do."

"Sis, you're onto something. Yeah, let's—"

Dead Carpenter appeared from the hallway.

"Uh, the door was locked, but it was so beat to hell that I just walked in. Hey, what's going on outside?"

Marilyn shook her head and said, "Oh, that's a little hard to explain. You see, we—"

Without a sound, a mountain lion sank her claws into him from behind, his eyes bugged out for a second, then he was dragged to the floor and back to where he'd entered. They heard the crunching of boards and ripping of flesh as he was dragged out through the ragged opening.

"And just like that, Sis, no explanation needed."

*   *   *

Dayzee retracted her barbs, dialed down the heat, and lay still on the Boss's chest, looking into his eyes.

"That's to die for, Dayzee."

"Usually is," she said with a grin. "On Earth anyway."

He tipped his head to one side and said, "I'm ready for more."

She pushed herself up, supporting herself with hands on his chest.

"Oh, what the hell? You are! Not as much as before, but still . . . damn."

"Give it a minute, Dayzee. It'll be ready to blow—"

"Even after all I just gave you, you're still looking for—"

"Blow up! I was going to say 'blow up!'"

"Oh. Not that I was complaining or anything. It's just that—oh, wait. How long have we been going wild down here?"

He looked at his watch, then grimaced almost as much as when he'd taken every bit of Dayzee's pleasurable wrath.

"Too long! We got to get out of here!"

She was still sitting on him, with her skirt hiked up, when a low wailing began somewhere in the darkness.

"Oh, boy."

"Damn Collectors, Dayzee?"

"Yeah. More of them. Just wonderful."

# Chapter 25 – Yapping About Lemonade

"That's a lot of steps, Boss," Dayzee said, then she looked up at the skylight high above.

"Yeah. We should try to figure out how deep that is."

Still looking up, she said, "And someday, dammit, I'm going to find that skylight."

She was about to take a step toward the closet, but the Boss grabbed her arm and stopped her.

"Dayzee . . . no, it can't be."

"What?"

"Could that be another portal?"

"What is up with this mansion? Sure, I can handle finding extra stairways. But then, we find out there's a portal way down in the . . . um, far underground. Now, we're thinking maybe there's another portal way up in an attic that no one's ever seen?"

He shrugged and said, "We might never know."

"No, maybe not. Let's go see what those gorgeous twins are doing to that poor barmaid."

"She's an actress."

"Oh, no. You too."

* * *

Dayzee led the way, punching and kicking at the last remaining shards of the closet door, and they stepped out into the mansion's interior.

"Follow the music," she said, and they walked toward the great room.

The first thing they saw was Kenzie, dancing topless.

"Alright, that's not bad. But where are the girls?"

A few steps later, they saw Marilyn and Sophia near the line of glass doors that provided passage to the nightmare backyard. They were laughing and waving their arms and just outside, several angry lions were jumping, roaring, and pawing at the glass.

"Hey, you two! Don't we have enough problems without you tormenting the lions?"

"No, Dayzee," said Marilyn, "we're trying to help. Come here and see."

"Hang on, Boss. Oh, you can enjoy the live entertainment."

"I believe I will."

Dayzee joined the twins and looked out at the lions and beyond them, the pandemonium of her estate.

"Girls, you're teasing these lady lions, and they're—"

"No, we're really not," said Sophia. "We're distracting them."

"From what?"

Both pointed past the snarling lions at another one, by herself, dragging a limp body toward the deathhouse.

"Who's that?"

"Carpenter," said Marilyn.

"Really, Sis? That's just lazy. Come on. Try again."

"Oh. Dead Carpenter, Dayzee."

"At least he showed up. Did he get anything done?"

Marilyn grinned and said, "You two were certainly gone long enough for some lumber to get delivered."

"Good one, Sis. She isn't wrong, Dayzee."

"Girls, there was something that was going to blow, and we—"

"That's almost too easy for a joke."

"Yeah, it is, Fia. But it's true too. We set the bomb, then—"

"Then, something got blown . . . up."

"Yeah, Mare," Dayzee said, laughing. "Something damn big too. Anyway, did he fix anything while he was alive?"

"Not a damn thing."

"He was just another slacker, Sissy."

"Alright," said Dayzee, "so he showed up, he got dead, and now he's getting collected. What's with these lions?"

"We got the gate open," said Sophia. "That's how Dead Slacker got in."

"Good name for him, Sissy."

"Okay, so . . . what's with the lions?"

"Jiffy," said Marilyn. "He can't dodge this many lions. We're trying to keep these girls busy so that he can get in here and film all of us upstairs when we try on some more—"

"Mare, no. As fun as that is, there's no time. This place is going straight to hell. I mean, look at my little guesthouse!"

She pointed past the jumping lions, past the lone lion dragging Dead Slacker toward the smaller guesthouse, which had flames jabbing out of all windows and doorways.

"It didn't even last long enough to become a deathhouse, Dayzee."

"Good observation, Mare. Thanks."

"The Dead Firemen are here, though," said Sophia. "They're at the gates."

"Yeah, Fia, I hear them. Maybe they erected a ladder up to help Jiff get down from his perch."

"That's funny, Dayzee," said Marilyn. "Might be true too."

"Well, they'll be back here soon to put out that fire. While they're busy with that, Jiff can get set up to—"

A loud pounding on the front door froze the girls and the lions.

"Oh, what now?"

"It might be the squid," said Marilyn.

"Probably," said Sophia. "The lions won't even eat that slop."

"I don't think anyone could knock like that with squishy flippers, Sissy."

* * *

With the Kildare Killers close behind her, Dayzee swung in the front door, which still wore a sheet of plywood.

"Oh, boy. Just wonderful."

"We—"

"How did you get in here?"

Dayzee leaned out and saw the entry gate open and a line of fire trucks waiting on the street. Their lights were busy, but the sirens were taking a break.

"Your gate opened and since the nice firemen were—"

"Dead Firemen, Sissy."

"Soon, Sis. Wait for it."

"Girls. Shh."

"They were busy trying to catch a large cat that—"

Marilyn giggled and Sophia scoffed and rolled her eyes.

"—that someone let out before it climbed a tree or something, and they told us that we could go on ahead and knock on your—what happened to this door?"

"Relax," said Sophia, "there's a carpenter around somewhere."

"Really all around, probably," said Marilyn.

"He's kind of a slacker, though," said Dayzee. "We're not expecting much from him. Alright, you didn't come here to critique my door. What?"

The woman sneered and said, "We've filed charges with the local police, and you will soon be forced out of Beverly Hills!"

"You just don't get it," Sophia said over Dayzee's left shoulder.

"Oh, Sissy, I think they will," Marilyn said over her other shoulder.

"What are those two bimbos talking about?"

"These two?" Dayzee said, tipping her head at one, then the other. "The Kildare Killers?"

"What? They're killers?"

"So are the lions," Sophia said, nodding at the woman.

"Oh, and the Collectors too. Kind of."

"Girls," Dayzee said, then leaned through the doorway and looked each way, "we should always remember to be overly polite with the kind and considerate people of our lovely neighborhood."

She looked each way again, then stayed inside to glance at her watch.

"We might even consider mixing up some tasty lemonade to show them just how pleased we are that they came all this way to visit, when they probably have so many better—"

Lions pounced from both sides, growling and ripping and shredding, and barely a one of them got a chance to scream.

Dayzee slammed the beat-up door and leaned her back into it.

"Oh, finally. I didn't know how long I could keep yapping about lemonade."

"Gotta love lady lions, Dayzee."

"Yeah, Mare. Oh, yeah."

"I'm so itchy that I don't even care if my first killer dose of killer potion is from that rude neighbor of yours getting crapped out of a Collector."

"You make it sound enchanting, Sissy. Me too."

"Count me in. Not a very pleasing visual, though. Let's get back inside."

"You're making lemonade?"

Dayzee grinned at Sophia and said, "Such a sweet kid!"

* * *

Before any of them could leave the foyer, the sirens fired back up, then the volume started increasing. Dayzee shook her head at the twins and opened the door again.

A convoy of fire engines, lights and sirens engaged, were rolling through the entry gate and taking positions all along the circular part of the driveway.

"Just wonderful."

"Do you see Dead Mack with them, Dayzee?"

Dayzee got up on her toes and looked all around.

"No, Mare. He's still dead at the Prism, probably."

"Oh, look," said Sophia, watching over Dayzee's shoulder. "There's Jiff."

"Yay!" said Marilyn. "Finally, we can get back to our show!"

"Really, Mare? We might have just a few distractions at the moment."

"Like them?" Sophia said while pointing past Jiff, who was crouched low and running alongside the fire trucks.

"Oh, boy."

A large pack of female mountain lions were swarming in through the open gate. Jiff would sometimes look behind him, scream really quick, then pick up his pace.

"Girls," Dayzee said as she held up her phone, "this is getting kind of ridiculous. The best we can hope for is to contain all of this."

"So right," said Marilyn.

"Yep. Lock it down, Dayzee."

She tapped her phone a few times, and the heavy gate swung closed and latched.

"What's the plan?"

"Mare, what do we always do when we have things to figure out?"

"We drink?"

"Yep. Lots of it too."

"We could at least film that, right?"

Dayzee thought for a second, then said, "You know, Fia, you're onto something. Yeah. That should be fine. The sirens in the background will give it some good mood."

"Can we make Kenzie keep being Topless Kenzie?"

"Does she like being Topless Kenzie, Mare?"

"Uh-huh. Topless all day every day."

"Hey," said Sophia, "that's a scene: we all try to get her blouse back on her. You just know she's going to struggle. The camera will love it."

"Fia, you're a film making genius. Yes, let's all go wrestle with that barmaid."

"Actress, Dayzee."

"Of course, Mare."

# Chapter 26 – Our Kollector Kitties

"I just bet all of those Dead Firemen are going to pound on this door soon," said Dayzee. "Why don't you two strut on ahead, get a drink or three, and see just what kind of entertainment that Moe girl is performing for the Boss."

"Sure, Dayzee," said Sophia. "Whatever it is, it's topless."

"Well, yes, Sissy, because she's Topless Kutie Kenzie!"

She took her sister's hand and they strutted, as they'd been instructed, toward the great room. And Dayzee grinned at the sight until they'd rounded a corner.

With an ear to the plywood, she said, "Huh. Nothing? I hear voices, so they're still at least kind of alive. Or could that be the Collectors? Do they talk while they're collecting—"

"Dayzee. Come look!"

"Coming, Fia."

Dayzee hurried out of the foyer, her heels clattering on the wood floor, until she could round the corner and step into the great room.

She scoffed at what she saw first: Topless Kenzie on the open floor, shaking her hips and everything else.

The next quick glance was to the Boss, who was slouching on a barstool with a whiskey glass in one hand, a cigar in the other, a huge smile, and two staring, unblinking eyes.

"Just wonderful."

"Dayzee, sometime today, okay?"

She said, "Sure, Mare," before turning to look, and she saw both twins, agitated and pointing out through the sliding glass at the backyard.

"Yeah, I know, girls. We have some minor issues that we—"

"Damn, Dayzee, not like this."

She started walking, tracing a path near Kenzie, and said, "Alright, Fia. I'm coming."

Kenzie bumped her with a hip and said, "Mm."

"Oh, boy. Hold that thought."

She stopped and turned to point at the Boss.

"You, don't hold anything."

He nodded, never lost his smile, and never stopped watching Topless Kenzie.

Dayzee rushed over and got behind Marilyn and Sophia, looking between them with an arm around each one's waist.

"What, girls? Where's the fire?"

"That's funny, Dayzee. You know where."

"Thanks, Mare."

"That's not funny, though."

Sophia pointed at a tight cluster of Collectors in the yard, surrounded by lions that were sitting calmly, their tails flapping lazily.

"Uh, some kind of Collector lecture, Fia?"

"You even made it rhyme!" Marilyn said with a few quick claps.

"Yeah, Mare. It just happened. But what's going on?"

In unison, all of the Collectors leaned toward a lion that had her back to the girls. With sirens blaring and flames raging in the nearby small guesthouse, all of them chattered, frozen in place like a Halloween display gone bad.

"What the hell?"

"Wait for it," said Sophia.

The Collectors all snapped to attention but kept chattering.

The lion slowly turned and seemed to be looking right at Dayzee and the twins.

Only her face was more yellow than before.

And her teeth were smaller. And brown.

And they were chattering like mad.

"Oh, this can't be happening!" said Dayzee. "What on Earth is going on here?"

"Earth. That's always funny, Dayzee."

"Thanks, Mare. Yeah, it kind of is. But that's not!"

"Are they Lion Collectors, Dayzee? Or are they Collector Lions?"

"Oh. Sissy raised a good question."

"Like I should know? Dammit, girls, this can't be—"

While the converted lioness sat facing the house, her brown teeth chattering, the Collectors all leaned toward another lion, who was sitting at attention and patiently waiting.

"They're messing with all the lions? Really?"

"It would seem that way," said Sophia.

Their work completed, the Collectors assumed an upright posture, and the newest lion with chattering teeth also turned and sat facing the mansion's glass doors.

"Oh, girls, only in Beverly Hills! I've been saying that forever but this time, I really mean it!"

They watched a third lion get the Collector treatment. She stumbled around and sat, staring toward the staring girls.

"They're not coming inside! Bad cats!"

Sophia snickered and said, "Bad Collector Cats."

"Wait a second," said Marilyn. "I just thought of something."

"What's that, Mare?"

"No, it would never work. That would be too easy."

"Come on, Sis, spit it out."

"How many times have we heard that, Sissy?"

Sophia laughed and said, "Never!"

"Girls, you got a little sidetracked. For the record, I never hear that either. Alright, Mare, what's the deal?"

She smiled pleasantly at both of them, shrugged, and said, "Litter boxes."

"Huh? Sis, are you getting as loony as Topless Kenzie?"

They all turned to look and since Kenzie had heard her name, she stopped. Facing them, she shook her pair from side to side.

"That's, um, that sure is topless," said Dayzee.

"Damn. Alright, Sis, what about litter boxes?"

"Simple," she said with a soft laugh. "We set out litter boxes for the big Collector Kitties. Then, we—"

"Hold on," said Dayzee. "We're at the beginning of something here, so let's do this right. Are those both with a 'K?'"

"Okay! Yeah!" said Marilyn. "They're our Kollector Kitties! Then, when they clean up blood and guts and slop—not that dreadful squiddy Cliff thing, though—we just scoop out our Godzilla potion!"

Dayzee looked at Sophia and said, "Who's Godzilla?"

Sophia shrugged, and they focused on Marilyn again.

"Did you get some extra Earth download you're not telling us about, Sis?"

Marilyn looked down and kicked at the floor.

"Mm-hmm. This is the first time I used any of it, though. Godzilla's just some big angry guy. Like a monster."

"Alright, that doesn't matter. We can figure that out later. The question now is: where do we find big litter boxes?"

They heard a loud, steady pounding on the plywood front door. A man on the other side yelled.

"Hey, whoever's in there, you got a problem!"

"It's the Dead Firemen. They probably have boxes."

"Mare, they're not dead yet. Give it a minute. And how are you so sure that they have boxes?"

"Oh. I don't know. I just thought about how they have hoses."

Sophia chuckled and said, "There isn't enough time for all the jokes after that one, Sis."

"Girls, we'll hear those jokes later. Right now, though, there's a Dead Fireman beating up my mansion!"

*  *  *

Dayzee grabbed a hand of each and got them all strutting toward the front door. Each one lingered for a moment, grinning at the shaking display that Topless Kenzie dedicated to them.

"She should have been topless long ago," said Dayzee. "Right from the moment we met her."

"That seems like an Earth century ago."

"Doesn't it, though, Fia? We've been busy."

At the door, Dayzee pounded on the inside and yelled, "Two can play that game!"

"Good one, Dayzee."

"Thanks, Mare."

"Lady? This ain't no game. You got some kind of fire out back. Open up, will you? We need to check the main house too."

"Uh . . . no. How do I know you're who you claim to be?"

"That'll teach him."

"Thanks, Fia. I'm stalling. You know why."

"Kollector Kitties to the rescue?"

"Exactly, Mare. I'd rather that puny little guesthouse burns to the ground. With the insurance money, I'll build a—"

"Full-size deathhouse."

"Yeah, Fia. You know it."

"Alright, lady, we'll just go around. Stay inside where it's safe."

"Dayzee, ask if they have hoses."

"Why, Mare?"

"Just because it's a funny thing."

"It is kind of funny, Dayzee."

"You two. Alright."

She pounded again and said, "Hey, do you all have hoses?"

"What? Of course, we do. What do you think we are?"

Sophia grinned, bugged out her eyes, and said, "Dead."

Marilyn nodded and said, "Soon to be collected by Kollector Kitties."

"Alright, never mind," Dayzee yelled at the door. "Do you have boxes?"

"What? Why do you want boxes?"

"We, um, we like to collect things."

"With a 'K,'" Marilyn said softly.

"No, lady. No boxes. Just stay inside, then. We're going around the house."

"Goodbye!" Dayzee yelled and gave the door a few raps.

"He was pleasant enough," Marilyn said with a gentle smile.

"And he doesn't have a clue what kind of amazing journey he's about to take so we can all dazzle."

"Oh, for sure, Fia. I just love you girls!"

*　*　*

An engine revved outside, then they heard men yelling and saw the truck's lights through windows as it was driven around the house and toward the fire.

"Dammit, he didn't say they were taking a truck back there."

"Men need their hoses, Dayzee."

"That's helpful, Mare. But my lawn. Somebody's paying for that."

"Huh," Sophia said with a scoff. "It won't be the dead guys."

When the truck was halfway between the front and back, the driver sounded the horn twice, and Kenzie became a half-naked statue on the great room floor.

She looked down and quickly crossed her arms, covering her bare breasts.

"She heard the two toots," Dayzee said, pointing toward Kenzie.

"And she covered her two—"

"Why am I dancing naked all the time? What are you all doing to me?"

"It's the house," Dayzee said while nodding. "It always has some kind of mayhem going on."

Dayzee and the twins started walking toward her, and Dayzee said to the Boss, "You must have seen enough by now, Boss. Why not give the girl back her blouse?"

191

"I never took it," he said, then looked down at it lying over one leg as he sat on a barstool. "Um, how did that get there?"

He tossed it toward Kenzie, and she quickly slipped it on and started buttoning.

"Blame it on the house," said Dayzee.

Sophia reached out to fluff Kenzie's hair back over her shoulders and said, "You just kind of go back and forth, don't you?"

"I have a joke for that, Sissy."

Kenzie squinted at Marilyn for a second, then relaxed into a smile.

"I was just trying to decide which of you twins is hotter," she said.

"Aw, thanks, Kenzie. I vote for Sissy."

"No way," said Sophia. "It's got to be—"

The fire truck horn blasted twice from somewhere in the backyard.

"I like two toots," said the Boss, then he grinned at all of them.

Marilyn slowly pointed at each of the girls, including herself, while her lips were moving quietly.

"Sis is counting toots."

"That's funny, Fia. She never bothered with that when we had the stunt double Moe upstairs, and she was—"

A rhythmic tapping and scratching on one of the glass doors got them all to turn and look.

A Kollector Kittie, one with bone and gristle hanging from her jaw, was looking in and staring blankly.

"See?" said Kenzie. "This is so much worse than ever."

"It's just a Kollector Kittie, Kenzie. She wants a litter box."

"That's fast," said Sophia. "She whipped up some . . . what was it, Sis?"

"Oh, I don't remember, Sissy. King Kong, maybe."

Dayzee said, "And that all starts with 'K?'"

"I think so, Dayzee."

"Alright," said Sophia, "This Kollector Kittie is delivering King Kong potion, and we'd better find some boxes quick."

"You're just not taking this seriously!" said Kenzie. "This is getting really bad!"

"Eh," said Dayzee. "Just another day in the Hills. Hey, let's go watch."

"It's not a sporting event!"

"Sure it is, Kenzie," said Sophia. "Is anybody rooting for the Dead Fire Guys? Hell no."

As the four girls were walking toward the glass doors, the Boss, still seated at the bar, said, "I'm rooting for the lions. I mean, uh, those Kollector Kitties."

Dayzee laughed and said over her shoulder, "Right. Because we'll use you and abuse you with all of that King Kong potion."

# Chapter 27 – Kildare in the Hills

At the sliding glass doors that led to Dayzee's backyard, all four girls stood in a line: Sophia on the left, then Kenzie, then Dayzee, then Marilyn.

And they watched a scene of death and destruction after the closest lion, the converted one that had called them over, turned away and joined her pack.

"She called us over to watch," said Dayzee. "Such a sweet cat."

"I think she's proud of her work."

"Yeah, Fia, and she should be."

"Oh, look," said Marilyn. "Is that your buddy, Jiffy?"

A man with a large camera was running around the pool, then toward the side of the house away from the fire truck.

"Oh my gosh," said Dayzee, "that's him. I bet he thinks the gate is still open."

"And when he sees that it's locked up, trapping him inside with all kinds of weird stuff, he'll—"

"Hurry back up onto that post by the gate. Yeah, Fia. We can only hope that he'll do some filming from up there."

Kenzie said, "You can't be serious. You'd want all of that,"—she swept her pointing hand from left to right—"as part of our reality show?"

"I like how she said 'our,' Sissy."

"Well, the credits will read 'Topless Kenzie,' so, yeah."

Kenzie said, "I'd rather use my full name: Topless Kutie Kenzie."

"That's all wonderful, girls," said Dayzee, "but Kenzie does have a point. I mean, look at all that."

They scanned in silence at prison yard guys in orange jumpsuits running from lions but never quickly enough, getting pounced on, then dragged toward the deathhouse.

Only a few film guys remained, and they were meeting the same fate. They were lucky if they at least had time to scream before being collected. Two of them had retreated to the top of a tall lighting pole planted in the yard, but a few lions were figuring out how to scale it. Throwing cameras and floodlights at them only annoyed them more.

A sloppy mess that looked like a runaway science experiment was trying to stand on two spindly flippers, but a lion dragging a body past it paused her work long enough to attack it and rip it into several pieces.

"Sheesh."

"Seafood, Sissy."

And rolling into the scene was the fire truck, lights working but silent.

"Oh, that's something we don't see too often," said Marilyn.

A headless Dead Fireman was still holding the steering wheel, and a lion, riding shotgun, held his dripping head by its scalp.

"She's helping him to still see where he's going?"

"Lady lions are a polite sort, wouldn't you say, Mare?"

"Oh, yes, Dayzee."

"This is a nightmare," Kenzie said as she dropped down to sit back on her heels.

Sophia looked over Kenzie toward Dayzee and said, "It's just that all of the lady lions have been converted to Kollector Kitties. I think that's what's bothering her."

"Sissy's right, Dayzee. If it wasn't for that, Kenzie would be okay with it."

They all looked down at Kenzie, who said nothing and only shook her head while watching the disarray.

A loud squeal got the three girls to view the backyard again. The brakes on the fire truck had locked up, stranding it close to the house and off to one side.

"Dead Fireman better not leave that damn truck in my yard," said Dayzee.

"Maybe Jiff will move it for you?" Marilyn said as she pointed at Jiff running toward it.

"Huh," said Dayzee. "I guess there's a lot of collecting going on in front of the house too. He got out of there quick. Oh, look, he's climbing up there."

Jiff waved to them before scrambling up onto a long ladder that was sticking out from the back of the fire truck.

"Come on, already-dead guy," said Sophia, "give the not-yet-dead guy some help."

He did. The lion on the front seat clawed at the headless driver, and he fell enough to hit a lever. The ladder began raising up.

"Whoa!" Jiff screamed, but he hung on and kept his camera with him.

"It's working!" said Dayzee. "Girls, it's just about show time!"

"You can't be serious," said Kenzie. "Show time how?"

"Well, not you. You'd be just a hot walking piece of lion chow. I meant these gorgeous twins and me. We're going out there to—"

Kenzie hugged both of Dayzee's legs and said, "Don't leave me alone in this haunted house!"

Dayzee looked toward the bar quickly, then said, "Uh, you won't be. The Boss will—"

"He'll rip my blouse off and make me dance again!"

"Well, who wouldn't?" Sophia said with a smirk.

"I would, Sissy. All the time."

"Girls, any of us would. That's not the point."

She turned toward the bar and said, "Boss, grab a bottle and get over here. Since I kind of have to, I'll stay inside and—no, not that one. Get one that's full. Yeah. Okay, that one."

"Kenzie," she said, looking down at the trembling barmaid, "I don't know what the hell is going on with you. Something—"

"With her brain?" said Sophia.

"That's not overly helpful, Fia."

Marilyn said, "It might really be your house, Dayzee. It's not exactly normal."

The Boss arrived and tapped Kenzie on her shoulder. She looked up, then stood up.

"Look, Kenzie," said Dayzee, "I'll stay inside and protect you from the Boss, who's got his own brain problems from a jumbo dose of potion."

"It wasn't even the King Kong variety," said Marilyn.

"I like that better than that other thing, Sis, the one that started with a 'G,' I think."

"Me too, Sissy. It can only help if we stay with 'Ks.'"

Dayzee looked from one twin to the other. Marilyn offered a pleasant smile, and Sophia only shrugged.

"Okay, that's settled. Now, Jiff looks like he has his camera ready to roll. Time for the Kildare Killers to ad lib."

"Also with 'Ks,' Dayzee!"

"We were way ahead of the curve on that, Sis."

"Yes, you two are amazing. Now, get out there, and give us some—"

"Kildare in the Hills?"

"Uh, no, Mare," Dayzee said as she looked around at the ongoing cataclysm. "Let's just try for—"

"Fountains," said Sophia. "Get that on film."

"You know," said Dayzee, "that's a remarkable idea. Yeah, grab some potion and go."

"Um, can I go with them?" said the Boss. "Just so, you know, in case—"

"Uh-uh. No way, Boss. You're staying with me to watch Topless Kenzie do a little dance, then—"

"I don't want to keep doing that, Dayzee!"

"Oh. Wonderful. Alright, my gorgeous twins, it's time for Kildare in the Hills!"

*   *   *

Marilyn, dressed in a short and tight white dress and white heels, and Sophia, wearing a short black skirt with black heels and a snug red blouse, unbuttoned low, stood just outside the closed sliding glass doors.

Dayzee pounded softly from the inside.

They turned enough to look and saw Kenzie, giving them an eye roll as she stood between Dayzee and the Boss, both of whom were reaching across to unbutton her blouse.

"Hmm," said Marilyn. "I'm not so sure they'll even watch us."

"Can't blame them too much. How about Jiff, though?"

They both looked up and saw him waving from high on the ladder. He'd tied himself in place with the camera's strap and pointed the lens down at them.

"He's got us on camera, Sissy. Got that potion?"

"Not King Kong, Sis, but it's still pretty good. Here's yours."

She handed Marilyn a small bottle, and they surveyed the area for two earthmen still alive enough to give them their fountains.

"Oh, you got to love these lady lions!"

To their right, there were two lions backing toward them, each dragging a chewed-up earthman, one in orange and one still holding a clipboard.

"Yeah, Sis. Perfect. Hey, are we sure that they won't attack us?"

"Oh. We don't know for sure, no."

"Let's find out. And remember to strut."

"Always, Sissy."

They strutted in a path to intercept the approaching mountain lions.

*   *   *

"Oh, I can't even fight this anymore," Kenzie said and raised her arms straight up.

The Boss worked on one button, and Dayzee was popping the one below it.

"It's just until the girls get things going out there," said Dayzee. "Really, though, admit it: Topless Kenzie has a good sound to it, right?"

They'd finished unbuttoning, and she dropped her arms. She answered while they were peeling it back over her shoulders to let it drop to the floor.

"Yeah, okay, I do kind of like it. Ooh, you both have cold hands!"

*　*　*

Marilyn glanced back at the house and said, "Sissy, Kenzie is Topless Kenzie again. Just like that."

Sophia turned to look and said, "Not dancing, though. Just kind of . . . standing there. Smiling."

"Not as much as the Boss. I'm glad we didn't really kill him, Sis."

"Yeah, just his clone. Hey, let's get to those lions. They have—oh, what the hell?"

The twins had gotten close enough to touch the lions' tails as they backed their cargo toward the deathhouse. Each of them let the twitching almost-dead earthmen drop to the grass and turned to look up at them will their teeth chattering silently.

"They're Kollector Kitties, Sissy. We should have known that."

"Well, we know it now. Hey, do they still not care about us because we're not from Earth?"

"Uh-oh. I don't know. Hold still, Sissy, they're coming to get us!"

The mountain lions padded closer to them, their heads angled up and their beady collectorized eyes staring, then they rose up on their hind legs.

A tense few seconds passed, all of them staring at each other, then Marilyn reached out to the nearest one and said, "Aw, you're a nice kitty."

She began scratching around her ears and rubbing the top of her head.

"That's the damnedest thing, Sis."

"Sissy, pet your kitty. You're going to make her feel bad."

Sophia hesitated, focusing on the quietly chomping brown teeth.

"Sheesh, no treats for you, girl," she said, then reached out to pet her cat.

"Dead bodies are their treats now, Sissy. Except for these two earthmen, who aren't quite ready for those creepy collectors yet."

"Sis. They brought them for us? They want us to get our fountains?"

Marilyn shrugged and said, "Maybe Jiff wrote a script real quick, and they wanted in on this show? Could that be?"

Sophia hooked a thumb toward the deathhouse that wasn't burning and said, "Sis, maybe it's those Collectors that are directing now?"

Marilyn looked toward the deathhouse briefly and saw many pairs of Collectors either stooped down and feeding on cadavers or walking toward them with chattering teeth.

"They do like their cadavers, Sissy."

The lions stepped in closer and put their paws on the girls' shoulders.

"Aw," Marilyn said as the patted the big cat's sides, "such a nice kitty."

"Mine too, Sis. Hey, we're touching our own kitties together. How about that?"

"Oh, Sissy. 'Kitties.' Uh-huh, I get it."

"Think they'll care if we use a couple of their dinners for fountains?"

"Oh," said Marilyn, "I don't think so. Maybe we shouldn't burn them down to dust, though? That would give those Collectors belly aches."

"Good thinking, Sis. Barbs, though, right?"

"Of course!"

* * *

"Ooh, that potion's kicking in again," said the Boss.

"Starting to hurt?"

"Yeah, Dayzee. Maybe you and Topless Kenzie could, I don't know, help a Boss out?"

"Maybe in a second," Dayzee said as she watched the girls nudge the lions to the side and straddle the two men who were only slightly hanging on to their lives. "I'm a little busy. Try Topless Kenzie."

Kenzie snapped her head toward Dayzee and said, "Dayzee! Topless dancing is one thing, but . . . but . . . I don't even know if this guy's from Earth."

"Earth?" said the Boss, chuckling. "What the hell is that?"

"Good one, Boss. Kenzie, no, he's not from Earth. Neither was Bruno. Remember that fun little escapade at my bar with him?"

Kenzie looked back out through the windows and smiled.

"Oh, uh, yeah. Sure. I was pretending to be a lion."

"And you liked being Bruno's lion girl, right?"

She sighed, then nodded and said, "Yep. Oh, okay then, Mr. Boss."

Dayzee unbuttoned her blouse and pulled it back over her shoulders while saying, "I'm next," then she took her place next to Kenzie.

"Okay," said Kenzie, "but I'm going to keep watching those Killer Kuties out there."

"Me too. You haven't called them that in a long time. Good one."

"Thanks, Dayzee."

*　*　*

"So glad they still have their heads, Sissy. If they didn't, where we would pour the potion?"

"Huh. Good question. Maybe we'd have to get a lioness to rip some other part of them open?"

"Oh, that could be it. Okay."

With the lions sitting close by, watching intently with vacant eyes, the Kildare Killers began their steady gyrations on the earthmen who'd suddenly stopped writhing from their many wounds.

They even started smiling.

"They like it, Sissy. And mine is . . . oh, I think he just died."

"Well, no need to stop. Mine's doing alright. He's just kind of staring up at . . . nope, he's gone too."

Marilyn looked up and pointed.

"But Jiff is still filming. I hope he has a good zoom on that thing."

"Of course, he does, Sis. Hey, I wonder if Dayzee and the—"

She turned and stopped talking, but she never stopped working up her fountain.

"Hey, Sis. I'm not complaining, but why is Topless Kenzie smashing her boobs into the window like that?"

Marilyn turned to look.

"Oh, my. Not just once, Sissy. She just keeps squeezing them into the glass again, and again, and—"

Sophia laughed and said, "Oh, of course. Look who's behind her. That horny Boss."

"I see him. He's been doing a lot of smiling lately."

"Dayzee's fine with it too. She has her boobs up on the glass, so she's probably next."

"It was very nice of her to let Topless Kenzie go first, Sissy."

"Well, Sis, she probably plans to have the Boss all to herself soon anyway. I think she and the Boss have something kind of serious going on."

"Oh, I did wonder about that. It's quite a sight to see their boobs all lined up like that."

"Let's join them next time—double the boobs. Hey, let's give them all something more to smile about."

Sophia slipped the nearest strap down over Marilyn's shoulder, then reached around her sister's waist and pulled her in closer.

"Mine's just about ready to give it up, Sis. I bet yours is too."

Marilyn finished dropping her dress, unbuttoned the last few buttons of her sister's blouse, then reached around Sophia's waist, and they held each other close as they continued a slow, steady bounce.

"Oh yeah, Sissy. Uh-huh."

"They're all watching. Hell, even these helpful Kollector Kitties are watching."

"Jiffy's camera too."

"All on film. Nice."

"So, we hug each other?"

"Well, yeah, but not just that. When our fountains go off, and our eyes are dazzling like they do, we should kiss until the fountains are done."

"Oh, sometimes that takes a long time."

Sophia nodded and grinned.

"I know, Sis."

Marilyn giggled softly and said, "Okay. But only because they're all watching, Sissy."

*   *   *

"God, what the hell is going on with those two?" said Topless Kenzie, one word with each bounce into the glass.

"Oh, that," said Dayzee. "They sometimes kiss just to amuse everyone."

"Well, it's working," said the Boss. "Damn."

"Not that," said Topless Kenzie. "Their eyes. What the hell is that?"

"That's the dazzle from something I like to call the fountain of youth. It's a potion thing when some lucky earthman gets to—"

"They're lucky? Really?"

Dayzee laughed once and said, "See their smiles?"

"Oh, yeah, now I do. Huh. Um, how long are they going to kiss?"

"You want them to stop?"

"Uh, um, I guess . . ."

"She doesn't," said the Boss. "I might have to stop, though, before I break her through the glass, Dayzee."

"Oh, what the hell, Boss. I'll just call another Dead Carpenter."

Kenzie tipped her head toward Dayzee and said, "He still has really cold hands."

# Chapter 28 – Even Meaner Torch People

"Mm," said Marilyn, leaning away from Sophia. "That was a special kind of fountain, Sissy."

"Yeah, let's remember that."

"For our next fountain?"

"Uh, sure. Then, too."

A loud scream echoed around the grounds from high up on the fire truck's ladder. The twins looked up and saw that Jiff had slipped from the rung, and his fall was checked by the camera strap winding around his neck. He hung there, gasping and kicking but still holding his camera.

"Everyone's dying, Sissy."

"He's not dead," said Sophia. "I think he's just kind of hanging there. Someone needs to get him down."

The two lions who had watched them so closely stood and ambled over to the truck, then up into the back area. Then, they started carefully climbing the ladder.

"Those are such nice kitties."

The lionesses had reached the level of Jiff's kicking feet.

"Yeah, they're just trying to—"

Each one bit on a shin, then let go of the ladder, hanging there with him.

"Uh-oh. That's not going to end well, Sissy."

"Nope. Even if we tried to run up there, we'd never—"

Like a bottle of red champagne uncorking, Jiff's head popped off, and two lions and two pieces of Jiff and one camera fell to the truck, thumping loudly.

"Oh, my. That's not good."

"No, Sis, he kind of needs his head. But those—"

"I was thinking about our reality show, Sissy. That poor camera."

The lions came trotting around from behind the truck, and one of them had an intact camera in her mouth.

Sophia pointed at the one carrying the camera and said, "No chattering, you. No chattering!"

"At least, not yet!"

The mountain lion brought the camera closer, and Sophia accepted it, then patted the beast's side.

"Good, kitty."

"Everyone we know from Earth is dead, Sissy."

"Huh? No, Sis. We still have Topless Kenzie."

"We do. And she's topless."

"And Dead Mack is kind of, well, I don't know. He's kind of alright."

"Sure he is, Sissy. Oh, we'd better get back inside. Come on."

Sophia looked quickly toward the house and saw that no one had remained at the windows to watch them. She looked at the camera in her hand.

"Sis, no one's watching anymore, but I think my dead earth guy might have found his second supply."

"Really, Sissy? That never happens."

She leaned in closer and said, "I know. Humor me."

"Mm-hmm. Okay, Sissy."

* * *

"Just sit here awhile, Kenzie," Dayzee said as she guided the dazed earthgirl onto a barstool. "You'll recover. Whiskey will help."

The Boss was already pouring, and he set a full tumbler in front of her.

"Wow," Kenzie said, then took a swig. "Buy me a ticket."

"Ticket to what?"

"Whatever sex-crazed world you're all from."

"No tickets," said the Boss. "Just portals. Speaking of which,"—he looked at his watch—"we're running out of time."

The glass sliding door screeched open, and Marilyn and Sophia rushed inside, then together slammed it shut.

"That was a wonderful show," said Dayzee. "Even that bit with your dazzling eyes."

"That's funny, Dayzee. It was Sissy's idea. Maybe I shouldn't have—"

"You should always listen to your sister. Alright, so what's the rush?"

"Almost all of the Dead Firemen are dead. And—"

"That's just silly, Sissy."

"Right. But they're mostly all dead, almost all of the lions have been converted to Kollector Kitties, and even Jiff is dead. His head popped right off."

"Do we know where it went?" said Dayzee, bouncing her eyebrows and grinning.

Marilyn giggled and said, "Uh-oh. He's looking for it, Dayzee."

"Okay, good. So, he's still kind of a normal guy. What else?"

"We saved the camera."

"Wait," said Dayzee. "He filmed that whole fountain deal you two had out there?"

They both nodded.

"Oh, my. Um, I think I have a theater in this enormous mansion. Let's see . . . now, where was that?"

"Dayzee," said Sophia, "we'll have to watch that later. There's something else: about a dozen of the Collectors are coming here from the deathhouse."

"Well, Fia, they probably want more cadavers. What's the big deal?"

"They're hands are burning, Dayzee."

"Mare, no. They're coming to burn down the house?"

"Sure looks like it," said Sophia.

"After all we've been through together? What with the lions, and dead guys, and cadavers . . . even that goddamn squid seafood dinner? Oh, I know what's going on."

"What's that?" said the Boss.

"They got their goddamn cadavers, now they don't want to poop out all that King Kong stuff for us. Not fair. Not fair at all!"

Marilyn pouted and said, "I want sex with King Kong."

Kenzie, her back to them, clunked down her empty glass and said, "Let me tell you a story about King Kong Jr."

"Never mind her," said Dayzee. "She'll recover. We need some serious help, girls. Not just to stop those freaks. I mean, think of the cleanup out there."

"Carpentry, too, Dayzee."

"Yeah, Mare. That too."

"Who are we going to get to help?" said Sophia. "Bruno would be good, but he—"

"That's it!" screamed the Boss. "Sophia, you're brilliant!"

"Um, my eyes, you mean? When I'm—"

"No, not that. I mean, yeah, that too. You two really spiced it up nicely too. You'll have to remember, next time, to—"

"Boss?" said Dayzee. "Collectors? Torches for hands?"

"Oh, yeah. I got a little sidetracked. Alright, listen up. Bruno is the key. When he—"

"He isn't coming back," said Dayzee. "Some sweaty mountain of a bearded woman took him back and made a sex slave out of him."

"Oh, Dayzee, really?" said Marilyn. "I didn't know that."

"We almost did that, Sis," Sophia said with a snicker.

"Girls. This is serious. Boss, how is Bruno any kind of a key to this mess?"

"Easy. Well, no, not easy. Watching those twins, the way they rode those fountains, that was easy. And it's all on film? And you have a theater somewhere in this—"

"Boss! Try to focus!"

He covered his eyes with both hands but couldn't lock down a giant smile.

"Okay. Here it is. You needed Bruno, and you got him. You all figured something out that brought him back. Something else you all did even got me back through the portal once. Remember that?"

"Oh my," Marilyn said with a soft giggle. "Yes. I was helpless on that pool table, and those fellows weren't really gentlemen at all. Oh, no. I—"

"You were bent over the table, Sis, and they held you in place. And the leader of that gang, he—"

"Pulled down your panties," said Dayzee, "which were white and really tiny. I remember that. They were so small that—"

"Hey!" yelled the Boss. "You were yelling at me? Come on already!"

"The Boss is right," said Dayzee. "The thing is, we did figure something out, and that brought someone through the portal."

"I don't think we could drive though that battlefield out there to get back to the Prism."

"No, Fia, not quick enough anyway. By the time we got back, those Torch People would have—"

"That's what we're calling them now?"

"I don't know, Mare. We're kind of just making this up as we go, you know?"

Marilyn nodded.

"The point is that there's no time. And that portal downstairs, it just isn't the same kind of portal. God knows what might come through."

"Maybe even meaner Torch People?"

"Sure, Mare. Hungrier, too. Yeah, that could happen."

"I don't think we have much choice," said the Boss. "That might be your only hope. We just need to figure out the plan."

# Chapter 29 – Some Kind of Twisted Sex

Dayzee said, "Kenzie, you're probably in no condition yet for any deep thinking."

Marilyn giggled and said, "She said 'deep,' Sissy."

"Yeah, Sis. That Boss man, loaded up on potion. That would sure go—"

"Girls, it's time for some drinks. We need them if we're going to figure this out in the next few seconds."

The twins turned to look out toward the deathhouse.

"Oh, they're not fast," said Marilyn, "but they kind of don't stop either."

"Yeah, Mare. They—oh, wait. What the hell is going on now?"

Visible from the bar, through the glass, they watched the last of the living Dead Firemen walking toward the Collectors. Three of them held a fire hose, and two others wielded large axes.

Sophia chuckled and said, "Yeah, boys, put out those Torch People. Forget about the tiny deathhouse."

"It never really had a chance to be a true deathhouse, Sissy."

"I wonder if we could bowl a head in there from Dayzee's patio. Then, we could call it a deathhouse."

"Girls, no bowling with heads. At least, not right now. Kenzie, we need the Boss to focus with us. Call Dead Mack and see if he can get here quick to tend bar."

Marilyn laughed and said, "Seriously, Dayzee? That's kind of silly. You know the Prism won't let him go at a busy time of day like this."

When Dayzee looked at Sophia, she saw her shaking her head and bouncing her eyebrows.

Dayzee said, "Such a sweet kid."

Looking at Marilyn, she said, "Mare, think about it: he probably has vacation time or something. And if he gets fired, I'll just hire him here."

"You did say you needed a Dead Butler."

"I, uh, don't recall saying exactly that, Fia. The point is, Kenzie, try to call Dead Mack. He's the greatest living bartender that—"

"Ha!"

"Oh, Fia, what am I saying? No, he's not quite the greatest—look, girls! They're hosing down those Collectors!"

While the three men with the hose were sweeping it around, trying to put out all of the torches, the two with axes had closed in on some of the Collectors. The water had no effect, and two Collectors calmly ignited two firemen, who ran screaming for the pool.

"Just how many dead things have been in that pool, Dayzee? Sheesh."

"We never could count all the dead things, Sissy. A lot."

"Girls, they're buying us some time, at least. That's their job."

"What the hell kind of job is that?" said the Boss. "Get burned by Collectors and jump in a squid tank just to buy a few seconds for Topless Kenzie to call Dead Mack to come tend bar?"

"He does have a point."

"That he does, Fia. That's not much of a career."

Kenzie held the landline phone receiver away from her ear and said, "Uh, I'm not topless at the moment."

"She has a good point, too, Dayzee."

"Sis, you're really setting the jokes up for me, aren't you?"

"Happy to help, Sissy."

"Kenzie?" said Dayzee. "Can he get his dead ass here?"

She put the phone down and said, "It's not looking good. They put him on the phone, and I asked him. But all he did was grunt."

"It might be like a different language when you're dead?"

"Could be, Mare. We'll hope for the best. In the meantime, Kenzie, let's get some whiskey poured. We have some serious figuring to do."

"Uh-oh," said Marilyn. "Another torched Dead Fireman just dove in the pool. I mean, squid tank."

Dayzee held the Boss's gaze, and they both smiled as the twins continued.

"He jumped, Sis. I think he was in a hurry and wasn't practicing his fancy stuff."

"Oh, that's understandable. Is that squiddy character back in the pool?"

"Part of him, Sis. Did you see that lion vomiting back by the shrubs? I think she tried to eat some of that chewy slime."

"I'm never ordering that for take-out, Sissy."

"Nope. Me neither."

Dayzee shook her head and said, "Twins, huh?"

"Gorgeous twins," he said. "Maybe they'd like a closer look? Like, right up against that glass?"

"You're a particularly horny kind of Boss. You know that?"

"Maybe you gave me too much potion."

"Hmm. I'm thinking it might not have been enough."

* * *

While Kenzie was setting full glasses in front of them as they sat at the bar, Dayzee said, "I hate to be a nag, Kenzie, but . . ."

Kenzie sighed and started unbuttoning her blouse. Everyone in a line, Sophia on the left, then Dayzee, then Marilyn, then the Boss, watched with big smiles.

She smiled back as she let it drop to the floor.

"Better?"

"That always helps," said Marilyn.

"Yep. That's nice. Since she's almost always topless, though, maybe we could save some time and just get back to calling her Kenzie?"

"Smart thinking, Fia. Alright, now, we're finally ready. I'll start."

"With an idea?" said Marilyn.

Dayzee laughed and turned to her left.

"Such a sweet kid."

She looked to her right and said, "No, Mare, with a drink."

She picked hers up and finished half of it.

The rest of them gulped down some too.

"Alright. Idea time. Girls, when we called the Boss, Mare was—"

"Surrounded by eager sticks?"

"That's true enough, Mare. But what was the theme of that little deal?"

"Sex."

"Right, Fia. That's important. We know that worked. Whatever we do, it has to involve sex."

"Easy enough."

"Yes, Sissy, because almost everything we do already involves sex."

"Girls, you're right. Alright, that part is a cinch. What else?"

Marilyn cleared her throat and said, "I still think everyone should have left me alone for a while at that pool table. You could have waited just a few minutes."

"Sis, no, you were getting into some serious danger, and you—"

"That's it!" said Dayzee. "Danger!"

"But when we called Bruno, when we were all stripping by that statue at the Prism," said Sophia, "there was no—"

Dayzee pointed at her and said, "Oh, yes there was, Fia. Remember all that garbage that the assassin was throwing at us?"

"Oh. Yeah. Now, I do. Good thing we had Kozy."

"I miss Kozy," said Marilyn.

Kenzie said, "And you wonder why my mind is more squishy than that squid fellow out there?"

Everyone stared. But just for a few seconds. They kept watching Kenzie, but they also got back to their drinks.

"I know I'm Kenzie. Uh, I'm pretty sure. But for a while, I think maybe I was Kozy? Then, I—"

"Then, you were Moe," said Marilyn.

"Well, just Moe's head, which is what the role required."

"Good point, Dayzee," said Sophia. "Kenzie, you volunteered for that one."

"I kind of did, didn't I? So, I guess I'm kind of wondering which one you all like the best? I mean, if my brain is shot anyway, maybe you should all just vote?"

"I liked Kozy the best," said Marilyn. "He sure liked danger."

"I'll go with Moe's head, Sis. Don't forget: we were planning to do some abusing up there with Moe's loose head."

"Girls, those are both good options. Maybe we should mix it up a little? Kenzie, could you be Kozy that sometimes volunteers to be Moe's head?"

Kenzie stared from Dayzee, to Marilyn, who clapped quietly, to Sophia, who smirked and studied her toplessness.

"How about if I just stick with insane? That's what I'll do. I'll just—"

"All of you," said the Boss. "Maybe we should get back to the topic at hand?"

"Right," said Dayzee. "The burning hands of those irritating Torch People."

Sophia nodded and said, "That's why he's the Boss."

"Yep," said Kenzie. "There's another reason too. A big one."

"So, we're making progress. We need sex and danger."

"Way to sum up life, Boss."

"Thanks, Sophia."

"My life anyway. Oh, and Sissy's too."

"Yeah, Mare," said Dayzee. "Me too. So, what's the plan?"

Mad scratching at the glass doors got them to spin around, and Kenzie looked past them.

Two lions were looking behind themselves quickly, then into the mansion as they tried to scratch through the door.

"Hey," said Dayzee. "Notice anything?"

"Teeth."

"Good, Fia. Keep going."

"Oh, not brown."

"Yeah, Mare. Anything else?"

"They're not chattering," said the Boss. "Dayzee, girls, those two haven't been corrupted by the Collectors?"

"That would make a good title for a book," said Marilyn. "*Corrupted by the Collectors.*"

"Mare, that's nonsense. No one would buy garbage like that. So, those two are kind of going crazy."

"They're afraid of the rest of them, I bet."

"Yeah, that's probably true, Fia. But it's not like we can let them in to hide. They're still pretty—"

"Dangerous!"

"Kenzie, such an outburst," said Marilyn. "You got yourself bouncing nicely."

The Boss said, "Hey, she's right, though. There's our danger. Those two."

"Danger, how, Boss?" said Dayzee. "We let them in, they rip us apart, they drag our bloody, twitching bodies to the deathhouse, then we come back as King Kong?"

"I don't know, Dayzee. Oh, wait! They don't want you. They don't want those twins either."

He turned slowly to look at Kenzie.

"Hey, wait a second," she said and held her blouse over herself. "What the hell are you thinking?"

Sophia grinned at Kenzie and said, "I see some prime lion bait, right there."

Kenzie's eyes opened wider.

"Oh, but Sissy, she has to have some kind of twisted sex too."

"Who said it had to be twisted?"

Marilyn giggled and said, "I did, Boss. Always choose twisted if you can."

Everyone got quiet and watched as Dayzee tapped her empty glass on the bar at a steady pace. She didn't stop when Kenzie poured more whiskey into it.

She held the glass still and looked up when Kenzie said, "I got it!"

# Chapter 30 – Space and Time Fracturing

"Do I have to be completely naked?"

"Yeah, Kenzie. Oh, wait. You're not."

"High heels, Dayzee? That's all I'm allowed?"

"I insisted on that one," said Sophia.

"Gee. Thanks, Fifi."

Marilyn elbowed her sister and whispered, "She's still calling you Fifi!"

"Just lie down on these couch cushions," said Dayzee.

She did.

"No, not on your side. Come on. You know better than that."

"Kozy would know better," said Marilyn.

"Even Moe's head knew better."

"So true, Sissy."

"There you go. That's better. Oh. It might not seem like an important detail, but . . ."

Kenzie spread her legs a small amount.

"Better. Sure, that's—"

She spread them farther.

"You have the best ideas, Dayzee," Sophia said, mostly to herself.

"Where's that yoga?" Marilyn said with a giggle. "Show us some yoga."

Kenzie made a better effort.

"Perfect. You really finished this idea off nicely, Kenzie, when you upped the sex angle."

"I like that, too, Dayzee. Kenzie, tell us again, just to be sure we got it."

"Fine. You three have to protect me from the lions, because they want to eat me."

"Damn," said Sophia. "Is there time for a comment?"

"No, Sissy. Tell us later. Every little detail."

Kenzie continued: "So, if you don't protect me, they'll rip me to pieces. But to make it more extreme, if you *do* succeed in saving me, I have to have sex with everyone here."

"I'm here!" the Boss yelled from the bar.

"Haven't you had enough?"

"Dayzee, that's just silly. He's still loaded with potion."

"True, Mare. Well, I don't know if the plan will work, but I'm sure as hell glad we're at least setting it up."

Kenzie looked up at her and said, "You don't know if this will work?"

Dayzee shrugged and said, "I guess we'll see."

"We should have been practicing."

"True, Fia. That couldn't have hurt. Okay, the rest of us need to form a circle around her. Boss, you get the honor of letting those two vicious she-lions in."

"And those two want to eat me?" said Kenzie.

"Sure," Sophia said with a grin. "I bet they're . . . hungry."

"Good one, Sissy. I feel like a hungry lady lion."

"Mare, try to keep pretending you're human, alright? Okay, Boss, I think we're ready. Let loose the lions!"

* * *

The Boss hurried over to the glass doors but turned to smile at Dayzee and the twins. Outside, three Dead Fireman floated facedown in the pool, burning, and the other two were fighting with the hose, spraying the Torch People with no success.

And up against the glass, the two unconverted lions waited.

"Sometime today, Boss? We're kind of on a schedule here."

"Oh, right, Dayzee. Okay."

He slid the door open just enough for one of the lions to get her snout in, then he ran back toward Kenzie and the girls.

"Join the circle, Boss. Those lions are fast."

"Hey," Kenzie said as she sat up, "I, um, I'm not so sure about this. I mean, what if they do get through your circle?"

"They'll eat you," Marilyn said plainly, then shrugged.

"You're set up like a tasty feast," Sophia said, with her eyes roaming all over her.

Kenzie started to get up, saying, "I changed my mind. I'm not—"

Sophia didn't hesitate. She pushed Kenzie down onto her back and straddled her, her knees pinning both arms to the thick area rug.

"Hey! Let me up, Fifi!"

"She's still calling you Fifi, Sissy!"

"Oh, no, Kenzie," Sophia said as she leaned over, keeping their faces close. "This is how you trapped me up in that bedroom, remember?"

"Yeah, but that was just for fun! No one was going to get eaten!"

Sophia scoffed and turned to look at her sister.

"She's funny, Sissy. I think she already knows that's just silly."

Sophia laughed and looked down at her again.

"Tell you what: if the lions don't, you can be sure that—"

"Mare, Boss, tighten up the circle! Here come the lions!"

Dayzee and Marilyn, each guarding near Sophia, backed up until they could go no farther.

The Boss positioned himself closer between Kenzie's legs, still facing away.

"Damn lions, Dayzee. Damn lions!"

"That doesn't help, Mare."

The lions crept toward them slowly and silently, stalking the circle of two girls and one Boss. They hid behind furniture, peeking over, while Kenzie struggled to free herself. Sophia held her in place, and the rest of them stared at the approaching beasts.

Dayzee, facing out toward the lions and away from the bait, said, "Fia, you got our girl under control?"

Sophia's knees still held down Kenzie's arms, and she was holding both of her shoulders. Kenzie frowned up at her and shook from side to side, bouncing her breasts around.

"Huh," said Sophia, "maybe way less is way better."

She let go of Kenzie's shoulders and when she rolled each way again, trying to escape, Sophia nodded at the sight. Marilyn turned for a quick look and clapped a few times before focusing again on the lions.

"Give the girl some freedom, and just look at that," Sophia said with a smirk.

"Oh, you like that, don't you?" Kenzie said with a snarl.

"Who wouldn't? Shake them all you want. Oh, but we'd better stay quiet. The lions are coming!"

Kenzie shook harder, Sophia smiled more, and Kenzie said, "Fifi, if I survive this, I'm—"

Sophia put one manicured finger on Kenzie's lips and said, "Shh, pretty girl. Shaking but no talking."

Marilyn didn't look back, but she said, "Sissy, you have a way with trapped naked girls."

"It comes natural, Sis. And you can just think up your own joke for that because—"

"Hey, you two!" Dayzee whispered loudly. "They're coming in for the kill!"

"Fifi!"

"Quiet, Kenzie!" said Dayzee "Or I'll come sit on you too!"

"Dayzee, most of Kenzie is already covered quite nicely by Sissy."

"True, Mare. But I'll find a place."

"Oh, yes, you would!" Marilyn said and dared to clap a few times.

"Uh-oh," Dayzee said softly and slowly as one lioness had gotten quite near and was staring into her eyes. "Oh, boy. Here we go."

Everyone got quiet, and Kenzie stopped bouncing things around to watch the staredown.

Dayzee's chest rose and fell with her deep breaths, and her breasts were hardly held in place with her blouse mostly unbuttoned.

The lion took a quick step one way, then the other way.

Dayzee shifted each time, blocking access to Kenzie.

Sophia placed a hand on Dayzee's back, then she placed the other on Marilyn's back.

The lion rushed back to Dayzee's other side and began a deadly swipe toward Kenzie, but Dayzee was quick enough to get in the way. A sharp claw snagged Dayzee's blouse between her breasts, and the beast snapped its paw back, ripping the cloth open.

"Just wonderful," said Dayzee.

It was all she had time to say because the lion swiped again, hooked a sleeve, and pulled.

"Hey, my blouse!"

The lion growled and kept pulling. Dayzee turned and let the lion rip the blouse completely off of her.

"This lion's undressing me!"

"Somebody had to do it," said the Boss. "I would have helped."

"Thanks, Boss. You and the lion."

The other lion was trying to find a way past Marilyn by feinting to each side of her while staring into her eyes.

"Don't let that lion get me!" said Kenzie.

"Shh!" said Sophia. "How do I keep you quiet for your own good?"

"Oh, Sissy, I have an—ah!"

The lion took a swipe, caught Marilyn's white dress with a sharp talon, and shredded it entirely down the front, leaving it flapping open like a robe.

"Sissy! I'm almost naked! Damn lion!"

The Boss laughed and said, "I guess these beasts are afraid of me, though, huh?"

One of the lions roared near his head.

"Yikes! I was kidding!"

The lion swiped again, hooked what was left of Marilyn's dress, and ripped it from her completely.

"Dayzee, now I am naked!"

"Well," said Dayzee, still staring into her lion's eyes, "naked looks good on you. Keep doing your job!"

Both lions roared and jumped from side to side, swiping down and across, ripping at anything they could find.

The Boss lost his shirt, and his pants were shredded.

Somehow, Dayzee's lion had poked a claw into her skirt and yanked that away. She and Marilyn were down to only their panties and heels.

Sophia laughed and said, "What the hell? I'm the only one with clothes?"

It didn't last long. Both big cats were successful at breaking through the defenses to strip Sophia of everything but her heels too.

Dayzee turned to see and said, "You were saying, Fia?"

"Alright, so I'm naked, sitting on Kenzie, who's also naked."

"That's true, Sissy. I'm just about naked too."

"Me too."

"I'm almost naked," said the Boss. "And horny. Just thought I'd mention that."

The lions padded around the circle, sniffing and growling, looking in at Kenzie, who stared back at them, her eyes bugging out.

"Hey, lions," said Dayzee, "you're done attacking?"

They both sat, one facing Dayzee and the other facing Marilyn.

"Mare, what's your lion doing?"

"She's just watching me, Dayzee."

"Mine too. Fia, is that lion bait still—"

"Hey, I'm an actress."

"That's funny, Kenzie," Marilyn said with a scared laugh. "Very true, too, though."

"Wait a second," Dayzee said, still staring into her lion's eyes. "You, she-lion . . . did you just want us all naked?"

Dayzee's lion grunted once at the ceiling.

"Oh my God. Girls, we have ourselves a little question and answer thing going on here with these lady lions."

"Dayzee, that's silly," said Marilyn. "Things like that just don't happen."

Dayzee turned enough to glance back at Sophia, who had placed her hand on her back again.

"Such a sweet kid," she said with a laugh.

Facing her lion again, she said, "Mare, think about all that's going on. Come on. It's not all that ridiculous."

"She's right, Sis," Sophia said, then she placed her other hand back on her sister's back. "Ask your lion something."

"Hmm. Lion? Is it raining in Kildare today? Because we—"

"Sis, that's good to know, but maybe something about this little party we're having?"

"Oh, okay, Sissy. Lady lion, why do you want us all naked?"

"Mare, she probably can't speak this Earth language like we've learned. Maybe stick to yes and no questions?"

"Oh, that's smart, Dayzee. Okay. Mrs. Lion? Do you—"

"She's probably not married, Sis. Try again."

Marilyn coughed once, then said, "Pretty lion, should we be doing anything special besides just being naked?"

"Good question, Sis."

Marilyn's lion roared sharply at the ceiling.

"I get it," said Kenzie. "Oh, and Fifi, my arms are starting to hurt."

"Oh, yeah, sorry," Sophia said, then moved her knees to the rug.

Kenzie took turns rubbing each arm, then said, "So, Fifi, you remember what this plan was about, right?"

"I do," said Marilyn. "Sex."

Sophia grinned down at Kenzie and said, "How could I forget? Yes, some kind of sex has to be going on to get someone or something through the portal to help us."

"Exactly, Fia," said Dayzee. "We have to at least get something started. But that's not all."

"Oh," said Marilyn. "Danger, too, right?"

"I'm not waiting," the Boss said while turning himself to face all of them. "I see my chance and I'm taking it."

He reached out both hands and began fondling Dayzee's and Marilyn's breasts.

"Oh, that's kind of nice, Boss."

"I like the way you're bossing me around," said Marilyn. "Sissy and Kenzie, you have to pitch in too."

Dayzee scoffed and said, "Even though neither of you want to."

"That's funny, Dayzee."

"Thanks, Mare."

"A kiss would be a good start, Fifi."

"Hmm. Can't argue with that."

"Uh-oh," said Dayzee. "My lion's snarling and coming after me!"

"Mine too!" said Marilyn. "She has big teeth!"

"This is perfect," said the Boss. "Dayzee and Marilyn, offer them your throats."

"What? Are you insane?"

"No, Dayzee, it's just that—"

"Boss, I like my throat! I want to keep it!"

"I don't think they'll hurt you, girls."

"Uh, you 'don't think?'"

"Yeah, Dayzee. Look, try it and see. It'll be alright."

"Oh, boy."

Dayzee looked straight up, leaving her throat open to be ripped apart.

"This is a bad idea," Marilyn said as she looked up at the ceiling.

"Really, Boss?"

He kept rubbing her breasts around and said, "It's for the plan, Dayzee. You know that. Oh, you'd better hold still."

Dayzee's lion placed her open mouth over her throat and held it there.

"I don't mind at all, Boss," said Marilyn. "If you weren't doing that, somebody else would—oh, my . . ."

Marilyn's lion had closed her razor-sharp teeth around her throat too.

The Boss kept fondling them and said, "Sophia, you know what you have to do for the plan."

She removed her hands from Dayzee and Marilyn and placed them flat on the rug on each side of Kenzie's head, who grinned up at her.

"You're doing this because you have to, Fifi?"

"Uh-uh. Plan? What plan?"

While the Boss was caressing and rubbing Dayzee's and Marilyn's breasts, and while Dayzee and Marilyn waited, terrified, as the lions were about to remove their throats at any second, Sophia leaned forward.

Then, her lips touched Kenzie's.

And the thunder of space and time fracturing erupted from the portal below them, shaking and rattling everything and everyone in Dayzee's mansion.

The lions retracted their fangs and jumped onto the couch.

The Boss kept rubbing.

Sophia kept kissing Kenzie.

"Boss," said Dayzee, "was that the bomb?"

"No, Dayzee. That bomb is telepathic. No sound."

"So, what the hell was that?"

"Trouble."

"Could you try to add a little detail, please?"

"Okay: big trouble."

"Oh, boy. Uh, the plan seemed to have worked. You could probably stop playing with our boobs now."

"I could. Yep."

He didn't.

Dayzee turned enough to see Sophia.

"Fia. You could probably stop too."

"Mm-hmm."

"Kenzie?"

"Mm-hmm."

# Chapter 31 – You Can't Burn my House!

A thundering herd of horses was pounding their way up the stone steps that led down from the closet to the portal under Dayzee's house.

Dayzee jumped up and played tug of war with a lion to get back her skirt and blouse. She won, the lion lay back down, and Dayzee started getting dressed.

"All of you, come on. That doesn't sound good."

"Horses, Dayzee?"

"Really, Mare? Have you been paying attention?"

"Oh. Maybe not enough."

She reached slowly for her dress and snapped it back from the lion's jaws, then held it up.

"It's all ripped. It's a robe now."

"Here," the Boss said as he handed her his belt. "Try this."

"You look pretty good with your shirt ripped off of you, Boss."

"Thanks, Marilyn. I think it might be that potion still boiling around in me. If there's time, you and I could—"

"You two," said Dayzee. "How about getting dressed?"

"Oh, alright," Marilyn said, pouting.

"Fine," said the Boss.

They stood and covered up as well as they could, then stopped to listen to the heavy hooves getting closer.

Dayzee shook her head at the shattered closet door, then looked down at Sophia and Kenzie.

"Mare, check it out."

"They must have heard the horses, Dayzee."

"Yeah, probably. They don't care. Hey! Fia!"

Sophia turned her head to grin at Dayzee.

Kenzie tipped her head, held Dayzee's gaze, and also grinned.

Dayzee said, "That's quite a sight, you two naked like that, and—"

"They do have heels, still, Dayzee. So, they're not truly naked."

"Thanks, Mare. Yeah, I guess that's true. But you two should—"

"Sissy's just keeping that lion bait ready in case we still need it."

Sophia and Kenzie both turned to look at Marilyn, who shrugged and smiled down at them.

"Someone has to do it, Sis."

She turned to look at Kenzie from very close, and Kenzie looked up at her.

"Damn lion bait," Sophia said, causing Kenzie to giggle.

"Really, though," said Dayzee, "we have problems. Maybe give each other a rain check on that?"

"Oh, alright, Dayzee, but we're just so damn itchy," Sophia said, then sat up, still on Kenzie's lap.

"We all are, Fia. Maybe get up all the way?"

"Fine, Dayzee," Sophia said while standing and extending a hand to help Kenzie up too.

Dayzee watched them searching for their clothes and said, "Well, that worked. Sex and danger seem to be the formula."

Marilyn took a step closer to the lions and slowly reached a hand toward them.

"Such good kitties."

They only looked at her calmly, so she petted one's head.

"Thank you for the danger. We needed that."

"Sex, too, Mare. We always need that."

"Listen to Dayzee, Sis. She's not wrong."

"I know, Sissy, and we're thankful that you two are such good actresses. It's the only way that scheme could work."

Sophia turned to meet Kenzie's gaze, and they shared a smile.

"Uh, yeah, Sis. Kenzie's a damn good actress."

"Fifi, too, Marilyn."

The hooves got louder.

"Okay, the awards ceremony needs to wrap up. Some horrible thing got sent through that portal when that explosion—"

"I don't think so," said the Boss. "Those horses must have—"

"They're not really horses, Boss," Marilyn said with a patient smile. "That's just silly."

He squinted at her for a second, then continued.

"I was saying that those things with hooves—"

"Torch People?" said Marilyn.

"Collectors?" said Sophia.

"Girls, whatever they are. Go on, Boss."

"They came through quietly, like the rest of them have. No, girls, whatever that noise was, that's something else."

Marilyn clapped and said, "Someone came to save us!"

"Oh, Mare, that's right. Yeah, that's why we had all that danger and sex."

"Huh," Sophia said. "Sure, Sis. That's why."

"Well, maybe not you and Kenzie, Sissy," Marilyn said with a soft giggle. "Oh, I could have played your role too."

"Sis, that's just—"

"Next time we have to do this," said Kenzie, looking from one to the other, "you're both in that role."

"Girls, wait. Something's happening."

The first pale face with quickly chomping rows of little brown teeth leaned through the closet door splinters and looked around. Its eyes moved in opposite circles until one, then the other focused on them.

The lions jumped behind the couch, then peeked up over the back.

Dayzee shook her head and said, "Just wonderful. What the hell is he—"

"Gray feather in the hat, Dayzee," Sophia said while buttoning Kenzie's blouse. "That's a girl."

"Me too, Fifi."

"Mm-hmm. Oh, yeah."

Dayzee sighed and said, "We know way too much about these creepy things."

The female Collector poked a hand out of the closet, showing long, slender fingers, each with one extra joint. Almost all of the fingers wore rings as white and grim as bones baked in the sun.

"Well, look at that," said Sophia. "She's waving to us."

"Say hi to Mrs. Collector, Sissy."

Dayzee raised a hand and shook it around, saying, "Allow me, girls. Hello, creepy Collector thing. Nice hat. Now, why don't you get your bony ass back down to—"

Her hand became a torch.

"Uh-oh, Dayzee. That's probably not good."

"No, Mare. Just . . . no."

She stepped out into the house and held her torch high.

Another followed, head first.

Marilyn pointed at its black feather and said, "Okay, this one's a—"

He reached out into the mansion's interior with a burning hand.

"Oh, boy. Boss, any ideas?"

He tipped his head each way to look past Dayzee, then said, "Those firemen are losing the battle out there. We can't even call them."

"Damn Dead Firemen," Marilyn said with a pout.

"We just need their hose," Sophia said with a smirk.

"Yeah," said Kenzie while finishing her blouse, "Fifi and I might want to play with a hose sometime."

The Boss snapped his head around and said, "We could—"

"Boss!" Dayzee yelled. "Stay focused, alright? Dammit!"

"Sure, Dayzee. Alright. Well, if it's only the two of them, we could—"

Two more stepped out, hands ablaze.

"Damn Torch People."

"That doesn't help as much as you think, Mare."

Two more joined the others in a tight huddle, each holding up a hand that was more of a torch.

"See, Dayzee?" said Kenzie. "This is just too much. None of you ever took it seriously. I tried to tell you!"

"You did," said Dayzee. "Yep. You're not just an actress or—"

"A barmaid," said Marilyn.

"Or a Moe head," said Sophia.

"Girls, may I? Thank you. Kenzie, you're also a very wise and beautiful girl."

"Aw, Dayzee, thanks. That was sweet of you to say."

The Boss said, "Uh, Dayzee, maybe hold back on all of that for a second. There's a lot of them coming up. Hear the hooves?"

They listened for a few seconds.

"And our sex and danger extravaganza didn't call them?"

"I don't think so. They probably already had tickets and were waiting to—"

"Boss," said Marilyn, "that's just silly."

"Okay. Yeah. But you know what I mean."

There were a dozen congregated near the closet. Each had a fiery fist raised up high, and no more hooves were pounding on the old stone steps.

"Oh, this is just wonderful," said Dayzee. "Hey! Who's your spokesman?"

"Dayzee," Marilyn whispered, "you're offending the ladies of the group."

"Sis has a point."

"Kenzie?" Dayzee said, "Want to weigh in on that too?"

Kenzie shook her head and said, "I just want to get undressed again."

"She's got the only plan that makes sense."

"Fia, really?"

"You said it was an extravaganza, Dayzee. Can't pass that up."

"Mare? You too? Oh, you girls."

She shook her head and turned back to the band of Torch People.

"Who's your spokesperson?"

"Close, Dayzee," said the Boss. "Better try again."

"Who's your spokescollector?"

"Eh," said Sophia. "You can do better."

Dayzee snorted a loud scoff, then said, "Who's your spokesmodel?"

"That should do," Marilyn said, then she turned to look at the Collectors.

So did the rest of them.

One stepped forward, his jaw violently but silently chattering.

His jaw stopped.

"We eat until we've eaten enough good eats and can't eat anymore. Then, we—"

Dayzee held up a hand and said, "Cut! I really can't take you guys anymore. Which one is your, um, woman?"

Another chattering, burning Collector stepped forward.

"Good. Finally. So, little lady, what's—"

"No need to be sarcastic."

"You're right, Mare. Alright, Collector, what's the deal? What the hell do you all want now?"

"Like he was trying to say, we have fed enough. Thank you all for so many good and nourishing cadavers."

"Okay. Sure," said Sophia. "But where's that King Kong stuff you promised?"

The rapidly chomping teeth stopped, and she said, "The King . . . who?"

Dayzee grabbed the Boss's crotch and said, "The damn potion! You promised!"

The male Collector stopped his teeth and said, "We lie around lying, then we lie about lying, too, and we—"

"Fine. Go burn the deathhouse if you want. I don't care."

The female looked all around at Dayzee's luxurious mansion interior, then leveled her beady eyes on Dayzee.

"Thank you. We shall."

At once, they all began marching in different directions, some toward the foyer and front door, others toward the kitchen and garage.

"This can't be good," said Marilyn.

"No, Mare. Nope."

Each touched his or her torch to anything that would burn.

"Hey, you can't burn my house!"

"They seem to think they can, Dayzee."

"You're not funny, Boss!"

Many of them walked calmly up the grand staircase and the extra one leading up from the kitchen.

"Hey, don't go up there!"

"So much for that trapeze."

"That is a shame, Fia. Damn. What are we going to do?"

The house was filling with soot and ash, Collectors were wandering everywhere, their quick teeth sometimes visible through the smoke, the two lions were running to try to escape through every door and window, but they were all burning, and everyone cowered together in the middle of the great room.

"Someone, grab the whiskey," the Boss yelled. "We're going to the portal! It's our only chance!"

He grabbed Dayzee's hand and got her running with him.

Marilyn followed quickly behind them, then stopped before going into the closet to look back.

"Sissy! Kenzie! Not now!"

Sophia turned to her sister and said, above the roar of flames and sirens and screaming outside, "I'm kind of hooked on sex and danger, Sis."

Kenzie smiled at Marilyn and said, "Oh yeah. Sex and danger for me too."

"You have to follow us! I promise, I'll make sure you both get lots of sex and danger!"

Sophia turned to Kenzie and said, "Such a sweet kid."

Kenzie smiled and said, "She makes a damn good offer, though."

"Oh, yeah. Let's make her pay."

Hand in hand, they ran toward Marilyn, and they rushed into the closet just as part of the ceiling, in flames, fell and blocked any chance of coming back out.

# Chapter 32 – Why Did You Call Me?

"We're down here!" Dayzee yelled from near the bottom of the stone stairway. "Wow, those damn Collectors sure know how to wreck some perfectly good steps."

Sophia leaned to look down into the darkness.

"We made it, Dayzee. Kenzie, Sis, and I are safe."

"Those are some very bad Collectors," Marilyn said.

"Yeah, Mare," Dayzee called up to them. "They're not really my favorite people anymore."

"She said 'people,' Sissy."

"Sis, what did she mean by 'anymore?' They used to be her favorite? What the hell?"

"Clearly, she's lost her mind, Sissy. It's all just too much for—"

They heard the lions howling through the blazing closet.

"They're trapped, Sissy. Those poor lions."

"They weren't so bad, Sis. Maybe because they didn't get a chance to become Kollector Kitties."

"No, they're still just cuddly."

"Oh!" Kenzie yelled, looking toward the screaming animals. "We might need them again, Fifi! For the danger!"

She took a step toward the back side of the closet, but Sophia stopped her.

"You can't go back there. You'll burn up too."

Marilyn stamped her heel once and said, "But they're nice kitties, Sissy. We have to do something!"

"Like what, Sis? Sure, we can get damn hot, but we can't walk through fire!"

Kenzie took another step, and both Sophia and Marilyn stopped her, and they didn't let go of her arms.

"Kenzie, come here."

Sophia reached around Kenzie's waist, and Marilyn did the same. They hugged her close in the dark, hidden place that was beginning to fill with smoke.

"There will be other danger for us, right?"

Kenzie shook her head and said, "Sharp teeth on a naked girl's throat? Like that, Fifi? I don't think so."

Marilyn nodded and said, "She's making sense, Sissy. That really is kind of hot."

"Sis, that doesn't help. Kenzie, there are lots of good ways to have sex and danger. We'll find them, I promise."

"She will," said Marilyn. "I'll help. Because I like it too."

Kenzie had tears in her eyes and said, "I want those cats. I want to keep them!"

She wiggled and fought until she was free of the twins, then she looked all around. Something caught her eye, and she hurried to one side of the room before either of them could stop her.

Walking toward her, Sophia said, "What are you doing, Kenzie? You can't just hide in the shadows while—"

Kenzie grabbed something high up, then stepped her high heel onto a rung that the twins hadn't seen before then. She began climbing the crude ladder built into the wall.

"Oh, Sissy, I don't know about this."

"The view's good, though, Sis," she said, looking up.

"Well, yes, but Dayzee's mansion is burning up. Where's she going?"

Kenzie was almost lost in the smoke and darkness, but Marilyn and Sophia could still see the skylight an unknown height above them in an attic that no one had ever visited.

Sophia pointed and said, "That's where."

"Girls!" Dayzee screamed from the bottom of the stairs. "Get down here while you still can!"

"She's right, Sissy. We'd better go."

Sophia was still looking up into the smoke and haze, where Kenzie wasn't visible anymore.

"I'll get her. She's not dying today, Sis."

Sophia began to climb, and Marilyn grabbed an ankle.

"Sissy, no! Look!"

They both looked up at sharp flames licking out from the sides high above them, sometimes blocking the skylight from sight.

"Kenzie!" Sophia screamed. "Sis, let go!"

She shook her leg, but Marilyn wouldn't release it.

"Sissy, no! You can't!"

"Sis, I have to—"

The solitary flames above them erupted into an inferno that spanned across the entire space, and the ceiling of fire showed no sign of retreating.

"Kenzie!"

There was only the sound of crackling and snapping as everything around them ignited. Parts of the mansion near them began to collapse, crashing to the floor.

Marilyn tried pulling on her sister's leg and said, "Sissy, please, you have to come back down!"

Sophia stared up at the wall of heat and shook her head, then began a slow climb down.

"We'll find her again, Sissy. I know we will. Somehow."

Sophia sighed and said, "Alright, Sis."

She took her sister's hand, and they began careful travel on the crumbling stone steps.

When just one more step downward would have blocked their view of the closet, which had become a wall of flames, they stopped at the sound of the two lions wailing and screaming.

Marilyn shook her head and said, "Those poor kitties."

Sophia touched her sister's arm, prompting her to look into her eyes.

"Those were good cats, Sis. Remember that a lion is faithful, but a woman never is."

"That's kind of jumbled up, Sissy, but I agree. Good one."

Sophia wiped at both eyes, then said, "I'll miss them too. Kenzie and those cats."

"Damn fires."

* * *

"What took you so long?" Dayzee said after the twins had gotten to the bottom. "And where's Kenzie?"

Sophia looked down and kicked at the dusty floor.

Marilyn gave that a glance, then looked up at Dayzee.

She coughed once and said, "She, um, wanted to save those lions. She's trying."

"How?"

Sophia looked up at Dayzee and said, "Remember that skylight? Way above the stairs? She climbed up there."

"Oh my. Is she going to be okay?"

Sophia looked down again, and Marilyn shrugged.

"Uh, we don't have much time for that bomb, girls," said the Boss. "We should probably get to the portal."

"She was trying to tell us."

"What, Fia? Who telling what?"

She looked at Dayzee and said, "Kenzie. She's been telling us that things were different. It's all going crazy like Kenzie said, and we weren't taking it seriously enough."

Marilyn nodded and said, "Sissy's right. So was Kenzie. Now, your house is burning, Dayzee."

Dayzee sighed and said, "And the yard is full of all kinds of dead things . . . even some kind of squid."

"The last I saw," said Sophia, "all the other Collectors and their Kollector Kitties were coming into your house. I think they all wanted to burn up together."

"All except one, Sissy. Remember that? With the burning head?"

"Oh, right, Sis. One escaped out to the Flats."

"That's one for the neighbors to enjoy."

Sophia scoffed and said, "Sure. The ones still alive."

Dayzee looked from one twin to the other, then said, "Well, that's nonsense. Why wouldn't the freaks just use the portal? The same way they got here?"

"The smell," the Boss said while looking at his watch and shaking his head.

"The smell of what?"

"The bomb. They probably smelled it when they came through."

"Oh," said Dayzee. "Yeah, that makes sense. So, what are they doing? Killing themselves?"

"I believe so. They probably don't want to leave any trace of their having been here."

"So," said Dayzee, "they're all going to incinerate themselves?"

"Yeah, I think so."

"And the lions and Dead Firemen and heads and everything else?"

"Probably, Marilyn."

"Even the squid," Sophia said. "All gone."

The Boss nodded and said, "Even your house, Dayzee. There won't be anything left. Just a smoldering pile on a quiet lot in the Flats."

Dayzee looked at each of them, her eyes big and not blinking, then she relaxed into a calm smile.

"Well, hell. I was getting run out of town anyway."

Marilyn tried a weak smile and said, "Only in Beverly Hills, Dayzee?"

Dayzee stared at her for a second, shook her head for a few more seconds, then said, "Nope. Not anymore."

"We have to go," said the Boss.

* * *

After racing through the tunnel, still hearing the roar from the flames above, and the lions screaming, and the sirens outside, they stood inside the dark room that contained the portal.

"Is that enough?" Marilyn said while pointing down at the briefcase bomb.

"Yeah, Marilyn. It's not big, but it—"

"It just needs potion."

"That's funny, Dayzee. But nothing else is."

He stooped down and popped it open, then stood to show it to them.

"It's a telepathic bomb," he said, showing them the screen. "It's an ungodly mix of sorcery crystals and sick brain cell telepathy. Weird, but it'll work. We hope."

Marilyn stared at the screen and said, "What's all that?"

"It picks up on the desires of anyone that's nearby. There are four of us, so there are four images."

That got Sophia to look up from the dark floor, and all of them gave the screen a good look.

Marilyn pointed and said, "I know that one's mine: I'm so worried about those poor kitties. That's a nice photo of them."

"It's not really a photo," said the Boss, "but I think you know that."

"These two," she said, pointing to two more images, "are just pictures of you and Dayzee. Why is that?"

He gave Marilyn a quick smile, then turned toward Dayzee. She was already looking at him. They leaned closer together and kissed.

"Aw, that's sweet," Marilyn said and clapped her hands softly.

Then, she tipped her head to look at the fourth image. Her eyes popped open wide and she grinned at it before looking at her sister, who was also grinning.

"Well, I don't have to ask who that is," Marilyn said with a giggle.

Dayzee and the Boss broke their kiss, and Dayzee squinted at the image, then smiled and pointed.

"Never saw just her lips before, though."

Marilyn laughed and said, "Oh, Sissy, that's sweet too. We'll find her again."

They all froze at the sound of growling and parts of the house near the closet collapsing.

"That's so sad! Those poor sweet kitties!"

"Wait, Sis. That sounded different, didn't it?"

Marilyn tipped her head, but the lions had gone silent. She straightened up and looked at her sister.

"You mean . . . maybe they got through? They got away from the fire?"

Sophia nodded and shared the first smile any of them had seen from her for a while.

"Yeah, Sis. And if they somehow survived, then—"

"Maybe Kenzie did too!"

A loud crash sent a cloud of smoke puffing toward them through the tunnel, but it mostly dispersed before filling their chamber.

The Boss looked at the timer and said, "Dayzee, and the rest of you, we need to go."

"Go where?" said Dayzee. "Do we even know where that'll take us?"

He shook his head and said, "Let's hope for the Prism."

"You're only hoping? Seriously?"

Another crash sent more smoke billowing their way.

"We're out of choices, Dayzee."

"Oh, boy. Just wonderful. And girls, there used to be a ladder out of here, but the damn Collectors destroyed it."

She pointed at the broken pieces lying all around.

Marilyn shrugged and said, "It's never easy."

"Wait a second, Boss," said Sophia. "That loud boom when we were all partying with sex and violence. That was—"

"It was sex and danger, Sissy. But I like your suggestion better."

"Good, Sis. Yeah. Put that on our list. But Boss, nothing came through—just more Collectors. They were already crashing through this damn portal."

"Oh, well, there's a time factor with these kinds of things. Kind of a delayed reaction. It's not very well-defined. That boom might have been setting things up, like opening up a doorway."

"So, all of that upstairs was for nothing?" said Marilyn.

Dayzee looked at Sophia and said, "Even with all this shit going on, she's still such a sweet kid. Mare, it wasn't for nothing. We'd all do that again just for the thrill of it."

"But we have to remember to add violence next time too," Marilyn said with a sigh.

Sophia looked at Dayzee and said, "Uh, she's not always so sweet and innocent."

"No, Fia."

"Okay, we're out of time. Marilyn, Sophia, you have to follow right after us. Time is running out but more importantly, that'll help make sure we all travel to the same place: the Prism."

"Okay, Boss," said Marilyn.

Sophia said, "Sure, Boss, we'll go right after you two."

"Good. Dayzee? Are you ready?"

"Oh, yeah. There's nothing left here. Let's go."

They embraced, and Dayzee turned toward the girls and said, "See you gorgeous twins on the other side."

Then, they lost themselves in a kiss and fell sideways into the shadows and gloom without a sound.

"Alright, Sis, we have to—"

Another loud crash sent smoke clouds down the tunnel and into the room.

And along with that smoke, the twins froze at the sound of agitated, angry growling traveling along the tunnel too.

"Uh-oh, Sissy. Kitties aren't so happy anymore."

"Would you be, Sis? Think of all they've been through."

"Oh, true. It's a bit much for such—"

"Hey, Sis!" Sophia yelled as she pointed down at the clock on the bomb. "We only have three seconds!"

The sisters hugged each other close, then turned to face the shadows that harbored the portal with their cheeks touching.

"Sissy, we'd better—"

A shock wave of soundless telepathic energy shook the room and its walls and knocked the girls a step away, but they didn't fall and they didn't end their embrace.

And they stared, their eyes bigger than ever, still cheek to cheek, as a tall, muscular man stepped out of the shadows and smoke and stuck his fists on his hips.

His black hair was shoulder-length and wavy, and his trimmed goatee was also jet black. Even his eyes were black, and they looked upon one twin, then the other.

Faded, ripped blue jeans ended in scuffed and gouged black work boots, and his bare arms, neither one showing a single tattoo but both crowded with lean muscles, remained motionless.

A black leather vest without buttons revealed an abdomen that could have been chiseled from rock.

Without a smile, he let his serious black eyes rest on Sophia's.

"Who are you?"

The girls stared and squeezed each other more tightly.

He moved only his eyes, and they drilled into Marilyn's.

He squinted at her and said, "Why did you call me?"

# Chapter 33 – Sis, What Is He?

The twins still hugged each other close, cheek to cheek, as they gazed upon the man who had come to them through the portal.

"Sissy, I don't think—"

"You're sisters?"

Neither one answered. They only kept staring.

Sophia coughed softly and said, "Twins."

"Face me."

They turned toward him, but each kept an arm around the other's waist.

He looked from face to face several times.

"I see it."

He leaned in closer, squinting at each for a few seconds.

"Different. Mostly the same."

His black eyes left their blue eyes and traveled slowly down Sophia, over her breasts squeezed into a tight red blouse, across the minimal cloth of her short black skirt, then even more slowly down along her bare legs.

He focused on her high heels. A grin appeared and left quickly.

But it made another appearance when he shifted his gaze to Marilyn's high white heels.

Again, devoid of a grin or any other sign, he let his eyes trace a leisurely path up along Marilyn's long, bare legs, then over the torn white cloth of her dress, held together by a single belt around her waist, then side to side a few times when he'd found her breasts.

He finished by looking into her bright blue eyes, then Sophia's equally bright eyes.

With a grim smile, he said, "This can't be Hell."

His smile, already meager, vanished, and he said, "I asked who you are."

Since his eyes were locked on Marilyn's, she said, "I'm Marilyn."

He did nothing but look into her eyes for a long moment.

Then, he tipped his head and looked into Sophia's staring eyes.

"You?"

"I'm . . . I'm Sophia."

He squinted for a few seconds, then nodded to each of them.

"I'm Risk."

No one said anything as parts of the upper floors of the house above them burned and crashed down, and heavier smoke found their secret chamber.

Growling lions, intent on surviving the conflagration above and driven deeper into the mysteries below Dayzee's mansion, drew nearer.

Risk looked down at the briefcase which had been left open on the floor near his boots.

The girls looked too.

They watched its timer, frozen from Risk's arrival, begin again and count from three to two.

"Uh-oh, Sissy."

"Dammit, Sis!"

Then, from two to one.

Risk scoffed and said, "Fuck."

The bomb that they'd set, the one formed from sorcery crystals and spiced-up brain cells, shook and rattled for a second, then fell over, sending dust up from the floor to join the increasing smoke.

He looked back up at them.

"Tell me something good."

Sophia cleared her throat, and he focused on her eyes.

She said, "Um, we planned to, um . . ."

Marilyn shook her head once, almost too slight to be seen, but his eyes quickly found hers.

"That portal was, um, our last . . . uh . . ."

He pushed between them so quickly that it could have been before the lion behind them had roared. With both arms, he held the girls behind him as they all stared at an angry lion that stared back.

A lioness crazed by the heat and smoke and singed by the snapping flames that had forced her to seek shelter there.

A ferocious beast crouched down and showing her still-bloody fangs—the only recourse that she felt she still had to the madness her world had become.

The mountain lion held her ground, snarling, her eyes locked onto Risk's.

Risk leaned toward the lion, even as he protected the girls behind him. Both of them had reached around him to hold on tight, neither speaking nor even breathing and only watching the beast bare her fangs in the swirling smoke.

Their arms were locked around him, but they couldn't constrain his steady, deep breaths.

None of them moved.

Only the lioness moved, her whiskers twitching with each low growl.

"Don't," he said to her, his voice calm. "You don't have to."

Then, she roared and jumped at him, sending a jaw full of razor teeth at the man from the portal.

And when he launched himself just as quickly at the lion, the girls lost their grip.

But they did see, through the churning smoke, a wild, savage tangle of claws and fangs from two beasts rolling and tumbling in and out of the shadows and smoke.

Two animals roared continuously in the dark space below the burning mansion in the Flats of Beverly Hills as their battle raged.

One shrieked, then whimpered, and the other made no sound.

Then, the whimpering became gurgling, then went silent.

The smoke drifted away to either side, and Risk, his mouth still closed on the lion's neck, remained low to the ground, teeth grinding as he snarled up at the girls, his breaths ragged and racing in and out as shiny blood flowed from his mouth and the lion's ripped throat.

Marilyn and Sophia hugged each other just as close as they could.

From near Sophia's ear, Marilyn whispered, "Sissy, who is he?"

They watched him as he released his kill, letting it slump to the stone floor, and rose to his feet. His black eyes looked into theirs, then around their smoke-filled chamber.

He held his hands down at his sides, and blood dripped from his fingers.

His neat black whiskers were red—and dripping onto his chest.

Sophia leaned closer and whispered to her sister, "Sis, *what* is he?"

Soft yipping and whimpering grew louder, coming from the thick clouds in the tunnel. The second lion appeared, just her head, and she studied the room and its inhabitants quickly.

But the staggering building above had pushed the flames all the way into the tunnel, and she snapped her head around behind her to see the fire that was about to claim her tail. She howled and leaped into the room.

From a low crouch, her wide eyes watched Risk intently as he, too, began to lower himself to the ground, keeping his black eyes fixed on the lion.

She looked once at her dead friend, slaughtered in that dark room, then she growled as she glared up at the man waiting for her to make her move.

Flames licked at her tail as Dayzee's mansion continued its collapse.

The lioness turned to see while whipping her tail to safety, screamed once, then looked again at her fallen comrade.

When next she looked into Risk's eyes, she began a low whimper, and it only grew when he raised both hands. He kept his palms toward her as he stood tall amid circling smoke.

"It's okay," he said.

She continued her whining, and she blinked her eyes repeatedly as she gave quick, panicked looks at Risk and the bloody lion on the floor.

But the man who'd killed that lion only said, "Shh, now. It's okay."

Her whimpering stopped, but she didn't move, even when he approached her, then stooped down, their faces close.

Risk held her head with both hands and looked into her scared eyes.

He tipped his head toward the dead beast and said, "She left me no choice."

The lion's eyes softened, and she began to pant lightly.

Still holding her head gently with his left hand, Risk reached farther with his right and patted her side.

"You, though, might have killed all of us," he said, rubbing her side.

She tipped her head to her right, resting it in his hand. Her long, rough tongue took a quick swipe at that hand.

He gave her side three solid taps, then said, "Thanks for being kind."

Then he stood, and his lion stood beside him, both calmly studying the Kildare Killers, who were locked in an embrace so tight that neither could easily breathe.

# Chapter 34 – Or We All Burn

Risk pointed at the blond Kildare Killer and said, "Marilyn."

She held her breath and waited.

"We can't stay here."

Marilyn nodded without saying a word.

He lowered his hand and focused on Sophia's eyes, their blue shining even as smoke engulfed them all.

"Sophia."

She nodded and got a tighter grip on her sister.

"Where's the exit?"

Sophia shook her head, cleared her throat, and said, "There isn't any. Not anymore."

With one hand rubbing the ears of the lion beside him, he raked his fingers through his unruly hair then looked around, then up.

"Not good."

Again addressing Marilyn, he said, "Where are we?"

Marilyn said, "We're, um, underground in a room that—"

He held out his free hand.

A few seconds passed before he pointed up.

"No. Up there."

"It used to be Dayzee's mansion."

Sophia gave a quick glance to the flames and thicker smoke trapping them as it blocked the tunnel.

Risk shook his head and said, "No. The place."

Marilyn said, "It's Beverly Hills."

He nodded, scratched at the lion's head, and said, "Good. I'll remember."

The twins looked at each other for just a second, didn't say a word, and looked back at Risk.

"Are we going to die down here?" Sophia said.

Marilyn took quick breaths while looking around them, then said, "We don't want to die here!"

He almost smiled at each of them.

"No one is dying here."

He looked down at the mountain lion still at his side, and she looked up at him.

A few seconds passed, then he said to her, "No. Not you either."

She panted while holding his gaze, then both of them looked again at Marilyn and Sophia.

"She wants a name," he said.

Sophia gave the lion a quick look, then said, "Huh? The lion?"

He nodded, then said, "She needs one."

Marilyn shook her head, then turned to say softly to her sister, "Sis, maybe Kenzie?"

Sophia's eyes blinked heavily, and she pointed them at the floor.

After several seconds, she nodded.

Marilyn said to Risk, "We can call her Kenzie, okay?"

He looked down at the lion, and she looked up at him. She snarled then opened her jaws wide, showing her sharp white fangs.

She snapped her mouth shut and focused on the twins again.

"Kenzie Cat," said Risk.

He tipped his head down toward the lioness and said, "Her idea."

Marilyn let out a nervous giggle, then said, "Can Cat be with a 'K?'"

"Sis!" Sophia whispered in her ear. "You shouldn't—"

"That's good," said Risk.

All of them watched as the flames reached the border between tunnel and portal chamber but went no farther.

"We have to go," he said.

"How?" said Sophia. "Everything's burning, and the—"

"And the portal is gone," said Marilyn. "There's no way."

He offered them the first true smile since they'd met.

"You must do as I say."

The girls looked at the advancing flames, bringing along more choking smoke.

Marilyn nodded and said, "We will."

"Yeah. Both of us."

"Good. Take out your knives."

They looked at each other, then back at Risk.

"Uh, we don't have knives."

He squinted at them for a second, then said, "An axe, then."

They both looked down at themselves, each wearing tight clothing that couldn't even hide their physical features.

Sophia shook her head and said, "Uh, sorry. Nothing."

Still patting Kenzie Kat's head, he wiped blood from his chin as he looked around.

"Oh, wait," said Marilyn. "Sissy and I are the Kildare Killers. We can—"

"You kill?"

"Yeah," said Sophia. "Easily too."

"How?"

Sophia kept a tight hold on her sister but raised up her other hand. It began to glow red hot.

Kenzie Kat yipped softly just once and pressed against Risk's jeans.

Risk nodded and said, "Good. Both of you?"

Marilyn held up her glowing hand and couldn't stifle her soft giggle.

"Good," he said. "Cool your fires."

They let their heat fade then quench altogether.

Risk nodded then held both hands out together, aimed at the twins. He slowly moved his arms out.

The girls gave each other a quick look, ended their embrace, and put some distance between them.

Risk looked first at Marilyn, then Sophia, then Marilyn again. He focused on Sophia for a few seconds, then looked down at the big cat.

He scoffed and said, "Yeah, either one."

The lion seemed to laugh up at him just once, then they both looked again toward the twins.

An explosion high above shook even the floor and walls of the room, and a wave of flames invited itself in, then branched to begin flowing around each way, encircling them.

"Dammit."

"Can we get the hell out of here already?"

"Sissy, he knows how, he just—"

"Too close," he said while scanning the hungry flames creeping along the perimeter.

"Can't do it right."

He held Sophia's gaze when she said, "What do you mean, 'right?'"

He ignored her question and studied Marilyn when she said, "Then, let's do it wrong! We don't want to die!"

He grinned for just a second, then patted Kenzie Kat's head and said to her, "Wait. Until."

Then, he said, "You," and took three solid steps to stand so close to Marilyn that she had to look up to see his eyes.

Quickly, he sent his left arm around her and held her head with his right. She'd barely had time to open her mouth for a gasp, and he covered her lips with his own.

Sophia stared from a step away, and Marilyn groaned softly and struggled, then relaxed in his arms.

Still kissing her, and still holding her head firmly in place, he began savagely ripping at her already damaged white dress. It came apart easily, and he snapped it back over her shoulders and down her arms, then tossed it to one side where the flames welcomed it.

She'd been weakly pushing against his shoulders, but she let her arms reach up over those shoulders, where she cautiously touched his hair with her fingertips.

He changed his hold of her, using both strong hands to hold her waist at its narrowest. Lifting her effortlessly, he held her there, still kissing her, until she wrapped her legs around him.

Breaking the kiss for a moment, he looked at Sophia and said, "You."

He waved one hand behind Marilyn, then said, "Here."

Sophia's eyes opened even wider, but she did as Risk had told her and stood close behind her sister.

Risk supported Marilyn with one arm, with help from her legs tight around him, and with his free hand, he began ripping at Sophia's blouse. He easily peeled it from her and let it drop.

She'd stared at him through it all, not saying a word.

When he pointed down, she only nodded and stretched her tight skirt over her hips and let it hit the dirty floor.

"Good," he said, looking over Marilyn's shoulder.

Then, he let himself ease down to the floor, taking Marilyn with him, until he was flat on his back and she was kneeling above him.

She laid her hands on the floor, which was warming up along with everything else around them, and leaned forward to continue their kiss.

He unclasped his belt and did whatever else was needed.

Marilyn tipped her head up, suspending the kiss, and he only stared into her eyes.

She nodded and found her place, right where he wanted her.

Sophia, still standing, watched with a shaking head.

Until he held her gaze and tipped his head down.

"Um . . . I don't—"

"Do it."

She coughed softly, then knelt directly behind Marilyn, who had begun to lose herself to the pleasure of riding him up and down, slowly and steadily, with her palms flat against his chest.

"Sex," he said, looking into Marilyn's eyes, and she never stopped.

Sophia squinted at him when he looked up at her and added, "And death."

She still only stared down at him as he crossed his right leg over his left. When she felt his hands at her waist in an iron grip, she looked down to watch as he forced her down onto that highest thigh.

She began to pant as he relaxed his downward shove, then forced her into it again, and she quickly found herself moving with his rhythm so well that when he released her, she continued on her own.

He got Marilyn's hips in his hands and said, "Sex and death. Same time."

Sophia was shaking her head, watching her sister mounted on a man or something else that had just come through the portal, while she kept herself more than busy behind her, holding Marilyn and rubbing on his leg.

He looked into Sophia's eyes and said, "No time. It has to be all of us."

"I . . . I'm already—"

"Touch her," he said.

She renewed her hold on Marilyn's arms near her shoulders.

He scoffed and said, "Forget sisters. Touch her."

Marilyn, engrossed in her own feelings, only grinned.

Sophia reached around and held her sister's bare breasts.

Risk looked from one held breast to the other, then back into Sophia's eyes. Then at her growing smile.

He shook his head, smiling himself, and said, "No. You have to mean it."

Marilyn said softly, "Sissy, we're actresses."

"No!"

Both pairs of blue eyes gazed down into a pair of intense black ones.

"Feel it. Want it."

Sophia sighed and began gently squeezing Marilyn's breasts, and Risk smiled at the sight of it.

When he aimed his smile up to Sophia and nodded, she began soft pinching and pulling and leaned close enough that her face was being tickled in her sister's wavy blond hair.

They all looked to Risk's side as Kenzie Kat lay close to him, rubbing her snout against his exposed ribs where his leather vest had fallen open.

"More," he said. "All of you."

Marilyn picked up her pace, and she reached her left hand up and behind her and began to touch her sister's black hair.

And she turned that way, too, just as Sophia leaned in closer, their noses touching as they gazed into each other's eyes.

No one looked at the lion as she started a low wail, her jaws working against Risk's side.

"Do it," he said. "Or we all burn."

They touched their lips, even as Marilyn continued her steady gyrations on him and Sophia kept fondling her breasts and riding a leg hard like rock with a soft wrapping of skin.

The flames had reached completely around them and were scaling the walls.

"More," he said.

Sophia gasped softly, then made their kiss as passionate as any other in her life.

The lioness snarled and began to bite at his ribs, sending thin trickles of his blood down into the dust.

Marilyn's eyes were closed as she felt the hot kiss and hands on her breasts, but she also felt him take her hand that was still on his chest. He moved it to cover his heart.

He tapped it and said, "When I say."

She nodded, and none of them stopped what they were losing themselves to.

The lion snarled and began a low growling.

Sophia shifted her hips forward and back quickly on him and focused on the playful pinching and pulling, giving both constant attention.

And Marilyn moaned when she first heard Risk say, "Ah!"

Having found nothing consenting to be burned on the walls, the circle of flames began tightening around them, as if they sensed the only fuel left for them to digest.

"Ah!" Risk said while Marilyn sped up, forcing herself down roughly, and Sophia kept squeezing and pinching Marilyn's breasts while kissing her deeply and grinding on Risk's leg, and Kenzie Kat began sinking her fangs through skin, then sinew, then bone.

Risk, his eyes squinting, curled himself up and reached for both girls. Their kiss didn't end until they were close enough to take turns kissing him, then each other again.

Marilyn gasped and stayed down on him, snapping her hips.

Sophia kept up her short, hard slides on his leg, her hands still grabbing and pulling roughly.

And they all kept kissing.

Until.

"Ah! Now!"

Marilyn didn't look at her hand that had instantly become glowing hot. She and her sister smiled at the smell of burning flesh, but the sex and violence would allow no escape and not the slightest retreat from what they'd all started.

Marilyn broke the kiss only enough to say, "I'm there, too, Sophia."

"God, me too, Marilyn. I can't even remember who you—"

Marilyn stifled her with a kiss, and all of them stayed locked in a menagerie of sex and violence as Risk reached the peak of his own pleasure just as Marilyn's deadly hand sank through his heart.

Adding death to a room already burning with sex and flames.

"Damn," he said, and the girls and the lion paused to look at his face, which was contorted from both the pleasure and the pain of Marilyn burning a hole through his heart.

They watched him smile as he lay back on the floor, then he tipped his head back, and it smoothly broke the surface of the stone floor like sinking into a frozen gray swamp.

A moment later, his entire head was in that stone muck.

Kenzie Kat resumed her biting, her wanton jaws snapping loudly through ribs while she shook Risk's torso from side to side, and she paused only to wail at the twins before renewing her attack.

And still, Risk kept sinking. And the girls sat up on him, never slowing. Still lost in their own ecstasy.

Their lips were still close, and they resumed their frantic kiss. Sophia savagely squeezed her sister's breasts, pulling her body into her, and they both shifted their hips desperately on their own parts of him.

They paused only when a scream from the lion got cut off, and they watched as Kenzie Kat, with Risk holding the scruff of her neck, got pulled into the floor along with all of him from his waistline up.

"Oh, Sophia, where the hell are we going?"

"With Risk and Kenzie Kat. Just don't stop."

"I can't. This is the strongest, sweetest one I ever—"

"No more talk, Marilyn!"

Sophia groaned and forced her lips into Marilyn's.

The Kildare Killers ended their time in Beverly Hills locked in a starving kiss, and their climaxes spiked as they sank with Risk and Kenzie Kat into a silent world of stone and darkness.

And flames just as insatiable as all of them—started by the torch hands of Cadaver Collectors that had ignited Dayzee's mansion in the Flats, then had eaten every floor and wall and ceiling, then had raced underground for any last prey to consume—claimed everything in that hellish pit.

Everything except the four who had escaped with their ravenous delirium of sex and death.

# Chapter 35 – Only in Beverly Hills

Dayzee looked at the inside of the Prism's heavy wooden door and said, "Where the hell are those gorgeous twins?"

She spun her barstool to face Dead Mack, who held a bottle in one hand and her washcloth in the other.

Beside her, the Boss said, "Sure, Mack. It should just be another minute. Another drink for the road would be good."

He started pouring onto the bar, and Dayzee scoffed and tapped her glass under the bottle.

Mostly to herself, she said, "Can't get reliable Dead Bartender help these days."

When her glass had been filled and then some, she nudged Mack's arm until the bottle was over the Boss's glass.

She laughed and said, "Well, that worked out," as the bottle emptied just before the glass would have been overfilled.

They both looked up at Dead Mack, who showed no sign of even thinking of moving ever again.

Dayzee waved a hand in front of his blank eyes and said, "Hey, maybe your other guests need things too?"

He rotated enough to focus his glazed-over eyes on her.

"Sheesh, as Fia would say."

He blinked once, then turned and ambled away, with no sign that he'd ever again wipe his hands with Dayzee's washcloth.

"Boss, they should have been here a long time ago."

They both turned to look toward the door when four vehicles, spaced a few seconds apart and with sirens screaming, passed along Sunset Boulevard from left to right.

"Your house, Dayzee."

"My beautiful house! There were rooms and hallways and staircases that I've never seen and now, I never will."

"You'll rebuild. Things will get back to normal," he said as he turned himself back around.

Dayzee sighed heavily while studying the closed door, then turned herself around too.

"Not without Mare and Fia, Boss. I'm done with Beverly Hills. And those Kildare Killers . . . if they . . ."

"Hey, don't talk like that. You know that portal was kind of squirrely. They probably got shot into a penthouse suite somewhere out there on Sunset."

"You think so?"

"Hell, yeah. They're probably busy with more fountains. I don't know if we can wait for them, though. We should probably—"

"I'm not leaving until I see that they're alright."

"I promise that we'll come back to Earth as soon as we can. But your promotion to general can't wait much longer."

Dayzee stared down at her whiskey as she swirled the glass around.

She sighed and said, "Yeah? And why's that?"

"Because if you don't report soon, you might get back on that termination list."

She turned to look at him, squinting and shaking her head.

"No way. Really?"

"They're a fickle bunch, Dayzee. Maybe from some background sorsciencery field energy soaking into all of them. They probably have all kinds of diabolical assassins that they'd love to send after somebody."

"Oh, boy. Just wonderful."

She looked past him and said, "At least we still have that big guy."

"Yeah," he said, looking that way too. "I still get a weird vibe from that guy. But his portal is damn reliable."

"Like he's guarding it."

"Yeah. Right man for the job. If you're ready, finish that drink, and we'll—"

They both grinned at the sound of the Prism's door opening, even though it let in the wailing of another siren, also heading toward Dayzee's property.

They turned to look.

Dayzee shook her head and stared.

The Boss laughed and said, "Perfect."

A Cadaver Collector stood in the bright California sunshine just outside the bar's entrance. He or she, no one could tell because its head was a torch, looked around the inside while its teeth chattered rapidly and silently.

"I guess we do have to go, Boss. Things are just ridiculous here."

A new barmaid was walking past with a tray of filled glasses. She stopped near the door and laughed at the Collector.

"Halloween is over, you loser."

The Collector stared, and the busy teeth never slowed.

"Okay, you asked for it. A little water will teach you."

She set down the tray while still looking at the Collector, then reached for a glass. She quickly threw all of it on the Collector.

"Oh, I'm so sorry! I really didn't mean to throw whiskey on you! Are you going to be okay?"

The candle only burned brighter, and the teeth were chattering like mad.

"Well, you could at least say something. God, the rude people around these parts."

She scoffed, picked up her tray, and continued to her customers. She'd left the door open, and the Collector hadn't moved.

"She dumped whiskey on that freak, Boss. How about that?"

"Yeah, now he or she or it is just burning even more . . ."

The flames began to dwindle.

". . . than, uh . . ."

The flames faded to nothing, and the Collector started to melt and shrink into itself.

"Well, what the hell?" said Dayzee.

The process continued until only a crumpled pin-striped suit lay on the sidewalk, topped by an unburnt fedora which the breezes rolled away.

"All this time, Dayzee?"

She held up her glass, gave it a long look, then focused on the abandoned clothing just outside the door.

"Huh. Whiskey? That's all it takes?"

"It seems so," said the Boss. "Well, live and learn."

Dayzee and the Boss spun back around and found that Dead Mack was waiting with a fresh bottle.

The Boss held his glass up toward Dayzee and said, "A toast."

She held her glass close to his and said, "Sure. To what?"

"Oh, come on," he said. "I mean, really, Dayzee? Just say it already, and we can be on our way."

"You're sure that Mare and Fia are okay?"

"I'm sure. Somehow. Nothing can stop those two."

"Alright, then."

She nodded and gave him a big smile, then they clinked glasses.

"Only in Beverly Hills!"

# Chapter 36 – Below the Bay

Risk gently rubbed the lion's ears as she lay sleeping beside him with her head on his lap. When she pulled in a deep breath and expanded her strong body, then let it out, followed by licking her chops comfortably, he smiled and said, "Good girl."

After Kenzie Kat had squirmed herself into a better position and rejoined whatever dreams had gotten her paws twitching, he looked toward his own boots where he sat on a rough, dirty tarp.

Just beyond those worn black boots, part of a white high-heeled shoe was revealing itself from under a thin canvas quilt.

He gave it a soft kick and waited. Watching.

Marilyn yawned first, and it never reached its full potential from her face being burrowed into the side of her sister's neck. Her blond hair and Sophia's black hair stayed lightly tangled when both yawned together, then opened their eyes.

"Oh, Sissy, what's going on?"

"I don't know, Sis. I just woke up when I felt you moving."

They stayed close, blue eyes looking into identical blue eyes, and neither smiled.

"I'm so tired."

"Me too," Sophia said, then squeezed her eyes shut again and flexed her legs, and Marilyn, her legs woven in with her sister's, stretched hers too.

Marilyn took a look down, then back at her sister. The edge of their blanket was pulled up high as the twins lay embracing against a mound of soft pillows.

"Thanks for the scratchy blanket, Sissy."

"Yeah, Sis, it is. Glad we have it, though."

"It's fine. Oh, I'm still sleepy."

They both closed their eyes and yawned, and Marilyn began adjusting the blanket up even higher, keeping them in a snug cocoon.

"Me too, Sis. We need just another few—"

"It worked," Risk said.

They both held their breath and looked all around them for the first time.

Behind the pillows against which they lay embracing, a wicker wall rose up. But it was a curved wall that looped around to form a circle the size of a generous California hot tub.

Across from them, Risk sat leaning against the bowl they shared, and the lion lay asleep next to him with her head on his lap.

He scratched between the lion's ears and focused his black eyes on the twins.

"Remember her name?"

"I do," said Sophia. "She's Kenzie."

"Kenzie Kat, Sissy. Not the real Kenzie."

Sophia reached above the blanket just enough to point at him and said, "You're Risk, right?"

He nodded and said, "Good. You woke up."

The twins looked at each other, then back at him.

Marilyn said, "Um, you weren't sure?"

His eyes were almost as tired as theirs, but he managed a meager grin.

"Nothing is guaranteed."

He looked them over, prompting them to lift the blanket and look at themselves too.

They saw that they were naked except for their heels.

"You'll get clothes," he said.

They looked up at the sound of crackling and saw a large metal pot with flames dancing above it. A gigantic balloon, open at the bottom, was wired in place above that and all around its edges, everything was blacker than a starless night sky. Thick ropes connected all of it to the top edge of their basket at even intervals.

Someone small, like a child, was hanging on up there, tiny gloved hands holding the taut wires and small, burlap-wrapped feet secure on a narrow wooden plank.

"Like a little trapeze," Sophia said to herself.

"For that kid, Sissy. He's probably a neighbor's—"

That kid snapped his head to look down on them. Round red eyes with centered black dots watched them intently from the sides of a thick, tapered beak that hooked down into a sharp point. The hood of his thin black jacket framed his feathered face.

"Our navigator," said Risk, unconcerned.

They looked back at Risk but pulled themselves closer together.

"Good eyes," he said, shooting a quick glance up.

"Um," said Marilyn, "we aren't in Beverly Hills anymore, are we?"

Risk shook his head, holding Marilyn's blue gaze.

"It burned. Remember?"

"All of it?" said Sophia.

He shrugged.

"Not us."

"Sissy," Marilyn said, leaning closer to her sister, "I'm starting to remember all that. I remember the sex and—"

"And the violence, Sis. Yeah, then you killed him."

"Oh, my goodness. I remember that now."

They looked back at Risk.

"You're not dead?"

"No, Marilyn."

"That lion, she—"

"Kenzie Kat, Sissy."

"Yeah, Kenzie Kat," said Sophia. "Hey, let's shorten that, alright? How about just K Kat?"

"Good idea," Marilyn said. "Risk? Is that okay?"

He looked down at the lion whose mouth had lazily opened wide into a gaping yawn, showing rows of razors. She snapped her jaw shut and looked up into Risk's eyes for a second or two, then back at the girls.

He looked at them too.

"She said okay."

Marilyn shook her head slowly, looking first at K Kat, then at Risk.

"Sissy and I didn't pack any clothes."

Sophia chuckled just once, very softly, and said, "That's funny, Sis."

"There are crafters," he said, his eyes blinking slowly.

"Where?"

He tipped his head up toward the edge of the basket, which was about chest high for the twins when standing, and said, "Down there, Marilyn."

"Not Beverly Hills shopping, though?"

"No, Sophia."

Marilyn frowned and started breathing more quickly. She pulled the blanket up under their chins.

"Where the hell are we?" she said.

Risk only smiled for a moment, then said, "That's what I first asked you."

"He's not wrong, Sis."

To Risk, Sophia said, "Seriously, though, where did you take us?"

He stood and stretched, opening his leather vest enough to show undamaged skin stretched over hard muscles, then leaned back with both hands out to his sides to hold the top rail.

"We all took us."

"Oh. All four of us. Together."

"Yes, Marilyn. When you called, I was here."

He tipped his head back quickly, then said, "Look."

The girls shared a momentary stare at each other, then reached up and behind them for the rail, using it to help themselves up onto their heels.

They held each other, still wrapped in their blanket, and looked out over the edge.

"Oh, my," said Marilyn.

"Sis, what the hell?"

Far beneath their basket floating from a balloon piloted by a small fellow with the face of a hawk, a dark city sprawled out to dim horizons in most directions.

Crooked streets, devoid of anything traveling them, crisscrossed all of it. Between the streets, there were buildings, some short and some taller, open fields, expanses that were still and smooth and black, and small groups of things with wings flapping over the low structures and around the higher ones.

Dotting the tops of buildings and along the streets, pinpoints of light flickered, dancing. And from each of them, a slender thread of light smoke reached high up into the blackness, barely moving in the still air.

"Fires?" said Sophia. "Just fires?"

They didn't turn toward Risk when he said, "Electric's out."

But they both got big eyes, looking at each other, when he said, "Damn reactor."

Sophia shook her head slowly, and the twins studied their surroundings again.

Directly ahead, far from them, a large fire burned, and clouds of things with wings were circling silently. Or they were too far away to hear.

Far to the left, they saw another fire, low and wide.

To the right, near the horizon, the world ended in a jagged cliff, with a sea of flames burning all the way to that horizon.

The girls held each other close, arms around each other's waist, as they studied a world that laughingly, horrifyingly, could not have been Beverly Hills.

"Risk," Marilyn said while her eyes tried to see all of it, "what is all that down there?"

They didn't look at him when he said, "There's no name."

Sophia turned to see him, and she saw that K Kat was standing up next to him, also studying her new surroundings.

"Well," she said, "what kind of place doesn't have a name?"

He pointed up and when Sophia looked up at the blackness, Marilyn did too.

They heard him say, "Far above, there's water."

"Okay," said Marilyn, "there's water. What water? Like rain clouds?"

"No. San Francisco Bay."

"What the hell?" said Sophia.

She looked around and swept her arm both ways.

"All of this is—"

"Below the bay."

"That's what you call it?"

He shrugged and said, "We can."

Marilyn blurted out, "How do we go home? I want to go home!"

"Sis is right. We don't belong here. How the hell do we go back home?"

He laughed once and said, "You already know."

Marilyn looked at her sister and wiped at her eyes.

"Sissy?"

"Sis, we do know. Think about it."

She nodded and said, "I remember sex."

"And violence, Sis. No, it had to be death."

"Oh, yeah, I remember when Risk said that."

They turned, still holding each other, when Risk said, "Remember it."

The twins stared at him for a moment, then faced each other, their arms around each other's waist.

They gazed into each other's eyes, like seeing their own blue eyes in a mirror, as seconds passed and they floated over the dark city under a bay.

Marilyn almost grinned and said, "I remember all of it, Sissy."

Sophia tipped her head and said, "I remember that acting doesn't work."

"Oh, no. It has to be real."

"We have to feel it, Sis."

"Yes, Sissy. Both of us. *All* of us. Even a lion if she's with us."

"It wasn't just for fun."

Marilyn sighed and said, "Not just for the cameras, Sissy."

A few seconds later, they shared their modest smiles with Risk.

"Good," he said. "Don't forget."

From far behind them, the sound of a sharp explosion roared past them and echoed off into the distance behind Risk. The girls turned to look. A massive fireball was rising from the far edge of the landscape and convulsing toward the black sky.

It began to fragment and fade when it struck that ceiling, and swarms of black dots flew away from the impact site and raced around it. And their screeching, like voices of men impatient for death, was loud enough to reach their vessel.

"Oh, Sissy, I don't know about this."

"Sis, we'll get home soon and—"

"Come here," Risk said. "Not much time."

They turned toward Risk and saw him waiting with his arms wide. K Kat was huddled close, standing next to him.

"Really," he said. "It'll hit soon."

He turned away and lifted his arms out as they rushed toward him, and each found a safe place, their arms around him, as he held the blanket around all of them. Even the lion was wrapped in there and standing with them.

Then, a sudden blast of hot wind shook the basket and jerked the balloon with it, causing the hawk boy navigator to squawk madly.

Risk's hair got snapped around, and Marilyn's wavy blond hair and Sophia's silky black hair fluttered out over the landscape beneath them. They all stayed pressed together under the blanket with bright sparks racing past and spiraling into the blackness.

Risk held the basket's rim, and the Killers held him, and all of them, even K Kat, looked out at the dark lands waiting for them Below the Bay.

# Enjoy the Story?

Thank you for reading! Please consider leaving a review and/or a rating at your favorite bookseller or with your favorite book club. Help your fellow readers meet Dayzee Dazzle!

For more about Edward Allen Karr and his books, visit:

www.LakesideLetters.com

What's Next?
We'll all find out someday soon in

# *Below the Bay*

Risk and the Killers
Book One

The sequel series to
Thrills N Kills in the Hills

# Have You Met Lin Finity?

She's the powerful star of her own series titled the Fringes Of Infinity. In the beginning, she's forced to learn how to control the unstoppable, magical power she earned at age fifteen. After killing her abusive uncle with her deadly new ability, she locked it away inside herself. Now, she's in her forties, and it's back. She calls it *Mayhem*. And it's done waiting.

Book One and the Novella are free in e-book format. Just visit https://www.lakesideletters.com

***Lin Finity and her Mayhem Rising***
***Lin Finity in Holding On***

## About the Author

Edward Allen Karr was born, raised, and continues to reside in Ohio, USA. His adult life has followed a meandering path, ranging from working an automotive assembly line to designing space flight hardware. And through all of it, he's seen that life is a captivating and ultimately unexplainable endeavor. His writing seeks to add a splash of wonder to a world already awash in it.

* * *

For more information, please visit:

www.LakesideLetters.com